DEADFALL

Shaun Jeffrey

DEADFALL
Published by Leucrota Press
40485 Murrieta Hot Springs Rd. Suite B-4 #131
Murrieta, CA USA

ISBN-13: 978-0-9824713-4-0
ISBN-10: 0-9824713-4-3

Cover art by Studio Tu On.
Cover and interior layout by Gilly.

First printing, March 2010.
Manufactured and printed in the United States of America.
Printed simultaneously in the UK and Canada.

http://www.leucrotapress.com

DEADFALL

Shaun Jeffrey

Also by Shaun Jeffrey:

The Kult

To Deb and Callum.
Words will never be enough. You rock my world.

ONE

An ear-splitting boom reverberated along the street, rattling shop windows in their frames.

Amber Redgrave moved with catlike grace, sidestepping across the pavement to position herself between the origin of the noise and the frail client whose bouffant hairstyle resembled a grey crow's nest atop her head.

Hand hovering over the bottom of her thigh-length dark blue jacket, underneath which the Glock Model 30 nestled in a holster around her waist, Amber surveyed the street. She knew the bang wasn't a gunshot—she would know the distinctive sound anywhere—and it took her a couple of seconds to work out the noise originated from the exhaust of a blue Citroen Saxo.

Small droplets of sweat beaded on the client's forehead, squeezing their way through a layer of industrial foundation that looked as though it had been applied to her wrinkled face with a trowel by an inept builder.

"It was just a car exhaust," Amber said.

The old lady peered along the street, her lips pinched, eyeballs bouncing in their sockets as she looked around.

"Are you sure?" she said, her bottom lip trembling. She tightened her grip on the Versace bag suspended over her shoulder.

"Yes, look." Amber pointed along the street to where the car waited at the lights, belching smoke. As soon as the light changed the vehicle sped away, unleashing a double-barrelled bang from its exhaust that made a number of shoppers along the street jump in surprise.

The old lady's hand fluttered against her breast. "Oh my goodness. For a moment there, I thought that was it."

Amber smiled. "Just relax, Ms. Hawkins. You're quite safe."

"Thank you, dear." She touched Amber's arm and squeezed. "It's so much easier having a female bodyguard than one of those brutish men I'm so often lumbered with."

The term *bodyguard* rankled Amber. She found the term *mercenary* even worse. She was a security consultant, her services available to the highest bidder.

The job to escort Ms. Hawkins arose at the last minute when the woman's usual guardian—ex-SAS man John Richmond— called to say something had come up which took precedence, and he asked Amber to step in. His exact words regarding Ms. Hawkins had been enlightening: 'She's a nutter, but her money's good.' Amber smiled to herself as she remembered the conversation. Although she hadn't seen him for over six months, the sound of John's voice brought back fond memories of their brief but explosive relationship.

But she didn't have time to dwell on it now. She had spoken to Ms Hawkins before venturing out, but the client was vague, saying only that her dear, departed husband had earned a number of enemies because of his business dealings, and despite him being dead, she feared for her safety.

As she surveyed the street, Amber's spine tingled and she shivered. Clenching her fists, she narrowed her eyes and scanned the crowd but couldn't see anyone staring back that might have given rise to the feeling.

With her concerns unfounded, Amber indicated they should

continue towards the large department store where Ms. Hawkins said she liked to shop.

The automatic doors slid open as they approached and they stepped inside.

Ms. Hawkins shuddered.

"It's nice to get out of that chill wind," she said, uncoiling the snakelike scarf from around her neck.

Amber nodded and scanned the shop. Racks of clothes stretched along aisles either side of the entrance, leading to separate display sections. Set out over eight levels, with each floor as large as a football field, a shopper could get lost for days among the items on display. Bright overhead lights illuminated the room, and scores of people wandered up and down the aisles, perusing the merchandise.

"Oh this is divine," Ms. Hawkins said as she fingered a blue cashmere cardigan. "It would go just wonderful with your eyes." She lifted the cardigan from the rail and held it before Amber.

Amber glanced at the cardigan and politely nodded. She hated shopping and would rather spend her time field stripping her large collection of guns, making sure everything was in working order.

"And if you'd just grow your hair out a bit," Ms. Hawkins continued, "then I'm sure this dress would look heavenly." She indicated a red floral, knee-length dress. "You have the figure for it. I would *die* to be so slim. Do you work out? Of course you do. Don't get me wrong, your hair looks lovely short, but I think just a couple of extra inches would make all the difference."

Amber knew the same was true of a few men, but she refrained from smiling.

As Ms. Hawkins wandered between the aisles, Amber walked behind her, slightly to her side, taking the best possible position to spot a potential hostile approaching from the front while still offering protection from behind.

She caught sight of herself in a wall mirror and did a double-take, the short black wig changing her whole appearance so that she hardly recognised herself. Her posture looked a little tight, and she allowed herself to relax a bit. Despite her line of work, she knew she didn't look like a security consultant; with her sculpted cheeks and slim physique, she more closely resembled a model. Someone once likened her to Keira Knightley, and she guessed there was a similarity if you only glanced at her.

"What do you think of this?" Ms. Hawkins said, placing a beret on Amber's head.

"I'm not really a hat person."

"Rubbish, it looks wonderful." She teased out the edges of Amber's short, black fringe. "There—very Parisian."

Amber bit her tongue.

"How about I buy it for you?" Ms. Hawkins said.

Amber shook her head. "Thank you, but I really don't thi—"

Ms. Hawkins put her finger to Amber's lips. "I insist. It's the least I can do." She tugged the hat from Amber's head and kept a firm grip on it as she wandered down another aisle.

From what she'd seen so far, Amber surmised Ms. Hawkins to be a lonely old lady. She wondered whether her request for bodyguards wasn't more for the company than the protection.

"They do a wonderful lunch in the restaurant on the eighth floor," Ms. Hawkins said, turning the corner round a display rack. "What say we have a bite to eat, and then let's really go to town?"

As a rule, Amber, who kept her presence low-key, didn't get asked to dine with the client, but she knew Ms. Hawkins wasn't going to take *no* for an answer. Come to think of it, she did feel a bit hungry.

"Only if I can pay for myself."

Ms. Hawkins seemed to consider Amber's statement for a moment, then she smiled. "Come on then, follow me."

She let Ms. Hawkins lead the way to the lift situated on the far side of the room. If left to Amber, they would use the stairs through a door on the opposite side of the room, but she couldn't expect an old lady to walk up eight flights. Not that Amber would mind. Hell, she'd run up. She loved the exercise, and saw any opportunity to keep fit as a godsend. There was also an escalator in the middle of each floor. Amber thought how good it would be to crank up the speed and try running up the one going down.

When they reached the lift, Amber pressed the call button and the door opened on a box capable of holding eight people at a squeeze. She ushered her client in and turned to stare out at the shop floor. As the lift doors closed, she noticed a figure snatch a dress from a rack of clothes. She only caught a quick glimpse, enough to identify the nondescript man as mid-thirties with short brown hair and broad shoulders. But a familiar hundred-yard stare caught her eye as he glanced across, which meant he would either make a good friend or a dangerous enemy.

She wondered what the man was doing looking at women's clothing. He didn't look like a transvestite—although she couldn't stake her life on it—and he didn't appear to be accompanying a woman. Of course he might be waiting for his partner to exit the changing room, or he might just be out shopping for his wife or girlfriend. But most men opted to buy flowers, chocolates or the usual unsuitable underwear designed more for titillation than comfort. What men knew about size never usually went any further than a woman's breasts, and they usually got that wrong, so a man out shopping for a dress made the hairs on the nape of Amber's neck prickle.

With just the two of them in the lift, Amber could smell her client's heady perfume. Amber hardly ever used scents herself, and she only applied enough makeup to disguise the bags that sometimes hung beneath her eyes. Fresh-faced, she saw little reason to disguise what nature intended with cosmetic slap, and she felt more at home in camouflage paint than foundation.

"Are you married?" Ms. Hawkins asked.

Amber shook her head.

"Sorry, I know it's none of my business. What you must think of me—"

Amber's lips curved into a faint smile. "I don't think many men would appreciate their wife following my line of work." The smile wavered as she remembered her break up with John—

when she'd chosen her profession over romance. She sometimes wondered whether she'd made the right decision.

The lift came to a shuddering stop and the doors slid open with a faint squeak. Amber stepped out first, glanced left and right, and then motioned Ms. Hawkins towards the restaurant on the far side of the room.

To reach the restaurant, they had to pass through kitchenware. The aroma of cooking food, rich with mouth-watering spices, was everywhere. Amber wondered whether the pots and pans were situated on the same floor as the restaurant for a specific reason—maybe to get those interested in cooking to eat before they made a purchase. The glass windows around the room offered a panoramic view of the surrounding city, the grey sky close enough to touch.

Just as she started to follow Ms. Hawkins, movement caught Amber's eye. She turned and saw a man moving her way from the top of the stairs—the man with the hundred-yard stare. To reach the top floor, he must have run up the eight flights, but he didn't appear out of breath. He gazed at Amber, and she saw his hand move towards the waistband of his trousers.

Sensing the imminent danger, Amber's pulse raced. Adrenaline coursed through her body. She positioned herself between the man and Ms. Hawkins, who, oblivious to the threat, continued shuffling towards the restaurant.

"Ms. Hawkins, get down," Amber shouted.

She didn't turn to see whether the client complied.

The man pulled a gun from his waistband. Amber couldn't be sure, but she thought it was a Heckler and Koch USP Compact.

So much for John's claim that Ms Hawkins imagined the threat, Amber thought. She should have acted upon her earlier assessment of the man, stayed in the lift and returned to the ground floor to escort Ms. Hawkins from the building.

Amber rolled aside, instinctively withdrawing her gun. Taking a bullet wasn't an option. She would be no use to her client dead.

The whiplash crack of gunfire rang out, and a bullet struck a saucepan near her head. Shoppers screamed.

Amber couldn't understand what the man was thinking, making his move in a busy store. It wasn't the best place to stage a hit—too many witnesses—unless the man was crazy or stupid, both of which seemed probable.

"Ms. Hawkins? Are you okay?" Amber shouted.

She heard movement to her side. "My goodness," Ms. Hawkins said, crawling towards her.

"Stay where you are," Amber said, holding her hand up as a signal to stay put.

Another bullet struck the pots and pans at her side, causing them to ring with a strange percussion sound. They swung to and fro as she stared through a gap in the aisle, scanning the area.

Where the hell are you?

Another shot rang out, but the acoustics of the room made the sound hard to trace.

She needed to pinpoint the man before she fired. Too many innocent people could be hurt otherwise.

Putting her cheek to the ground, she stared through the gaps under the shelving lining the aisles. She saw the shoes of people running towards the exits, but then about three aisles to her left, she spotted the sand-coloured boots of someone standing still, facing her.

It had to be the man with the hundred-yard stare.

A display of plates and dishes exploded over her head as another shot rang out, and shards of crockery rained down. A dish shattered on the tiled floor, sending slivers of porcelain flying like shrapnel. A number of the pieces embedded themselves in Amber's cheek. She ignored the pain, her senses working at hyper speed.

She turned, looked at the ceiling where the fire sprinklers blossomed. She knew the principle behind the sprinklers. Each sprinkler contained a glass tube filled with a liquid that expanded when subjected to heat. When the tube broke, it allowed the pressurised water to push out the plug. She also knew that, unlike what was shown in most movies, setting off one sprinkler wouldn't activate the others—and one sprinkler wouldn't provide much of a distraction, but it might unbalance the man enough to give her a shot.

With ten rounds in the Glock, she knew it might take most of them before she hit the sprinkler above the man's head, then she might not have enough time to reload. In a shooting encounter like this, it wasn't the first round fired that won the engagement, but the first *accurately fired* round. She needed a clear shot, so it was a risk she was going to have to take.

"Stay down," she said to Ms. Hawkins. "I'm going to try to draw the man out."

"Be careful, dear," Ms. Hawkins said.

Adrenaline coursed through Amber's veins, supplying her with added strength. She took a deep breath, steadied herself, then she stood up, aimed at the sprinkler above where she had seen the man standing, and fired seven rounds. The gun kicked in her hand. She saw the man in her peripheral vision, heard the bark of his gun as he returned fire, and she dropped to the ground. After a moment, she heard the satisfying hiss of water raining down; thought she also heard a muffled voice say, "Shit," but she wasn't sure.

Although it wasn't empty, she ejected the magazine, letting it clatter to the floor. She inserted a fresh magazine into the well, using her index finger to guide it in, something she'd practiced until she could do it in seconds—blindfolded. With a round still in the chamber, she didn't need to release the slide, which made reloading that much faster.

Hoping the water distracted the man, she crawled to the end of the aisle, braced herself, rose to a standing position, used the shelf as a support, tensed her finger on the trigger and aimed— but the man wasn't anywhere to be seen.

Cursing under her breath, she scanned the shop floor. A crowd of people cowered in the far corner of the room, while other people charged for the stairs, knocking others patrons out of their way as they ran.

The place looked like bedlam. Water from the sprinkler rained down, splattering a pile of pots and pans like an impromptu dishwasher.

Where the hell are you? Amber narrowed her eyes, tried to calm the racing thud of her heart. Gun clasped between both hands, she stalked through the aisles, scanning the faces of shoppers, trying to spot the target.

A deathly silence descended, as if everyone in the store were holding their breath in anticipation.

That's when she heard it. A slight click followed by the sound of hollow metal bouncing off the ground. The target was reloading.

Amber spun towards the source of the noise, and saw the man propped against a display cabinet full of crockery. With no time to hesitate, she aimed and fired two rounds.

The first bullet disintegrated a bone china cup at the side of the man's head. The second struck his right shoulder, knocking him back and twisting his body. Someone screamed. The man's left hand flew to the area of impact, staunching the flow of blood. He bared his teeth, grimaced, and dropped out of sight.

Amber couldn't lose the initiative. She ran along the aisle and found the man crouched on the ground, gun propped between his knees, trying to reload with one hand.

"Give it up," she said, aiming at the man's head.

The man glared up at her; his blue eyes looked haunted. He spat a wad of phlegm in her direction.

"Go to hell, bitch."

"This isn't worth dying over."

"Who said anything about dying?"

Before Amber reacted, the man launched himself towards her, using his legs as a springboard. He extended his good hand, fingers clasped like a claw, ready to gouge her face.

Acting on instinct, Amber fired a single shot. The bullet passed through the man's eye, leaving a vacant socket and putting an end to his hundred-yard stare. For a brief moment, she saw straight through the man's skull as the bullet tore a chunk of bone from the back of his head. Blood and brain sprayed the ground, creating a macabre puzzle, and the man crumpled to his knees and then fell forward, his head smacking the floor.

Sweat beaded on Amber's forehead and her hand was shaking as she returned her pistol to its holster on her waist. Taking a life was never easy. But she had to put it out of her mind and concentrate on the client—had to act professional—so she turned and hurried back to Ms. Hawkins. As she reached the end of the aisle, she noticed Ms. Hawkins still lying on the ground.

"It's okay, you can get up now," she said.

Ms. Hawkins didn't respond and a cold stab of fear prodded Amber's stomach.

"Ms. Hawkins? It's safe. The man's dead."

She took a couple of steps closer and saw the pool of blood seeping from underneath Ms. Hawkins' chest.

"*Jesus.*" She ran towards the prone figure and crouched down at her side. Blood dribbled from the corner of Ms. Hawkins lips, leaving an exclamation mark down her cheek. Amber felt for a pulse, but couldn't feel one. The hit-man's bullet had found its target.

She bit her bottom lip. Took a deep breath. This was bad. This was *very* bad. She closed Ms. Hawkins eyes and rocked back on her heels. Death never got any easier to accept. She pictured her brother Simon in her mind, saw the rictus of pain etched across his face, the rope pulled taut around his neck, creating a second chin below his cherubic features, his body swinging below the landing, as though rocked by unseen hands, the banister creaking in sympathy. She never forgave him for committing suicide. Everyone had problems. If only he'd talked to her about them, they could have sorted it out.

The chatter of shoppers brave enough to venture from their hidey-holes brought her out of her reverie, then she heard the slap of feet heading her way and looked up in time to see armed police exiting the lift.

She knew she couldn't afford to be found at the scene. Unlike some other countries, it was illegal to carry a firearm in public in the UK.

She wiped the hint of a tear from her eyes, then stood and ran towards the stairs.

"Stop," someone shouted.

Amber ignored the command and dove through the doorway, banging her shoulder and losing her footing as she careened into the wall. Ignoring the pain, she picked herself up and fled down the stairs to the next floor.

She heard the sound of officers in pursuit, their footfalls echoing down the stairwell.

Pulse pounding at her temples, she crashed through the door on the next level, her gaze taking in the racks of clothing. While the ground floor comprised the cheaper clothes, this floor housed the more expensive designer brands.

The crowds on this floor didn't know what had happened on the floor above, and they continued shopping unconcerned. Amber dodged between the aisles, walking fast. She headed towards the changing room, picking up a couple of tops on the way. Once she arrived at the entrance, a teenage girl counted her items and gave her a plastic token with "2" imprinted on it.

Amber glanced back, biting her lip when she saw the police swarm into the room. She thanked the girl and hurried past her.

The changing room consisted of a short corridor with curtained-off areas along either side. Near the entrance there was a rack with clothes people had tried on but didn't want. Amber snatched a long blue coat from the rack and ducked behind one of the curtains into a small cubicle containing a mirror and a bench.

Looking in the mirror, she pulled off the short black wig and shook out her wavy, shoulder-length strawberry-red locks. Then she reached into the pocket of her jacket, took out a small penknife and cut the security tag off the sleeve of the coat.

She put the coat on, stuffed the wig in the pocket, slid the tag under the bench, picked up the tops, left the cubicle, and handed the tops to the girl on the way out.

Head bowed, she walked to the escalator and made her way to the exit before the police had the foresight to lock the place down.

Outside, police cars were parked haphazardly across the road. Amber kept her head down and walked around the corner at the side of the building; then she ran.

As fast as she could.

TWO

Amber slammed her fist down on the wooden desktop, ignoring the resultant pain. The sound echoed around the room, made all the louder by the lack of fixtures and fittings.

"What the hell happened, John?" she snapped.

John Richmond leaned across his office desk and held his hands up, his swivel chair squeaking as he moved. "I think I should be asking *you* that question."

Amber fought to control her temper, hands clasped together to stop her from punching out. "'She's a nutter but her money's good,' you said. 'A rich old woman who got a little spooked after her husband died.' Well I guess she wasn't so fucking mad, was she?"

"Calm down. You're a professional, so act like one. What happened is unfortunate. No one could have seen it coming. But don't come in here barking at me just because things went bad."

Amber shook her head. "*Unfortunate*? She's bloody dead." She ran her hands through her hair, exhaled loudly, took a deep breath, and collapsed onto the padded high-backed chair opposite John.

In the six months since she'd last seen John face-to-face he'd lost weight; his once-athletic body looked at least fifteen pounds lighter, making him probably about twelve stone. Either he'd been working out too much, was ill, or something had affected him emotionally. And as he didn't look ill, that left only two alternatives.

His cheeks were sunken a little more than usual, eyes shadowed by his prominent brow, spiky brown hair gelled into place. He pursed his pale, narrow lips. She liked his lips, liked the feel of them crushed against her own, and despite her reservations, she still felt the original attraction that pulled them together.

She glanced around his office. Papers were stacked on top of a filing cabinet in the far left corner of the room and there was a general disorganised feel to everything, from the clutter on the desk to the jacket thrown across the back of the chair next to Amber. The only things that seemed organised were the photographs of John in military uniform adorning the walls.

Bands of light beamed through the long window behind John, creating a corona around his head.

Amber leaned forward. "So have you found out anything about the shooter?"

"So far, no. For all we know, he might have licked one too many stamps down at the post office."

"No. He was a professional. Not a competent one, but a professional all the same."

"Well we haven't got time to analyse it now. A situation's come up. It's time sensitive and it's going to require some finesse. But I promise—as soon as I get back."

"I want to talk about it now. Not when you get back."

John raised his hands in a placating manner. "Amber, I understand where you are, but you of all people should know that you shouldn't try to make sense of these things. Death is just a part of our line of work."

Amber bit her lower lip. She knew he was right, but she didn't want *him* to know that.

John smiled, and for a moment she saw the man she had fallen in love with.

"So what's this job you're going on?"

A slight twitch afflicted John's right eye. He put his hand in front of his mouth and coughed. "I can't tell you much as it's confidential, but the client's desperate, and they're paying a hell of a lot above the going rate. I'll be back tomorrow all being well, and we'll talk then."

Amber put her hands on the desk. As she did so, John reached across and grabbed her hands firmly but gently. He ran his thumb across her knuckles.

"I'm sorry it went bad. You know I wouldn't put you in a situation if I thought anything would go wrong."

Amber swallowed, felt her cheeks flush with colour as a spark of the old electricity flowed through her. Then John withdrew his hands and Amber stood up and walked towards the second story window, looked out at the busy street below.

"So how much is 'a lot above the going rate?'"

John shrugged. "I'm not certain of the exact details. All I know is that this job's going to make me a fortune."

Amber continued to look out the window. She knew John well enough to know he was lying. He wouldn't be going on a mission without knowing all the details. She turned back to look at him.

"You need some time off," he said. "You've been through the grinder today. We'll talk tomorrow—when I get back—if you want." He paused. Licked his lips. "Maybe, you know, we could go away together after this job is finished."

Amber saw a slight flush creep into John's cheeks. Was the old fire still there? Or was she mistaking his friendship for something more?

The mobile phone on his desk rang. He picked it up and accepted the call. "I need to take this," he said, covering the mouthpiece with his hand. "I'll be back in a minute." He stood up and walked out of the room, closing the door behind him.

Amber sat back down and put her feet up on his desk. Was there a chance they could rekindle what they once had? Of course she still had feelings for him, but in their chosen profession, relationships were doubly hard to work at.

The phone on the desk rang. Amber looked to the door John had walked through, then at the phone.

Thinking it might be something important, she leaned forwards and picked it up. "Hello? John Richmond's office."

"Could I speak with Mr Richmond please?" the caller asked, a London accent detectable in his voice.

"I'm afraid he's busy taking another call at the moment. Can I take a message?"

The caller hesitated. She heard him breathing down the line. "Tell him it's Christopher Finch. It's important that I speak to him."

"Well like I said, he's busy. I can have him call you back."

"I can't wait. I've got a meeting to attend to. Do you work for him?"

Amber pursed her lips. "Yes, you could say that."

"Well tell him one of the men he's arranged for tonight's team has pulled out. We need to find someone else, fast, otherwise the job's off."

Amber drummed her fingers on her thigh. She knew the job must be something important, and if it paid as much as John said, he wouldn't want to lose it. Besides, she owed him. Despite targeting him with her anger for Ms. Hawkins' death, she knew the only person to blame was herself.

"As long as you don't have any complaints about a woman taking the man's place, then there is someone who could step in," she said.

"A woman?"

"Highly trained. Three years as a Specialist Firearms Officer with the London Metropolitan Police. Before that she served five years in the army. Now she works as a security consultant."

"And how can I get in touch with her?" Finch asked.

"You already are," Amber replied with a smile.

THREE

By the time Amber arrived at the rendezvous point Finch had given her over the phone, darkness had smothered the light from the sky. The feeble glow of the moon illuminated the edges of baleful clouds overhead, but did little to lighten the surrounding countryside.

She knew she should have told John about what she'd done, but after what happened earlier, he might not be so keen on having her tag along, so she'd decided to keep quiet. Now that she was here, it would be too late to arrange for anyone else to take her place.

The potholed track leading to the farmhouse played havoc with the suspension of Amber's silver Audi TT, and she cursed each bump.

She saw Ms. Hawkins in her mind's eye, and chastised herself again for not preparing for the job, and for letting John convince her there wasn't any real threat. She should have known better. Her lapse in judgement and preparation had resulted in an unnecessary death. How could she have been so stupid? She had let both Ms. Hawkins and John down.

A couple of parked vehicles came into view, their bonnets peeking from the entrance of a dilapidated old barn. One appeared to be a new black Range Rover, the other a silver Porsche.

She parked alongside the barn, switched off the ignition, killed the headlights, and exited the car. The chill wind made her shiver. Several oak trees surrounded the property, their branches creaking in the breeze like arthritic old limbs.

Beside the barn stood a couple of outbuildings, in which most of the glass windows were broken.

She walked around the side of the barn and headed towards the house, her feet squelching through mud. A faint light shone around the edge of a boarded-up window in a ground floor room. Although she couldn't see anyone, she had the distinct impression of being watched, much like the feeling she'd had before Ms. Hawkins' demise. She hesitated, peered around.

A glint of light caught her eye, and she stared into the trees where she noticed a figure standing, watching her. The figure held a rifle of some sort—telescopic sight twinkling—which meant they didn't feel the need to stay hidden, otherwise the gun would be camouflaged and the optics covered. She guessed the person had been monitoring her since she drove towards the house. She spotted another figure silhouetted against the night sky on the roof of the outbuilding. The presence of armed guards—however inept—meant the people involved weren't taking any risks.

From the location, she knew the 'job' would be something clandestine, otherwise there wouldn't be any need for the out-of-the-way meeting place, which she had found with the help of her car's GPS system.

The farmhouse appeared rundown and uninhabited, the windows boarded-up. She noticed a couple of tiles missing from the roof, the guttering collapsed on one side. A couple of aerials bristled on the chimneystack, next to a satellite dish. At a quick guess, and going by the size of the place, Amber thought there were at least three or four ground floor rooms, and an equal number of rooms upstairs.

Once she reached the building, Amber noticed that despite the structure's general dilapidated appearance, the front door seemed new. The shiny screw heads on the boarded-up window beside the door also belied the rundown state.

Although hidden from the main road by a copse of trees, someone wanted to give the impression the building was abandoned, and to a casual observer, it might appear so.

Amber was unsure whether to knock. But before she could decide the door swung open.

"You must be Miss Redgrave, please come in," the man standing in the hallway said, stepping aside. Amber recognised the voice—the man she'd spoken to on the phone.

"Mr. Finch," she said, passing through the door.

He stood an inch or so shorter than Amber. His straight, shoulder-length brown ponytail accentuated his high forehead and the angles of his face, and the small dimple in his prominent chin looked like a thumb impression. Amber noticed an air of confidence about the man, apparent in his posture and expression, the thin gash of his lips a Plimsoll line on his face, which she guessed to be the only way to gauge his level of interest, as the rest of his face remained stoic.

"Next door on your left," Finch said as he closed the door behind her. "Go straight in."

The interior of the house kept with Amber's assertion that the outside was a ruse, the smell of fresh paint irritating her sinuses. Decorated in neutral colours, blue with white skirting boards, the nondescript hallway wouldn't look out of place in a newly built property, like any of those estates springing up all over the countryside.

Quiet chatter bubbled out from the room to the left. When Amber walked in, the occupants fell silent.

She recognised a couple of faces. Barry Adams, his bulky frame filling the leather chair by the boarded-up window, trademark Havana cigar glued between his lips. Amber had worked with Barry in Iraq, where the need for private security contractors meant there were rich rewards—rewards that far outweighed any risk involved. She didn't know a lot about Barry's history, but she remembered he used to be a member of the Parachute Regiment, the Airborne infantry element of the British Army, and was a good man to have on your side. She recognised another face: Lars Andersen, an ex-French Foreign Legion soldier built like a bull. She'd worked alongside Lars while protecting visiting dignitaries from Saudi Arabia. With his blond hair and chiselled Eastern European good looks, he could pass for a model. He stared at Amber, his blue eyes unfocused before he seemed to recognise her.

Both Barry and Lars nodded a greeting, the former raising his hand in recognition. But there was no sign of John, and her heart sank a little.

Amber did not recognise the other four men in the small, square room. One man sat in a chair at a long pine table cluttered with papers. He had a pockmarked forehead, black hair and almost toad-like characteristics. A nondescript man leaned against the wall on the left. Instantly forgettable, he would blend well into a crowd. The other two stood at the back of the room. One was a Slavic-looking man with piercing blue eyes, and the other was a bald man with a scar running through his lips that gave him a down-turned expression.

The room itself was decorated in magnolia, modern. Numerous up lights created warm illumination on the ceiling. The furniture consisted of two brown leather chairs. The long pine table was covered with a set of diagrams and maps. Nine metal high-backed chairs sat pushed underneath the table. The blank screen of a television inlaid in one of the walls cast a dark reflection of the room.

"Big Red, I didn't expect to see you here," Barry said, exhaling a cloud of cigar smoke. An ashtray rested on the arm of the chair at his side.

"You know what they say, Barry. You can't keep a good woman down."

"This is bullshit."

Amber turned to face the speaker: the tall bald-headed man with the scarred lip. He had a can of beer in his hand.

"I don't work with women," the man said, glaring at Amber.

Barry removed the cigar from between his lips. "Calm down, Eddie. Big Red's on the level. She knows the score."

"Bollocks. Women are only good for two things. No, make that *one* thing. Half of them can't cook for shit, which is why all the best chefs are men, and I'm not having a piece of skirt watching my back."

Amber stared at Eddie and smiled. She'd endured more than her share of egotistical men during her career. "Well, having one use is better than having none."

Eddie stood up straight. "What are you saying?"

"I should think that's obvious unless you're as stupid as you look."

Eddie squeezed the can of beer in his hand and foam poured over his fingers. "You cheeky bitch."

"Gentlemen—and ladies," Finch said, walking into the room. "We're all professionals here. Let's try to keep it civil."

"Professional? She's a woman."

Amber didn't need this shit after what happened this morning. "Although Dome Head's powers of perception are uncanny, you'd better tell him to keep a lid on it."

Eddie narrowed his eyes and glared at her. "No woman tells me what to do."

"I'd be surprised if any woman would want to come close enough to try it," Amber said.

She noticed the other men in the room watching with interest. They looked the sort to take bets on the outcome and, apart from Barry and Lars, the wry grins on their faces said they wouldn't be betting on Amber.

Barry guffawed, spewing a cloud of smoke from his mouth. "I think I'd quit while you're behind, Ed."

"Stay out of it. This is between her and me."

"On your own head be it." Barry tapped ash into the ashtray and settled back in the chair.

"Can we get on with the reason why we're here?" Lars said.

Finch clasped his hands behind his back and walked to the far side of the table. "Of course. My name's Christopher Finch. I work for…well, considering the circumstances, someone who would rather remain anonymous for the time being."

"Circumstances?" Amber said.

Finch motioned towards the table and chairs. "If everyone would like to take a seat, I'll fill you in on the details."

Barry pushed himself out of the chair and strutted across to seat himself at the table. The other occupants of the room did likewise. To her dismay, Amber found herself sitting opposite Eddie.

Finch sat at the head of the table, fingers tented on top of it. "I'm not going to beat around the bush. My employer is a wealthy businessman, and his two children have been kidnapped. My employer received a ransom demand for fifty million pounds for their safe return."

Eddie whistled through his teeth.

"Then I take it your employer doesn't want to negotiate," Amber said.

"Precisely. He feels that if he pays the ransom, then the kidnappers will execute his children."

"Based on what?" she asked.

Finch paused, his expression deadpan. "There was a similar incident a few months ago. It was all kept very hush hush, but a child was kidnapped from a private school in the Home Counties. The kidnappers requested that the parents not inform the police, otherwise, they'd kill the child. Taking the kidnappers at their word, the parents delivered the money to the location they were given. In return, they got their son back. Unfortunately, he was delivered in two pieces."

"The cruel bastards," Barry snarled.

"That's the reason you're all here. My client has instructed me to organise a rescue operation for his children before it's too late."

"Just like that," the nondescript man said. "And where are we supposed to start looking?"

"Before I go into details, I need to know that nothing I say now will go beyond these four walls."

Something didn't feel right about this. Amber tried to put her finger on what it was, but couldn't pin it down.

Why fabricate the building to look abandoned? Who owned it? Why were armed guards posted outside? Wouldn't it have been just as easy to convene in a room in a hotel?

She wondered whether the morning's fiasco had heightened her anxiety. Noticing Finch staring at her, she nodded. "Mum's the word."

"Speed is of the essence, so everyone who accepts the mission will have to leave tonight."

"Tonight?" the man with the pockmarked forehead said.

"The kidnappers have given my client twenty-four hours to gather the money. Almost twelve hours have already passed. When the time's up, they are going to ring to arrange where to drop the ransom. We need to act before that call is made."

"Who's to say the kids aren't already dead?" Amber said.

"That's a risk my employer is willing to take. If any of you don't wish to participate, then I suggest you leave now."

No one moved.

"Excellent," Finch said. "My employer threw some bait into the water, and we managed to get a bite. With such high-profile kidnappings, the kidnappers would have difficulty keeping their movements secret, but when someone offers a large sum of money as an incentive, you can virtually acquire their life history." He picked a remote control up off the table, pressed a button and the lights dimmed. He pressed another button and the television burst into life.

"These are the children: Robert and Lindsey," Finch said as the pictures of two kids flashed across the screen. "The girl's twelve and the boy's ten."

Amber fidgeted in her chair. They were cute. Both blond-haired with big, toothy grins. It sent a pang of anger through her to think they'd been kidnapped.

The screen went white before another picture appeared, showing a soldier with a mean glare. A series of shots followed, all of men in military garb.

"These are the most current pictures of the kidnappers that we were able to acquire. They are all extremely dangerous."

"So why not just inform the police and have them round the kidnappers up?" Amber asked. "They have people trained for this sort of thing."

The television screen went black and the lights came on.

"Hey, big mouth, are you trying to lose me my job?" Eddie snapped.

Finch held his hands up. "In normal circumstances, you're right. But my employer is not a happy man. He wants the kidnappers...how shall I put this...eliminated."

"So this isn't a rescue mission," Amber said, "it's a hit squad."

Eddie grinned. "What's the matter, babe, you squeamish? The sight of blood make you feel ill? I knew this was no job for a woman. They haven't got the bottle for it."

Amber stared across the table, the blood draining from her face. Her fight instinct kicked in and she felt her heart pound. "If you've got a problem with me, then I suggest we take it outside," she said, trying to keep her voice calm.

Eddie leaned back in his chair and laughed. "You? fight me? I don't fight women—all that scratching and hair pulling." He looked around the table for support.

"Why not? The way you act, you're more female than me."

Lars chuckled. The nondescript man laughed.

Eddie sat up straight. "If you weren't a woman, I'd—"

"You'd what?" Amber asked.

Finch shook his head. "Can we please concentrate on the task at hand? Lives are at stake. It doesn't serve any purpose fighting amongst ourselves like children." He paused. "Perhaps you're not the professionals I thought you were."

Eddie grunted and took a drink from his crumpled can of lager. "I'm the best you can get."

Finch stroked his chin. "Well, I hope your nickname of Crazy Eddie has more to do with being passionate than being foolish."

"I'm passionate all right." He stood up and thrust his hips forwards. "One hundred percent love machine. You ask any woman I've slept with."

A couple of men chuckled.

Amber rolled her eyes. She thought she would be hard-pressed to find any woman to back his claim up. "He didn't mean passionate that way, dumb nuts."

Eddie glared at her. "I know that. Can't you take a joke?" He sat back down.

"If we can get back to the details," Finch said. "From the information we gathered on the kidnappers, we've ascertained there are at least seven of them, all of whom have military experience, so we're not dealing with amateurs. These are professionals—men who will shoot first and ask questions later."

"What sort of military experience are we talking about?" the man with the pockmarked forehead asked.

"From what we know, these men were together in the army. When they left, they used their experience to plan these high-profile kidnappings, realising their talents could be put to monetary gain.

"They're holed up in the remote, abandoned lead mining village of Kilnhill. If you'll look on the table in front of you, you'll find plans for the town which we managed to obtain from library archives."

Amber opened the plans, which turned out to be an ornate old ordinance survey map, drawn in pen and ink. An area called Burnham Forest surrounded the village. Other names on the map included Peatland and Bogside written in stylised script. Hills averaging a thousand feet in elevation surrounded the area. There was also a modern version of the map, which didn't show the village of Kilnhill at all.

"So is the village still there?" the Slavic-looking man asked.

Finch nodded. "From what we can gather, it's fallen into ruin, but there are still buildings left intact."

Lars leaned forwards and studied the plans. "Looks pretty remote. What's the insertion plan?"

"As you can see, the area is surrounded by trees and the landscape is rugged, which is going to make progress difficult. Insertion is going to have to be by helicopter, with the landing zone about ten miles away from the target."

Amber looked up from the maps. "*About* isn't much good. For an operation like this, details need to be accurate."

Finch leaned across and prodded his finger at the map. "This circled area is the landing zone. As you can see, there's a river running almost all the way to the village."

"What about that road?" Barry asked, indicating a snaking line on the map.

"We expect the road, which is more of a track, to be monitored. It's not an option."

"What about this marshland?" Amber said, indicating an area on the map to the west of the village. "Your landing zone means we would have to traipse through the marsh."

"Yes. I think it will be the point of least resistance. If the kidnappers get wind of the rescue operation, they will figure the road to be the probable point of entry. They won't expect anyone to come in from the rear."

"I don't mind doing a bit of rear entry work," Eddie said with a smug grin.

"I presume you mean on men," Amber said, "as I doubt any woman would let you eat her shit, never mind prod it."

Eddie bristled. She saw him clench his fists. A couple of men laughed.

"Back to the mission," Amber said before Eddie responded. "Is there any reason to assume the kidnappers would be expecting a rescue operation?"

Finch shrugged. "One should always assume the worst case scenario."

"Which is?"

"That they know about the plan and have fortified their defences, or that they have withdrawn from the site, or that they have already killed the hostages."

Amber sat back and gazed over the maps. The terrain looked terrible. The forest and hills provided plenty of ambush sites, and the marsh would slow them down. Warning bells went off in her head. Although it might mean it would put the mission in jeopardy, after the Ms. Hawkins debacle, she wasn't about to commit herself to anything she didn't like the look of—not when she didn't have the time to plan ahead.

She stood up from the table. "I'm sorry, Mr Finch, but I think I was wrong. I'm not the right person for this job, so if you'll excuse me." She turned to walk away.

Eddie clapped.

"But—Miss Redgrave, we haven't gotten down to the nitty-gritty yet," Finch said.

Amber shrugged. "I think I've heard enough."

"For someone with your weapons training and military experience, this would be right up your street. I did a check on you. I was impressed enough with your credentials that I want you to head up the team."

"No way," Eddie said. "I'm not having a woman tell me what to do."

She ignored Eddie and looked at Finch. It would be good to accept—just to rub Eddie's nose in it. But it wasn't worth the hassle. "I'm sorry. I guess I'll just cut my losses and run."

"Yes, losses to the sum of one million pounds."

Amber rolled her shoulders. "Shared out between however many are onboard, it's not worth it."

Finch frowned. "I think you've misunderstood. That's one million pounds—each."

FOUR

Amber stopped dead in her tracks. A couple of the men whistled in surprise at the sum mentioned. She stared at Finch. One million pounds would more than boost her retirement fund. Hell, it would triple it.

"That seems a lot of money," she said, narrowing her eyes.

"It is. My client wants the best, and he's prepared to pay for the privilege."

"The deadline makes it risky. There's not enough time to plan, to acquire the equipment we would need," the Slavic-looking man said. His fair skin and blond hair were illuminated in the glow of the overhead lights, giving him an almost albino appearance.

"The equipment's not a problem," Finch replied.

Eddie stood up. "Look, if she's onboard, then I'm out of here."

"Mr. Bloor," Finch said, "think about it—one million pounds."

Amber could almost see the pound signs light up behind Eddie's eyes. He licked his lips. Swallowed. Stared at Amber.

"Why put her in charge?"

"Because she's qualified to do it."

"I'll vouch for that," Barry said. "You won't hear me complaining."

Before anyone else could comment, Finch stood up and headed towards the door. " Follow me and I'll show you what sort of equipment you'll be issued with."

Lars shrugged and followed Finch out the door, as did the man with the pockmarked face. The young Slavic-looking man walked out too, as did the nondescript man. Barry stood.

"Well, Big Red, you coming?" he asked.

Amber looked across at Eddie before nodding. "What the hell. May as well see what toys they've got."

She and Barry walked out of the room, along the hallway, and out the front door. She heard Eddie following close behind. He was going to be trouble. His sort always was.

Outside, the breeze tussled Amber's hair. She stared around. *Where was John?*

Finch stood in front of one of the outbuildings and fumbled with what appeared to be a brand-new padlock. After a moment, he undid the lock, slid a large bolt across and yanked the door open before disappearing inside.

Seconds later, light shone out the door, none of which radiated through the broken windows, which suggested the room was barricaded inside. Amber watched the men enter, then followed.

Once inside the room, she stared in awe at the shelves piled high with weapons. At a quick glance, she saw assault rifles, sniping rifles—including a Serbu .50BFG and a Dragunov SVDS—M203 grenade launchers attached to M16 rifles, H&K MP5 machine pistols, LAWs antitank rockets, scores of handguns, and cases of grenades and claymore mines. On top of that were piles of ammunition, webbing and other equipment.

The men walked along the shelves, taking down guns and checking the actions.

Amber whistled softly through her teeth. "You planning on equipping a small army?"

Finch shrugged. "Take what you want, courtesy of my employer."

"This employer," Amber said, "why would he have so much artillery?"

"He's a man who likes to be prepared."

"I'll say he's more than prepared," Barry said, picking up an M16.

"Holy shit," Eddie said, selecting an MP5. He held the machine pistol at arm's length and targeted down the site, aiming at Amber. After a second he grinned, tilted the gun, and blew imaginary smoke from the barrel.

Amber didn't like having guns pointed at her—even unloaded ones—which she couldn't be sure the MP5 was.

"So I take it everyone is onboard," Finch said.

Numerous heads nodded. Eddie added a "Hell yes."

Amber hesitated. Despite the money, the choice of team, primarily Eddie, needled her. She needed people who would watch her back—people she trusted. She recalled the images of the two grinning children, the pictures of the kidnappers.

Those poor kids must be terrified, she thought.

"Mr. Finch," she said, "you wanted me to take charge. Well, I have a few conditions before I agree. Number one, I want *him*," she pointed at Eddie, "off the team."

"No way, bitch," Eddie said.

Amber sighed. "You see what I mean?"

Finch shook his head. "Everyone's been chosen for a purpose. The choice of who goes and who doesn't isn't yours to make."

"Then what good would I be to you as a leader if I can't make a decision?"

"Once you're out in the field, you're in charge. Everyone who chooses to go, *will*"—he stared at Eddie—"follow your orders to the letter."

Eddie mumbled something incoherent.

"Now what other conditions have you got?" Finch continued.

"For one, I want to make sure there's a good extraction plan in place."

"All of that's in order."

Amber stared at him. "So, what is it?"

"As I said, you will be flown in by helicopter. Then, when the hostages have been rescued and the kidnappers have been dispatched, you will make your way to a point where the helicopter is able to land. The closest place is about four miles away from the objective."

"Then why don't we start there if it's closer?" Eddie asked.

"Because it's near the road and at night the kidnappers would probably hear you coming too easily. They would certainly hear the helicopter. There are hills and valleys between them and the present landing zone, which will muffle any sound. Any other questions?"

"How will we get the money? And what happens if any of us are killed? Will the money go to our next of kin?" Barry asked.

"The money will be transferred into an account of your choosing. Half will be transferred in immediately upon you accepting the mission if you have the details on hand, the rest on a satisfactory completion. And yes, if anyone is killed, the money will still be paid."

The door opened, and John Richmond stepped into the room.

"Sorry I'm late. Got held up at—" When he saw Amber, he stopped dead in his tracks.

Amber smiled, tried to make it nonchalant, but her heart started beating faster. "Surprise."

His right eye twitched and he clenched his jaw. "What the hell are you doing here?" he asked, anger in his voice.

Amber clasped her hands together, feeling slightly embarrassed. This wasn't the reaction she expected. "Mr. Finch called while you were on the phone earlier. He said someone had dropped out of the team, and he needed a replacement, otherwise the job would have to be abandoned. I knew how important it was to you, so I volunteered my services."

"And we're very glad she did," Finch said.

John shook his head. "No way. Not after what happened this morning."

"John, you know that wasn't my fault."

"It doesn't matter. You need time to get over it."

Eddie held his hand up. "Whoa. Is someone going to let the rest of us in on the secret?"

"Secret?" John said.

"About what happened this morning."

Amber swallowed. "It's none of your goddamn business."

"If it affects this mission, then it *is* my business."

"It doesn't affect anything," Amber snapped.

Finch looked at Eddie and then John. "I checked Ms. Redgrave's credentials, and I'm more than happy for her to take part. In fact, I'm so impressed, I've asked her to lead the mission."

John shook his head. "No way. Forget it. The mission's off."

Finch stared at each man in turn. "We haven't got time to make other arrangements. My employer's children are going to be killed. Even if you aren't bothered about that, then the money should be incentive enough to put your personal feelings aside."

"I'm in no matter what," the Slavic-looking man said.

Barry nodded. "Me too."

Eddie snorted loudly. "I'm not happy about having a woman in charge, but I can't afford to lose a million pounds."

John glared at him. "You have a problem with Red, you take it up with me."

"I can fight my own battles," Amber barked, although deep down she found his defence of her encouraging. It implied he was warming up to the idea of her being involved in the mission.

"I know," John replied. He looked at Finch. "Just give me a moment to talk to her alone."

Finch glanced at his watch. "We haven't got time. Either you're in or out. I'm sure we can manage without you."

John bit his lower lip, gazed at Amber, then back at Finch. He nodded. "I'm in."

* * *

The Bell 430 helicopter swooped over the trees. Amber stared out the window at her side, her stomach lurching. Darkness pervaded, the skyline a smudge against the cloud-filled sky.

The jet-black helicopter had arrived within minutes of them accepting the mission, landing in a field to the rear of the farmhouse. Amber hated flying in helicopters—they always made her feel queasy.

During the journey, she acquainted herself with the team. Aside from Barry, Lars, Eddie and John, she met Six-pack, the nondescript man who apparently acquired his nickname not for his physique, but for his ability to drink. TJ, the po-faced man with the pockmarked forehead and Scott Hunter, the young Slavic-looking man who assured everyone he was a hunter by name *and* nature.

From first impressions, they all seemed professional, but she didn't know if she would trust her back to any of the new faces. Barry, Lars and John she already knew well enough to trust. The others would have to earn that faith.

She watched as they applied camouflaged paint to their faces, the markings of the modern warrior, then she applied her own.

She noticed John kept glancing at her, but he didn't speak during the journey. He was probably angry that she'd answered his phone and invited herself along, and that she'd been selected to lead the team, but she was sure he'd get over it.

Amber wasn't happy with the setup. She would have preferred to know more about the strength of the enemy, more about their army experience, the weapons available to them and their state of readiness. Now she felt they were going in unprepared, and the sickly feeling in her stomach wouldn't settle.

About twenty minutes later, the helicopter touched down in a clearing among the tall trees and the team disembarked and offloaded the equipment.

Rain hammered down, and Amber ran a hand across her face to remove some of the moisture, squinting against the darkness.

As the helicopter took off, the team remained still and silent, giving them time to adjust to the environment, allowing them to switch their mindset to combat mode.

Amber's stomach began to settle, her eyes adjusting to the dark, allowing her to see the trees, the leaves rustling in the downpour.

Finch's voice emanated through Amber's earpiece. "Good luck, everyone. I'll be monitoring your progress. As soon as you've completed the task, I'll send the evac helicopter in. Out."

TJ donned a set of thermal imaging goggles.

"You see anything, TJ?" Amber asked.

"Nothing. Seems quiet enough to me."

Amber scanned the trees. Although she couldn't see anyone, the hairs on her neck prickled. It was a sensation she had quickly come to dislike. She chewed her lip and spun around. "TJ, you sure we're clear?"

"Positive. There's no one in the vicinity."

"What's the matter, Red?" Barry asked.

"Yeah, what's the hold up?" Eddie snapped.

Amber shrugged the feeling away. Not wanting to look spooked in front of Eddie, she put it down to delayed jitters and the flight. "Nothing. Just being cautious." She took out the handheld GPS system and checked their coordinates. "Right, we're ten miles away from the target, that's about sixteen clicks. Let's check the communications before we go any farther." She listened as everyone acknowledged themselves using the microphone and earpieces they all wore. "Okay, that's fine," Amber said. "TJ and Hunter, you scout ahead and see if you can see anything. Report back every two minutes."

She watched the two men disappear into the night. "Right, the rest of you follow me." Weighed down by a backpack and an assault vest crammed with grenades—both regular and stun—and ammo, she scooted across to the tree line. She had an

MP5 SD submachine gun fitted with a suppressor slung across her side, and an M9 9 mm Beretta pistol with a fifteen-round magazine strapped to her waist. When she reached the trees, she crammed a magazine into her pocket where she could reach it, felt the Zippo lighter nestled at the bottom. Although she no longer smoked, she always carried the lighter. It had been her brother Simon's and was the only thing of his she kept after his suicide—it meant a lot to her.

The patter of rain struck the leaves above, bringing down a potpourri of fragrances from the pine trees. Her heart pounded. Nothing else in the world gave the same adrenaline rush that accompanied life or death situations.

"What we waiting for?" Eddie hissed.

Amber glared at him, then pointed to the M-72 Light Anti-Tank Weapon strapped across his back. "You just be careful that you don't shoot yourself with that penis substitute, and leave the leadership to me."

Barry and Lars guffawed.

Eddie snorted loudly.

"Let's move out, single file," Amber said. "Six-pack, use the other set of thermal goggles and take point. Eddie, you follow, then me, then John, then Lars with Barry bringing up the rear."

"I want to take point," Eddie said.

Amber shook her head. *What is it with this guy? Is he determined to piss me off?* "It's not up for debate. Six-pack's taking point, now move out."

Eddie grumbled something, and then followed at a distance behind Six-pack.

The wind whipped through the fir, pine and larch trees, their branches creaking in response. Pine needles crunched underfoot, making silent movement difficult, and the uneven ground became more precarious as depressions full of foliage and needles turned into natural traps.

Using the landscape as cover, the team progressed through a gulley cut by heavy rainwater. They proceeded slowly, the ground difficult to navigate at speed. Amber placed her hands against tree trunks as support, the bark rough against her palms.

She thought back to the meeting at the farmhouse, and wondered why anyone would maintain such a well-stocked arsenal. It seemed like excessive paranoia. Along with the weapons, they'd been equipped with boots, combat clothing, webbing, communications equipment, GPS systems, food rations and water bottles. Everything they needed for the mission. If she didn't know better, she would think their employer gathered the equipment for just this purpose.

An owl hooted somewhere overhead. A moment later, she heard the muffled beat of its wings as it took flight. Amber signalled the team to halt. She wanted to make sure the owl hadn't alerted anyone to their presence.

"Come on, this isn't a ramble. It's going to be light before we get there," Eddie grumbled through the earpiece.

"Who's in charge here?" John asked. "It isn't you, so button it."

Although independent by nature, Amber appreciated having John on her side. She turned and nodded her thanks, wondering whether he still felt the same spark as she did, whether they could resume their relationship when this was over. The sex had been great. Better than great. The memory sent a delicious shiver down her spine. God, when was the last time she'd had sex?

She blocked the thought out. Now wasn't the time to get horny. She looked at Eddie, and the feelings floated away. *That creep could make a fortune as a contraceptive*, she thought. *His stare is better than a bucket of cold water.*

After a moment, she signalled they should move on. Textbook perfect, she guided the team across hills three-quarters of the way up to reduce any silhouette, and traversed clearings at their narrowest point.

Hunter and TJ radioed in every two minutes, but so far, everything seemed quiet.

Six-pack and Eddie were ahead of Amber, picking their way through a patch of ferns. She spotted movement forty feet or so in front of them. Hard to see in the dark, but she thought she saw something brush through the ferns.

"Six-pack," she whispered into her mouthpiece, "what's happening up there?"

Six-pack turned. "Nothing. Everything's clear."

"I thought I saw something moving—eleven o'clock."

Six-pack turned back and scanned the area she mentioned with the thermal goggles. "Nothing—"

A figure crashed out of the ferns, heading straight towards Six-pack. Bathed in darkness, it was hard to identify the figure as anything other than a moving shadow.

"Six-pack, look out," Amber said. She raised her gun, finger tensed on the trigger. Unable to identify the figure, she couldn't risk firing unless certain the person proved hostile.

She felt the beat of her heart, her temples throbbing in anticipation. Her breath was short, eyes straining to decode the puzzle of shadow as it loomed closer, crashing through the undergrowth with no concern for silence or stealth.

"Stop!" she barked. "Who's there?"

"Fuck this shit," Eddie said. A second later, a burst of automatic gunfire shattered the silence as Eddie opened fire with his Steyr Aug on full auto, unleashing a torrent of bullets that ripped through the undergrowth, obliterating everything in their path. Low-lying branches exploded upon impact, leaves dancing in the air. The figure bucked, flailed, fell without a sound.

Amber wheeled, ran towards Eddie and punched him in the face. Not expecting the blow, Eddie's head flew back. Recovering his stance, he held his weapon in one hand, pointed the muzzle at her stomach, and rubbed his chin with his free hand.

"What the fuck do you think you're doing?" Amber said, trying not to shout. "No one told you to open fire, you idiot."

Eddie glared at her. "Do you want some?"

Lars smacked Eddie's gun aside. "You dumb motherfucker. You've probably alerted the kidnappers to our presence."

"That *was* a kidnapper," Eddie replied.

"How can you be sure?" Amber spat. "It might have been a backpacker for all you know."

Eddie hesitated for a moment, and Amber saw a flicker of what she thought might be uncertainty.

"It wouldn't be a backpacker out here in the middle of the night," Eddie said.

Amber rolled her eyes, exasperated. "Lars, Barry and John, check the perimeter to see if there's anyone else around. Hunter, TJ, you okay? Over."

"Yeah," Hunter said through her earpiece. "We heard shooting, everything okay back there?"

"Someone's been a little trigger-happy. Are you sure you didn't spot anyone when you passed through?"

"Area was clean as a whistle. Why, what's up?"

"Someone just rushed out of the undergrowth, and Crazy fuckin' Eddie decided to make mincemeat of them."

"Was it one of the kidnappers?"

"I'm going to check on the body now. You guys keep a good watch and report anything unusual straight away." She turned to Six-pack. "How did you fail to spot whoever it was through the goggles?"

Six-pack shook his head. "I swear to God, there was no one there."

"Are those things working?"

"They're working fine."

Amber bit her lip. "Keep an eye on Eddie."

Eddie spat on the ground. "I don't need a babysitter. Shoot first, ask questions later. I've just saved your ass, and this is the thanks I get."

"Just watch him, Six-pack."

She crouched low and picked her way through the underbrush towards the body, brushing ferns aside as she went. Eyes now well accustomed to the dark, she found her night vision adequate to see the result of the gunfire. Leaves animated by the bullets drifted down around her. Some of the broken branches dripped resin, and part of a tree trunk bore the brunt of the attack. Its bark was shredded, the wood pulped and torn open as though punched with a pneumatic drill.

A full magazine on the Steyr Aug held 42 rounds, and by the looks of it, Eddie had emptied the lot. She knew he was going to be a liability, but this...

She sniffed the air, catching the unmistakable aroma of rotting meat. The closer she came to where she thought the body fell, the more powerful the stench became, and she wrinkled her nose. It smelled like something left out to rot, lying undiscovered in the undergrowth.

Knowing the devastation bullets wreaked on flesh and bone, she wasn't too keen on seeing the results of Eddie's mayhem, but she needed to identify the person.

She moved aside a fern with her foot, and spotted a hand clenched shut where she was about to tread. She crouched down and brushed the foliage aside to find the hand severed at the wrist. A stub of bone protruded from the meaty pulp, and closer to the ground, the horrendous smell clung to her nostrils and made her gag as it stuck to her throat.

A clump of broken ferns a couple of feet in front indicated where someone had fallen. Amber moved towards the patch, parted the foliage, and choked at the sight of a man's torso chewed by bullets, leaving jigsaw puzzle pieces in their wake. Entrails and guts slopped from the stomach cavity, the purple viscera snaking into the ferns as though trying to slither away.

The dreadful smell caused her eyes to water and forced her to cover her nose with her hand.

One of the bullets had torn the man's lower jaw off and ripped the flesh from the side of his face, leaving him with a grotesque, toothy grin. The separated portion of jaw hung on by a few threads of flesh, and the visible bone of his skull glistened in the dark.

Movement caught her eye, and she stared down at the corpse, stunned to see what appeared to be white maggots trickling like grains of rice from one of the bullet holes in its shoulder. She leaned closer, unsure whether her eyes were playing tricks, and the body suddenly twitched.

Amber jumped. Took a deep breath. Her heart thudded against her chest. Thinking it must be a death spasm as the body settled, she ignored the movement and prodded the entry hole with the muzzle of her gun, stretching the flesh to see more maggots wriggle out. Shocked and disgusted, she pulled back.

The figure sat up.

FIVE

Amber let out sharp breath and stumbled, almost losing her footing. Her skin crawled with revulsion. How in God's name was the man still alive? His lower jaw swung back and forth on a strand of flesh, glassy eyes regarding her with a look of hunger. As the man staggered to his feet, more entrails slopped from his stomach. Some of the bullets had torn straight through his body, leaving gruesome peepholes into the viscera.

Damaged beyond repair at the thigh, the man's left leg buckled underneath him and he crashed back down. Splintered and broken under the impact of a bullet, she heard the supporting bone crack.

On the ground, the man started crawling towards her, clawing at the dirt with his fingers. He cocked his head, stared up at her, teeth gnashing together. He didn't seem to register the pain of his open belly and shattered leg, didn't seem concerned that his insides trailed behind him like a leash, that his jaw dangled off and his useless leg dragged like an anchor.

Amber raised the muzzle of her MP5 and fired three shots in quick succession. Due to the silencer, the click of the action sounded louder than the muzzle burst that made a soft *phut phut*

phut sound. The bullets slammed into the man's head, shattering what remained of his skull and turning it into a bowl of bone.

Amber coughed and rubbed her eyes with the back of her hand. Wondered whether she could believe what she had just seen.

"What's taking you so long?" Eddie said in her earpiece, making her jump.

Amber turned and stared back through the foliage at Eddie and Six-pack. From where they stood, she knew they wouldn't have seen what just happened, the undergrowth too tall and thick. And even though sound travelled at night, the silenced gun would have sounded more like a sigh than a shot.

She looked back down at the body, prodded it with her gun to see if it moved. When the corpse didn't react, she crouched down, wrinkling her nose at the grotesque sight and holding her breath against the strange smell of putrefied meat. She did a quick search of the corpse's pockets but didn't find anything.

Fighting the gag reflex that made her throat tighten, she grabbed the man by the arm to turn him over. His flesh felt cold and clammy and she released her grip as though he had bitten her.

Amber frowned and shook her head. *It wasn't possible. He should still be warm.*

She turned away to take a fresh breath. A fly buzzed around her head. She tried not to wonder where it came from.

Not wanting to touch him again, and satisfied there wasn't anything else she could do, Amber stood up and hurried back towards Eddie and Six-pack.

"Who was it?" Six-pack asked.

Amber shook her head. "I don't know. There was no identification on him."

Six-pack sighed. "Do you think it was one of the kidnappers?"

Amber bit her lip. She stared at Eddie. If she told them what she had just seen, they would think her mad—and in their place, she'd be inclined to agree. For one thing, it would dispel their confidence in her as a leader. The man *couldn't* have moved. He *couldn't* have still been alive. No one could survive a hail of bullets like that. Jesus, the events surrounding Ms. Hawkins's death must have affected her a lot more than she realised. Out in the field, they called it shellshock. Out here, she called it fucked up.

"I can't be sure," she said.

"Who else could it have been?" Eddie said, as though her doubt vindicated him.

"We haven't got time to worry about it now." She activated her microphone. "Lars, Barry, John, you see anything out there?"

"Nothing," Lars replied.

"Ditto," Barry said.

"Quiet as the grave," John added.

"Okay, you guys, fall back in line. We're moving out."

Moments later she heard movement in the bushes as her team members stepped out.

John came up beside her. "I heard what you said," he whispered. "Couldn't you really be sure who he was? If he was one of the kidnappers, they'll probably expect him to report back."

Amber shook her head. "To be honest, I don't think it was a kidnapper." She opened her mouth to tell him what she had seen, then thought better of it. John thinking she was going crazy was no way to rekindle a relationship. "Whoever he was, he's dead now. There's nothing we can do for him. Come on, we've got a job to do."

She noticed John run his tongue around the inside of his gums, as though deliberating. "You mean he might have been some poor sap out rambling?"

"He was in the wrong place at the wrong time."

"You can say that again. Eddie's got a lot to answer for."

"Save it for later. Whoever he was, he's dead and there's nothing we can do. Now we have to concentrate on saving the hostages." She pressed the button to activate the microphone. "Everyone, let's move out."

Steady rain pattered against the leaves above. Where it dripped through the foliage, the ground squelched underfoot, the leaf mulch and soggy vegetation laid down over years trapping the moisture below.

The invigorating smell of pine filled the air, welcome relief after the aroma of rotten meat. That is, if she could trust her senses. Perhaps her sense of smell was as messed up as her perception. Perhaps there hadn't been a rotten smell. Perhaps now there was no smell of pine. Perhaps she imagined it all.

She tried not to let her mind wander down that path, because madness lay at the end. She needed to gather her wits. Pull herself together. Ms. Hawkins was old. She would have died sooner rather than later anyway—*but not by a bullet*. She chastised herself on the callous thought, knew it was no way to reconcile herself to a death caused by her own incompetence. *If only...* Two little words. She imagined there wasn't anyone alive who hadn't muttered them at some time.

The ground underfoot turned to marshland; the flatulent mud tried to steal her boots, making progress slow, and the air smelled pungent with rotting vegetation. Cotton grass nodded under the onslaught of the rain and in the distance, the hauntingly shrill call of a curlew rang out.

Amber continually wiped rainwater from her face, spitting out any that rolled into her mouth.

Combined with the odd rustle of furtive night time creatures, she worried old trigger-happy Eddie would open fire again. She'd met his sort before, hotheads who engaged their mouth before their brain. If he did anything like that again, she knew she would have to do something to assert her authority. But that was a bridge she would cross if, or rather *when*, it arose.

A quick check of the GPS revealed that they'd covered five miles. Comparing the distance travelled with the time taken, she worked out that if they continued at that pace, it would take another two hours or so to reach the abandoned mining village.

Then the real action would start. She felt her insides tie themselves in knots, and a sick feeling resided at the back of her throat. Perhaps she was getting too old for all this.

Not that she really believed that. She'd always been unconventional. As a child she'd preferred playing cowboys and Indians—with her holding the gun—rather than doctors and nurses. She made up for that with the adult version, remembered a raunchy episode with John where things got out of hand in the heat of the moment, and he ripped beyond repair the rubber nurse's uniform she'd bought. The thought brought a smile to her face.

The sound of a breaking branch snapped her back to reality. Her earpiece clicked.

"There's something up ahead," Six-pack said.

Amber dropped into a crouch and signalled the team to follow suit. She had visions of Eddie opening fire again. This close to the village, that would be a disaster. They could kiss goodbye any hope of taking the kidnappers by surprise.

"Everyone *hold* fire," she whispered, trying to put a menacing inflection to her voice. She scanned the marsh. "Six-pack, what is it?"

"I'm not sure. It's giving off a heat signature, and it's moving. Coming towards us at ten o'clock."

Amber tensed her finger on the trigger of her gun. She hoped the beat of her heart wasn't loud enough to reveal her presence.

She moved her head and looked towards the ten o'clock position, saw grass sway, heard something moving through the vegetation.

A cold sweat beaded on her forehead. Anyone who said they didn't feel fear was a liar. Fear kept you alive. It provided the adrenaline needed to survive. Her heart thudded inside her chest, her temples throbbed.

She held her breath. Muscles tensed. Eyes and ears straining to detect movement and sound.

"It's got to be more kidnappers," Eddie whispered in her earpiece.

"Hold your fire," Amber repeated, trying to make her whispered words sound menacing enough to prevent any rash action on Eddie's part.

The foliage up ahead rustled. She spotted Six-pack a few feet in front and to her left, the barrel of his gun pointed in the direction of the noise.

Something rushed out of the undergrowth. Amber's heart stopped. Her throat went dry. She fell back onto her bottom with a splash. The stock of the MP5 pressed tight into her shoulder. She tensed her finger on the trigger, the selector still set at three-round bursts, more than enough to dispatch whatever it was.

Two glassy eyes peered at her. As Amber assimilated what she saw, she relaxed her finger on the trigger.

"Don't shoot. It's only a badger," she said.

Probably more scared than she was, the creature waddled back into the undergrowth.

Amber exhaled. Panted for breath. *Jesus Christ.*

She heard someone laughing in her ear, but couldn't tell who. She *really* didn't need this shit.

SIX

The kettle came to the boil on the gas oven ring, whistling as though in pain.

"Samuel, what's the point of putting the kettle on if you're not going to take it off when it's boiled?" Jill Peters said, removing it from the cooker.

Samuel Green, otherwise known as Lofty due to his height of six-foot-four, looked up from the kitchen table, tugged his goatee, and mouthed a silent apology. He knew if Jill called him Samuel, he was in trouble. It had been the same when he lived at home with his parents. Most of the time they called him Sam, but whenever they needed to stress their anger or displeasure, it became Samuel—with an emphasis on the initial Sam.

The piercing through Jill's tongue clicked against her teeth as she tutted. She shook her head, the snakelike red dreadlocks slithering across her shoulders, a bright contrast to her pale features. She narrowed her green eyes, accentuating the dimples in her cheeks.

"Did you put it on for a reason?" she asked.

"Yeah, you know, I was going to make a brew."

"So what stopped you?"

Lofty peered over the top of the newsletter that had kept him engrossed for the last fifteen minutes with its various reports on animal welfare and comments on animal liberation.

"I was reading. You know what I get like. You can make it if you like."

"Can I now? What did your last slave die of?"

"Probably thirst." He grinned, revealing pearly white teeth that he knew accentuated his square-jawed face and deep blue eyes.

Jill feigned exasperation. "Now I know why you didn't take to the stage."

As though he hadn't heard, Lofty pointed at an article in the newsletter. "Jesus! Did you know there's an animal testing place near here?"

Jill arched her eyebrows. "Really? Where?"

"Outside the city. Says here they've been operating for years."

Jill sat at the table next to Lofty and snatched the newsletter from him. "This close to us! How come we didn't know about it?"

Lofty stroked his goatee. "That's what I was thinking."

"This is outrageous. People need to be told."

Lofty continued to stroke his goatee, lost in thought, his gaze fixed on the pile of dirty dishes in the sink. The pile grew taller by the day, neither of them willing to concede defeat in the ongoing battle over household chores.

"Did you hear me?" Jill said.

"Yeah. I think we should go look at it."

Jill frowned. "You know what happens when you act without thinking."

"I only said I want to look at it."

"That's what you said last time." She raised an eyebrow. "Remember?"

Lofty shook his head. "That was different."

"Different! You glued yourself to the slaughterhouse door."

"Well, it worked didn't it? It made a few people think and it gave some animals a few extra hours of life."

"Yes, you made the front page, but you were only supposed to glue up the lock. You cocked up. They had to get the fire brigade out and everything. *And* you ended up with a fine which, I might add, we're still paying."

"Yeah. I should refuse to pay it."

"Oh no you won't. You're on probation, remember? It's bad enough mum and dad thinking I'm shacked up with a militant leftist without you going to prison, too. Mum would have a fit."

"Your mum likes me. She'd be cool."

"If she liked you that much, how come she always makes you enter the house through the back door?"

Lofty rolled his shoulders, eyebrows raised. "What you saying?"

Jill sighed. "Forget it."

"No, I want to know. Are you saying she doesn't like me?"

"It's all about appearances. She would have a fit if the neighbours saw you entering the house. You've seen what she's like with me. She makes me wear a hat when I call round so they can't see my red dreads. She calls you a tattooed rapscallion."

"A rap what?"

"You know, a rogue."

"Yeah, but a lovable one." Although he tried to make light of it, he was hurt to think that Jill's mother thought of him that way. He'd always thought she liked him, and had just assumed that he had to use the back door because he never took his boots off, and they didn't want dirt on the carpet.

Jill put the newsletter down on the table. "Sorry. I shouldn't have said anything."

Lofty shrugged. "Anyway, I wouldn't mind going to have a look at that place. See if we can find out any more about it."

"I think it'll be enough to print some leaflets up and post them through letterboxes to let people know what's on their doorstep."

"Saying what? The reporter in the article says he doesn't know the extent of the experiments, never mind what goes on.

All he says is that they've had regular deliveries of dogs from that breeding supply company, you know, the one we demonstrated outside. And you know what that means."

Jill arched her eyebrows. "You mean the building we demonstrated outside when we actually found the right place? Trust you to have us start demonstrating outside a knicker factory. That security guard thought we were crazy."

"Well they shouldn't have had so much security. How was I supposed to know it was farther down the road?"

"Because you should have checked first."

Lofty grinned. "What do you think I want to do now? I want to find out more about the place. Think of those poor animals."

"I *am* thinking about them. But it's the middle of the night, and what are we going to find out from the outside?"

"I don't know what we'll see, but there'll be less people around to spot us. Come on, it's only about fifteen minutes away."

"The way you drive, more like four hours away." Jill grinned and crossed her arms.

"Come on, it'll be fun."

"Look at me. I haven't even washed my hair."

"It looks fine to me. Besides, no one's going to see you." The expression on Jill's face told him he had her convinced. He smiled. "It won't take long. Just a look. Then we can catch last orders at The Star and have a pint—Stan'll have a lock in. He always does."

"And you're sure you know where the place is?"

"Positive."

Jill narrowed her eyes and glared at him in mock anger. "You'd better be."

"Trust me." He stood up. "I'll even make us a brew before we go."

He squeezed past Jill to reach the kettle. This wasn't exactly the life he'd imagined for himself, and even though they had only been together for a year, he wanted to give Jill more—a nice house with a garden to grow their own vegetables. But with house prices in the city more than the bank balance of some small countries, he didn't see how he would ever afford it on his pittance of a wage working in the late shop four days a week. God, he hated that job. Jill was studying to be a graphic designer at the university, and they only made ends meet through frugal use of her student loan.

The sparse bed-sit consisted of a second hand kitchen table and two chairs liberated from a skip down the road and a double bed made warmer by all the clothes scattered across the duvet. They also had a small fridge freezer bought for them by Jill's parents, and a two-ring cooker barely adequate for cooking on, and which they had used to warm the room in the winter when the industrial scene outside the window became a cold mosaic through the frosted glass.

Jill squealed. Lofty wheeled around.

"Spider," Jill said. She sat with her legs tucked beneath her, arm extended to point towards the scurrying arachnid.

Although it wasn't a large spider, Lofty wasn't fond of them himself. He crouched down and shepherded it onto his hand. The black spider ran across his palm and up his arm, tickling the hairs. Lofty cringed and tried to coax the spider back down. Jill backed as far away as possible, arms wrapped around her legs.

"Kill it," Jill squealed.

Lofty shook his head, opened the window, and blew the spider outside.

"It'll only come back again," Jill said.

"And if it does, I'll put it out again."

Jill relaxed and let out a small sigh.

Lofty took the teabags from a wall cupboard beside the sink. The bags of rice and lentils were almost empty, which meant a walk to the cheap supermarket a couple miles away. He made a mental note to write a shopping list in the morning.

* * *

Lofty steered the orange VW camper van through the streets. Rescued from a scrap yard and lovingly restored over four years—when he could afford parts—the vehicle was his pride and joy. He would like to use it more, but the price of fuel made it an impossible dream. He knew one day he might have to sell it, but for the moment he put the thought out of his head.

Jill sat beside him, using the interior light and a small handheld mirror to check her makeup. When she finished, she sat drumming her fingers on her knees to the sound of "Killing in the Name" by Rage Against the Machine blasting out of the stereo cassette player. Lofty liked to play this tape whenever they were 'on a mission.' It fired him up and got his adrenaline pumping.

Rain beaded the windscreen. He activated the wipers to clear the view.

A car horn sounded as Lofty pulled out of a junction without looking properly. The vehicle came right up behind him, the driver flashing his lights in annoyance.

"Bloody hell, are you trying to get us killed?" Jill said.

Lofty shook his head. "Sorry." He rolled his window down and put his hand up to the driver behind to acknowledge his mistake. Next minute, the car pulled out and drew alongside. The driver ducked down and peered up at Lofty, mouthing obscenities and gesturing with his hands. Lofty mouthed a silent apology, and the car sped in front, braked suddenly to reassert his position, then accelerated away.

Lofty exhaled and tapped the steering wheel as if to reassure the vehicle that everything was OK and that he was sorry for the near-miss.

The gaps between streetlights grew more pronounced, plunging the camper van into darkness for long periods of time. The few houses alongside the road eventually gave way to industrial units, then to fields. The headlights illuminated the leaves of the high hedgerows, chased shadows through the fields beyond.

"It's going to be too dark to see anything," Jill said. "Why don't we just go to the pub instead?"

"We're almost there now."

A hundred feet farther on, Lofty indicated to turn left. Once he navigated the turn, he switched the headlights off.

"You *will* get us killed," Jill squealed. "Turn the lights back on."

"I don't want them to see us. I think the place is just up ahead." He leaned forwards to peer through the windscreen, his eyes not yet accustomed to the dark. "There's a lay-by here somewhere."

"I'm not going to ask how you know," she said, hands braced against the dashboard as though she feared the worst. "This is crazy."

Up ahead, a sign indicated the stopping place, and Lofty pulled in and switched the engine off. The music ceased playing when he killed the power, and the engine made a plinking sound as it cooled. He heard Jill exhale. By the sound of it, she wasn't happy.

"I think it's just up ahead and around the corner. There's a unit there, used to be a car components factory I think, but they shut it down years ago. I'm assuming they bought it."

"So how do you know this area so well?"

"Erm, I just do, I guess."

"I want to know."

"No, you don't."

"You used to come here with Dawn, didn't you? Tell me the truth."

Lofty tapped his fingers against the steering wheel. This wasn't the time to be talking about his ex-girlfriend—he especially didn't want to tell her that she used to drive him out here to have sex when they had nowhere else to go. He needed Jill to be on side. If he admitted that to her, she would get in one of her jealous moods and that would be that. He knew she often thought he had started seeing her on the rebound as they started dating only a couple of weeks after he split with Dawn, or rather, she split with him, but that wasn't the case at all.

"I know the area because my dad used to drive me out here to pick mushrooms in the fields opposite, you know."

Although hardly able to see Jill in the dark, he felt her staring at him. She didn't reply. The silence was ominous. Then he felt her hand grab his knee and squeeze.

"Sorry," she said. "You know I don't like that cow. Just the thought…"

Lofty leaned across and kissed her on the cheek. "I know, but you've got nothing to worry about. I'm with you now."

Jill squeezed tighter, her fingernails gouging through his jeans. "Good, because if I thought you were lying to me—"

Lofty grimaced and lifted her hand off his leg. "You know I wouldn't dare." He let out a small sigh, rolled his eyes, then opened his door and exited the vehicle before the inquisition restarted.

The air was cool. Lofty shivered and gooseflesh erupted along his arms. Tall trees lined the lay-by, their branches rustling in the slight breeze. Raindrops pattered against the canopy above. The drops that navigated the leaves tinkled on the camper van.

Lofty stuffed his hands in his pockets and stared along the road. He sucked his bottom lip in as he considered what to do next.

"We may as well get this over with," Jill said, stepping out of the vehicle and shutting the door behind her.

Pleased to hear that Jill wanted to proceed, Lofty nodded, then reached through the open door and withdrew a small rucksack.

"What's in there?" Jill asked, walking around to his side.

"Just a few things. You know, my camera."

"Big bag for a camera."

"Well it's not just a camera."

"What else?" She stood akimbo, giving him one of her challenging looks.

"I didn't empty it from the other month, you know, that Korn concert we went to, so it's still full of shit. I just couldn't be bothered to sort it out. I threw the camera and a torch on top."

"I'm sure you get lazier by the day."

"That's why it's good I've got you to look after me." He grinned. "Come on, let's go."

SEVEN

"It's not on the map," Amber said, frowning as she stared through the trees at what appeared to be a derelict farmhouse.

Eddie snorted. "It's got to be on the map, unless you're reading the map wrong. You sure you've got it the right way up?" He sniggered.

Amber ignored him and stared at the farmhouse TJ and Hunter had reported coming across a couple of minutes earlier.

Through gaps in the overhead canopy she saw clouds scudding across the sky, the faint glow of the moon a smudge in the blackness where the cloud cover thinned. The wind chased through the trees, picking up any loose leaves and animating them into life, making them look like scuttling insects. The rain had stopped for the moment, leaving the aroma of fresh ozone and foliage in the air.

She imagined that during the day the forest would look beautiful, full of greenery highlighted by dappled sunlight. But at night, it became a grey canvas upon which the imagination painted chilling scenes. A place of nightmare and illusion, where savage creatures sought out prey.

"TJ, have you seen anyone around?" she asked into the microphone.

"No one," TJ replied in her earpiece.

She couldn't see TJ or Hunter, but she knew they were hunkered in the undergrowth somewhere to her left.

"Six-pack, you reading anything?"

"Nothing. There's no one here."

After the earlier debacle, Amber wasn't taking any chances. She sensed someone watching her, and she scanned the surrounding trees, eyes narrowed to see in the feeble light. "You positive?"

"Take a look for yourself if you don't believe me."

Normally, Amber would take the man at his word, but not this time. She held her hand out. Six-pack handed over the thermal imaging goggles, his lips pinched tight, eyes narrowed.

"I'm sure you know what you're doing, but I just want to be doubly sure," she said. "We've been thrown together at the last minute. None of us knows much about each other. And at the end of the day, our lives are on the line."

"Well, if we're going to gel," Six-pack replied, "then you need to trust me."

Amber twiddled with the goggles in her hand. She stared at Six-pack in the gloom. With Eddie already opposed to her leadership, she needed to keep everyone else on side, and questioning their word wasn't the way to go about it.

"You're right," she said, handing him back the goggles.

Six-pack took the goggles and nodded. "If this is about earlier, I don't know what happened, but I swear on my son's life, that man didn't register. It was as if he weren't there."

Amber remembered the maggots falling from the corpse and she shivered. Had she really seen them? Had the man really still been alive after being shot so many times? She knew the mind played cruel tricks in times of stress. She wished she could be certain about what happened.

"So what now?" John asked.

Amber pinched her bottom lip between her thumb and finger as she considered their options.

"John, follow me. We're going in to take a look around. The rest of you, cover us."

"We haven't got time to be messing about here," Eddie said.

"Being thorough isn't messing about. What if the kidnappers are using this place as a lookout post? We've got to make sure."

"But if Six-pack says the place is clear, then we know there's no one here. So let's go."

Amber turned on Eddie and said, "Just watch our backs. If you fuck up again, then you'll have me to answer to."

Eddie shrugged, unimpressed. Amber knew if she didn't rein him in, then he would get even surlier, undermining her authority at every turn. She crawled towards him on her hands and knees, then reached out without warning, grabbed his jacket and brought her face close enough to his to smell the faint trace of shaving foam beneath the camouflaged paint.

"*I'm only going to say this once. You do what I say, or you're out of here*," she hissed.

Taken by surprise, Eddie stared at her wide-eyed. After a moment, his eyes narrowed and he nodded, jaw tensed.

She could tell he didn't like being told what to do by a woman, but that was his problem. The same sexual discrimination had blighted the whole of her life. In terms of equality, some were more equal than others. All of her jobs had been in male-dominated worlds: the army, the police, and now security consultancy. Every day was a battle for recognition to show that she could do her job as well as any man, which was why, in one sense, she was secretly pleased Finch had put her in charge.

Amber turned back to face the farmhouse and indicated to John that they should make a move. The sensation of being watched intensified, but this time she knew its source—thankful the daggers were only in Eddie's eyes and not in his hands.

Earthy aromas filled the air. Scattered among the tall trees, the dense boughs of common juniper provided cover, but also made movement difficult. Amber brushed the undergrowth aside. At a higher elevation than the farm, she had a good view where the foliage thinned out. A rough track led away from the house, and a number of outbuildings, all of which looked beyond repair, bordered the forest.

Taking the lead, she crawled through the dense undergrowth. Sharp pine needles on the ground stabbed her hands and knees, but she ignored the pain as she kept her eyes and ears alert.

It started raining again, sounded like it sizzled on the foliage. Although the inclement weather made movement uncomfortable, it helped deaden any noise they made as they crawled down the bank towards the farm.

The ground felt moist under her hands, squelched in places. She remembered the cold, clammy texture of the dead man's flesh and shivered, repulsed by the memory. Damn it. If only she could go back and double—even triple—check the corpse. She imagined it lurching through the trees behind her, entrails snagging on the dense undergrowth. But the man couldn't follow her. He was dead. A stream of thoughts ran through her head. She had never felt this way before, was usually in control. Now she felt… What did she feel? She expected to feel tense on a mission, even a little uneasy and scared, but what she felt now went beyond that. Chilled to the bone was the best way she could describe it. The more she thought about it, the more she believed she'd seen the man move. That he had started to stand. Impossible as it seemed, she didn't think she was going mad.

"Are you listening?" John asked.

Realising he had been speaking, she said, "Sorry, what did you say?"

"I asked if you could see anything."

"Nothing," Amber replied. "Let's get a little closer."

Although rundown with missing tiles and cracked windows, the two-story building offered a defensive firing position for anyone hiding inside. They approached with caution. Amber didn't want to expose them to sniper fire, so she made full use of the terrain, using structures for cover: an old, rusted green tractor, an overflowing water butt, the side of a barn, long-abandoned farm machinery. Once she reached the farmhouse, she ducked beneath the window on the front of the building so as not to be seen by anyone that might be inside.

The glass in some of the windows was smashed, but the paint-cracked red front door was intact and closed. She motioned to John to stand aside and kicked the door, splintering the wood and sending the remains flying inside the building. Without hesitating, John switched on his torch and rushed into the house, the barrel of his colt commando sweeping left and right, his finger tensed on the trigger, ready to open fire with a weapon that unleashed 750 rounds per minute.

"Clear," he shouted.

Blood surged through her veins, breath short and fast. Amber switched on the torch attached to the underside of her weapon and followed him in, sweeping the light around the room. There were a few remnants of furniture, including a threadbare settee, a desk, and a footstool. Apart from that, the room was empty. Pungent fungal growths sprouted from the tattered carpet, and part of the ceiling had collapsed. Water dripped down, indicating tiles missing from the roof, the upper stories fallen through, the wood rotted by years of rain, giving the building a damp atmosphere.

Amber picked her way through the debris to the door opposite, and followed the same procedure of kicking it open, allowing John to rush through. If anyone were inside the house, the noise they made entering alerted them to their presence, so they needed to act fast, checking each room as quickly as possible.

Four rooms later, Amber announced the building clear to the rest of the team. From the state of the place, she didn't think it had been inhabited for several years—at least. Dust coated most surfaces, and where the building lay open to the elements, plant life crept inside. A small tree sprouted from the corner of the room.

"We'll have to make up time after this," she said to John. "But I had to be certain, didn't I?"

He nodded. "I'd have done the same."

She didn't know why she felt the need to hear him vindicate her action, but his response lifted her spirits. She smiled. "Do you remember that day in Paris?"

John grinned. "How could I forget?"

Her smile faded. "I made a mistake, you know when I broke it off—"

"We can talk more when this is over." He put his hand on her shoulder, squeezed.

Amber felt a lump in her throat and her heart did a little summersault.

"If you lovebirds have finished, we've got a job to do," Eddie said, standing in the doorway, grinning.

Amber shone the beam of her torch at him, making him cover his eyes with his hand. She wanted to wipe that sanctimonious smile from his face. She clenched her fist, tightened her grip on the gun with the other hand, took a deep breath, and exhaled slowly.

"Let it go," John whispered in her ear. "He'll get what's coming to him sooner or later."

"Probably sooner the way he's going." *One bullet, that's all it would take. Who would know?* The callous thought made her shiver, made her wonder how far she would go if pushed to the edge. She looked down, noticed her hand trembling. She swallowed, switched the torch off to allow her night vision to return, turned and walked past Eddie and out of the room. "TJ and Hunter, continue up front," she said into her microphone. "The rest of you, hold your position, we're coming out."

Outside, she breathed in the aroma of the trees, welcoming the cool breeze and the chill of the rain as it spattered against her face.

A bang caught her attention, and she spun around, noticed the door to the barn flapping in the wind, almost beckoning. She stepped towards the structure, the corrugated panels clattering.

Although she couldn't see the rest of the team, she felt them watching her. At least she hoped it was only the team—the niggling sensation still gnawed away at the back of her neck, giving her a chill.

"Amber, what's wrong?" she heard Lars ask in her earpiece.

"I'm just going to check out the barn," she replied. "Cover me."

With her vision still affected by the torchlight, she couldn't see too well, but she noticed the glint of metal inside the structure. As she approached, the shape of a vehicle materialised from the dark.

When she reached the door, she reached out to stop it from banging. The wood felt cold, wet and brittle. The vehicle inside the barn turned out to be an old Land Rover peppered with rust. Amber stared at it for a moment. She wondered whether it worked, but didn't have time to find out now. Straw covered part of the ground, and old farm implements hung from the back wall, among them a sickle and pitchfork. A ladder led up to a second floor. The ladder looked liable to break if anyone used it, so she decided no one had been foolish enough to climb up to hide.

After another quick look around, she retreated from the barn. "Okay, let's get a move on," she said into her microphone. Although she loathed admitting it, Eddie was right and they needed to make up time.

She watched him traipse out of the farmhouse, a smug look on his face as he scurried back into the tree line. *One bullet. One goddamn bullet. That's all it would take,* she thought, following behind.

EIGHT

The spotlights bordering the research facility illuminated the drops of rain, turning them into balls of silver fire. Lofty peered through the hedge and stroked his goatee.

"There's no way we're getting anywhere near that place," Jill said. "We may as well go straight to the pub now."

Ignoring her, Lofty continued staring at the building. A high fence topped with barbed wire encircled the clinical looking property. If it wasn't for the fence, the security cameras posted at every corner, the guard on the gate and the spotlights, the building would be nondescript, a green shell similar to thousands of industrial units up and down the country.

"Samuel, are you listening to me?"

Lofty turned to Jill and frowned. "What?"

"I said we may as well go. There's no way we're getting anywhere near there."

"We haven't looked yet."

"Looked at what? It's lit up like a Christmas tree, and it's got more cameras around the place than Big Brother, so unless you're looking to get caught, we'd better go. *Now.*"

"Let's at least have a look now that we're here."

"A look at what? The inside of a cell? That place is shut as tight as your wallet."

"How can you say that?"

"You've got eyes. Look at the place."

"No, I mean about my wallet. When have I ever been stingy? I spend every penny I earn in the late shop helping support us, you know that."

"I was being flippant. Lighten up."

Lofty stared at her in the dark, just able to make out her features in the wan glow of the spotlights. Despite declaring her remark off-the-cuff, he felt it signified something deeper, perhaps some resentment to the way they lived. He wondered if it meant she was falling out of love with him. The thought brought a lump to his throat. He thought the world of Jill. Even though they argued, he felt they had a rapport. He'd never met anyone he felt as much about, and he knew most of her comments were impulsive. That's just the way she was.

He swallowed. "I love you, you know."

Jill nodded, her dreadlocks dangling. "I know."

Her lack of reciprocation caused a lead weight to settle in his stomach, intensified his fear of losing her to someone else, someone with a good job, with prospects, not someone scraping a living serving the deadbeats and drunks wandering the streets at night.

Tears moistened his eyes and he wiped them away.

"Come on, let's go," Jill said, starting to crawl back through the hedge.

"Wait a minute. We're here now. Let's take a quick look around. I won't do anything stupid."

"This is just typical of you, Samuel. You drag me out here in the middle of the night, in the pouring rain, and you haven't got a clue what you're doing."

"If you're not going to do it for me, think of the animals suffering in there right now. We owe it to them to at least have a look around. No one can stop us looking around the outside because it's public property."

Jill stopped. She peered back at him, her face almost hidden by leaves. "One quick look," she said, "then we're out of here."

"I promise."

He exhaled a relieved sigh and turned his attention back to the building. An illuminated red sign stood on the grass beyond the entrance: *Strident Industries.* Floral displays blossomed on either side of the sign.

"There's a road along the side," Lofty said, pointing through the thicket. "If we keep on the other side of this hedge, we can make our way around without being seen by the guard. If we're lucky, there might be a window. I've got the camera, and we could get some shots with the zoom lens."

"We've probably got a better chance of winning the lottery than getting any meaningful pictures."

"Yes, but we don't play the lottery. This is real. We're here now, and we won't know unless we try. Come on, follow me."

Besides shielding them from view, the tall hedge also blocked out the light from the spotlights. Lofty hunched his shoulders against the weather and trudged through the wet grass. Not dressed for the conditions, his trainers were soaked through.

Jill squealed. Lofty's breath caught in his throat and he spun around.

"What's happened?"

"I'm stuck in the mud, that's what's happened. My boots will be ruined. I knew I shouldn't have come."

Lofty smiled to himself, then reached out and grabbed Jill's arms. He tugged, heard a squelch as her feet pulled free from the mud, and the quiet curses muttered beneath her breath.

"It's only a bit of mud," he said. "You're happy enough to slap it on your face, you know, with those mudpacks." As soon as the words left his mouth, he regretted not engaging his brain first.

"That's special mud, not this stinking pile of—"

Lofty covered her mouth with his hand. "Keep it down," he whispered. "Someone might hear."

Jill batted his hand away. He heard her breathing, the sound relaying her peeved disposition.

"I didn't mean it like that," he said.

"I know what you meant. You meant I spend too much money on makeup—which I only do to try to look my best. Would you rather I look like a dog, like *Dawn*?"

Lofty grimaced. How in hell had she twisted the conversation back onto his ex-girlfriend? "Of course not. I didn't mean it like that."

A loud agonised howl pierced the night, originating from the vicinity of Strident Industries. Jill reached out and squeezed Lofty's arm.

"Jesus, did you hear that?" she said.

Lofty nodded. The hairs along his arms stood to attention. "My god, what are they doing in there?"

"Let's find out."

Before Lofty responded, Jill proceeded through the field. "Come on, hurry up," she hissed over her shoulder.

Lofty couldn't believe the rapid change in her interest. His only regret was that it took the suffering of an animal to bring it about.

The long grass soaked the bottom of his jeans, the damp spreading through the material as though it were litmus paper, turning his lower legs blue with cold. He shivered, trying to block out the feeling as he concentrated on the sound of the animal—like it was being tortured. The last time he'd heard anything remotely similar was when he'd demonstrated outside a slaughterhouse where they killed the pigs, their cries like those of babies squealing.

When she reached the end of the field, Jill stopped and waited. Lofty caught her up, breathing heavy after the exertion of trudging through the swampy ground.

"We'll need to crawl under the hedge and cross the road," Jill said, breathless.

Lofty nodded, unable to believe the chain of command passed over so easily. "Just let me catch my breath," he said.

"You haven't got any water in that rucksack by any chance?"

"I don't think so." He slipped the bag from his shoulder and rummaged inside. "Hold on, what's this." He pulled out a bottle and held it up. It felt about half-empty. "There's a bit of this Lucozade left."

"How longs that been in there?"

"Since the Korn concert I suppose."

Jill shook her head, dreadlocks whipping Lofty's face. "Any other time I would moan about your lack of tidiness, but not now." She leaned forwards, kissed him on the cheek, and took the bottle from his hand. After a moment, she handed the bottle back. "Here, I've saved you some."

Lofty accepted the bottle and took a swig.

"Come on then," Jill said, "let's get this over with."

He put the empty bottle back in the rucksack, then watched as Jill crawled on her hands and knees through the mud, getting as low to the ground as possible so she could slip through an opening in the hedge.

He followed Jill through the gap. His nose bumped her bottom as he caught her up, and lustful thoughts entered his mind. The thoughts made him think of a warm bed and sex. Then again, it didn't take much to make him think about sex, but the thought diminished as the foliage scratched his face, making his cheeks prickle.

Once on the other side, they hunkered close to the hedge. Lofty rubbed at the scratches on his cheeks, felt the thin lines etched into his face by the nicks and winced at the sting. He held his fingers up and saw what appeared to be blood. He wiped his cheeks on his sleeve and glanced back towards the research facility entrance. Although a light blazed in the security gatehouse, there was no sign of any guard.

He wiped rainwater and sweat from his brow, caught a faint smell of body odour from his moist armpits, and wished he'd applied some of the natural deodorant he used.

His heart beat fast. He swallowed, yearning for something more to drink to moisten his dry throat.

He pulled a couple of leaves from Jill's hair and said, "Come on, let's go," then stood up and ran across the road. He didn't know why he felt so nervous. It wasn't as though they were trespassing—the road was a public highway. But nonetheless a tremulous feeling rippled through his body, making his muscles feel weak. When he reached the other side, he squatted behind a telecom junction box and took a deep breath. Jill reached his side, leaned against the cold oblong structure.

Lofty peered around the side. The rain glistened in the spotlights. He wished he knew where the security guard had gone, wondered whether they should wait for him to return.

Another distressed howl emanated from the building. Lofty winced. Jesus. From this close, it sounded as though they were sticking red-hot pokers up the creature's backside.

At his side, he heard Jill whimper. He put his arm around her shoulder, hugged her close, and kissed the top of her head, grimacing at the taste of wax she used to maintain her hair.

He stared along the road that ran alongside the building. saw It didn't lead anywhere; the end was blocked by a pile of rubble.

A warehouse stood opposite Strident Industries on the side road, its white, sheet-metal-corrugated walls offering little in the way of cover. A couple of large waste bins on wheels stood about thirty feet farther along the road.

The fence surrounding the research facility stretched without end to encompass the whole complex. From what Lofty could see, there were no windows on the side of the building. More cameras kept silent vigil from each corner of the roof, angled between the fence and the building.

"So much for getting pictures," Lofty said. "The place is sealed tight."

"Perhaps there's something around the back."

"Could be. Only way to be sure is to go and look. Are you okay with that?"

"After what we just heard, I can't turn back now. Whatever they're doing, it sounded... I don't know, barbaric."

"Come on then, let's head towards those bins."

Aware of how exposed they were, he charged along the road, pumping his arms. He hoped he could stay out of the cameras' field of view.

It seemed to take ages to reach the bins, the loud, hard slap of his footfalls filling his ears. Once he reached the bins, he ducked behind the nearest one, setting it rocking on its wheels as he banged against its side.

The bin squeaked as it rocked, the noise amplified by the still night. Lofty cringed. Jill reached his side seconds later and squatted beside him. She gasped for breath.

"Jesus, I need to get more exercise," she wheezed.

Lofty knew what she meant. Sweat coated his forehead and his back, making the T-shirt stick close to his skin. Uncomfortable, he reached around and peeled the shirt free, but as soon as he let go, it stuck again. He gave up.

The pile of rubble provided the next cover. Lofty stared at it, guessed it to be about thirty feet away, which any other time would be no distance at all. But at night, with his heart racing and his body bathed in sweat, it looked a lot farther. From what he could tell, the pile consisted of dirt and bricks set out like the excavated earth from a First World War trench.

He looked at Jill and smiled, hoping she could see his facial encouragement in the near dark. He squeezed her shoulder.

"I'm glad you're here," he said.

He thought he saw Jill smile back, the momentary flash of white teeth in sharp contrast to the darkness behind the bin.

"You ready?" he asked.

"As I'll ever be."

"Then let's go." Lofty stood and ran as fast as he could, the driving rain stinging his face. Once he reached the pile of earth, he scrambled up the side and threw himself over the top. Turned to mud by the downpour, the man-made bank collapsed beneath his weight, sending him sprawling face first into the muck on the other side. Lofty spluttered and spit out a mouthful of mud. He ran the back of his hand across his mouth, smearing the mess.

This is typical, he thought, knowing where luck was concerned, he came near the bottom of the ladder.

Something was sticking in his back, and he shuffled aside and picked up a slim piece of metal about a foot-and-a-half long and an inch or so wide.

Jill scooted over the bank behind him.

"What happened to you?" she asked.

He held his arms out to indicate the mess. "I think that's obvious." Even though he couldn't see her very well in the dark, he knew she would be rolling her eyes and silently cursing his talent for attracting misfortune.

About to plead his own defence, he noticed a light scythe through the dark and he lunged forwards and pulled Jill down to the ground.

Jill gasped as the beam of light swept their way, illuminating the ridges of the pile of rubble and sending stark shadows across the ground to their rear. Lofty's stomach tied itself in knots. He covered Jill's mouth with his dirty hand, tried to push her closer to the ground, felt her struggle, indignant.

"Shush," he said. "There's someone there." Although he spoke louder than he intended, he hoped the rain would dampen the sound.

He knew they weren't breaking any laws, but he also knew their presence might lead to awkward questions, and he couldn't afford to run into trouble again if the police were involved, not after the incident with the glue and the slaughter house. Being on probation, he was supposed to stay out of trouble.

Jill stopped struggling and Lofty removed his hand from her mouth.

The light swept closer, coming from the direction of the building on the other side of the fence. Lofty felt a lump in his throat, but couldn't swallow to clear it. He reckoned with the fence between them, and from their position, they could make a run for it and be away in the camper van before the guard reacted.

Jill seemed to have the same idea. "Come on, let's get out of here."

She started to rise but Lofty heard the jangle of keys. He put a hand on her shoulder, pulled her back down and then peered over the pile of rubble. His eyes narrowed as he watched the person with the torch unlocking a gate in the fence. *How the hell did I miss spotting the gate?*

Hidden behind the beam of the torch, the security guard remained a shadow in the dark. The torch light flashed across the ground as the guard struggled with the lock.

Next minute, the gate swung open with a slight squeal and the torch beam played across the gap to illuminate the pile of rubble once more.

Lofty ducked back down, heart in his throat.

"He's coming across," he whispered, a slight tremor in his voice.

"This is just typical of you," Jill said.

Lofty swallowed. He didn't know what to say.

A disembodied voice spoke out. "Who's there?"

Lofty gulped. He wished he'd listened to Jill and just gone to the pub.

NINE

Amber leaned against a tree trunk, using it for cover. She chewed her lower lip, eyes scanning the abandoned mining village down below. Although she couldn't see them, she knew TJ and Hunter were over the far side of the small valley, while the rest of the team stretched out along the tree line on the surrounding hillside.

Numerous buildings hunkered against the dark background, half of which were shells. The skeletal frameworks were all that remained after years of onslaught from the harsh weather. A main road split the village into two halves, narrow alleyways running between the buildings.

"Can anyone see anything?" she asked.

A number of negative responses filtered back through her earpiece.

She didn't like it. Even the most inept kidnappers would post sentries, but to all intents and purposes, the village seemed deserted. In many ways it reminded her of an old Western cowboy town. She half expected to see a tumbleweed roll past.

Those buildings still intact were constructed from the local dark stone, which slotted together to form almost perfect seals. Their slate roofs glistened under the pouring rain. Numerous trees had seeded themselves throughout the village, a few of them now so large, their expanding trunks demolished whole buildings. Some of the trunks even grew around parts of some of the structures, assimilating everything in their path.

She strained her ears but heard only the patter of rain striking the leaves above. Nothing moved in the village down below. Whatever intel Finch had received, it was wrong. There was no one here. They'd been sent on a wild goose chase.

She checked their coordinates, then studied the map, but it only confirmed what she suspected—that they were in the right place.

Damn it, she thought, *where* are *they?* Her whole day had been a royal fuck-up. This was only the icing on the cake. She didn't think things could get much worse.

Farther up the hillside behind the village she spotted the dark maw of the mine entrance, next to which sat a building with a tall chimney. A narrow railway track led from the mine entrance and snaked down to the village. A couple of discarded carts were visible at the side of the track, and farther above the mine entrance, the trees held dominion.

Amber tapped her fingers against the stock of her gun. A bad feeling hunkered in her stomach, making her feel a little nauseous. She wondered where the two children were being held hostage, because it sure as hell didn't look like they were here. She checked her watch—time was running out.

She tried to imagine how terrified the boy and girl would be right now, remembered their cheeky grins from the picture Finch showed them, wondered how they might feel being locked in a dark room, uncertain, not knowing why they'd been ripped from their family. *Did the kidnappers abuse them?* The thought sickened her, made her nausea feel worse.

Goddamn it, where are you?

She scanned the buildings, narrowed her eyes to see better in the gloom. Down in the village of Kilnhill, nothing moved, the place as quiet as the grave.

"TJ, Hunter, you guys see anything at all? Any sign anyone's been here?" she asked.

"It don't look as though anyone's been here since the place was abandoned," TJ replied.

"It's too quiet," Hunter added.

Amber knew what he meant. She swallowed to clear her throat then licked her dry lips. She expected to see footprints or litter, anything to suggest habitation, but there was nothing. If it weren't for the thought of the terrified kids, she'd abandon the mission here and now.

"Okay, we're going to have to check the place out," Amber said. "Hunter and TJ can provide cover, while the rest of us pair up and head down into the village."

"No guesses who you'll pair up with," Eddie said, sniggering.

Amber clenched her fists. "Yes, Eddie, it looks like you've drawn the short straw, because you're coming with me." She heard him take a sharp intake of breath and then mutter something unintelligible. "Have you got a problem with that?"

"Hell no. I'm sure me and you can find something to do together."

John scrambled across to her side. "You sure you want to go in with Eddie?" he asked. "I can come with you if you like."

It was tempting, but Amber shook her head. "I can manage. Besides, I'd rather have him where I can see him." She triggered her microphone. "Barry, you go with John. Lars, you go with Six-pack. Look sharp, men. The place may look deserted, but appearances can be deceptive."

John squeezed her shoulder. "You be careful," he said, before slipping away into the undergrowth.

"Eddie, get your arse here now," she said. Moments later, she heard movement and Eddie appeared at her side.

"Hey doll, if I knew you had a thing for me, you know—"

"The only thing I've got for you is a magazine full of lead if you don't shut that gob of yours."

"Treat 'em mean to keep 'em keen." His shoulders bobbed up and down as he laughed.

Amber rolled her eyes.

"Come on hotshot, let's go," she said.

Amber started down the incline, using the bushes and foliage for cover. Eddie followed her down.

"Fan out," Amber said into the microphone. "John and Barry, start at the east side. Lars and Six-pack, move in from the west. Eddie and I will head straight down. Stay alert, guys."

The small hairs on the nape of her neck tingled. She knew Hunter sat higher up the hill in the tree line somewhere, sighting them in the lens of the Dragunov SVDS sniper rifle, which might account for the sensation.

As she slipped towards the wall of the nearest building, she caught a whiff of a foul aroma. She wrinkled her nose. The smell reminded her of the disgusting odour surrounding the person Eddie shot earlier—the stench of death.

"Can you smell that?" she asked.

Eddie screwed his face up in disgust. "You ain't shit yourself with fear have you?" he said.

Amber sighed. "What do you think it is?"

"Smells like something's crawled up its own backside and died."

Eloquent wasn't the word she would use for Eddie's turn of phrase, but he about summed it up.

Rain hammered down, turning much of the ground into a mud bath. Amber slinked along the side of the building, her feet making a slurping sound each time she dragged a foot from the mud. She wiped water from her face and hunkered at the corner of the building to peer along a weed-riddled stone track purporting to be a main road. Eddie leaned against the wall at her side.

"Jesus, that smell's getting worse," he said.

Bricks dislodged by an expanding tree trunk lay scattered at her feet. The wind whistled through the gaps left by the missing bricks at her side. If she listened close, the blustery weather sounded like someone screaming through the ragged remains of a bullet torn throat.

No matter what she tried, she couldn't get the thought of the man Eddie shot out of her mind. Everything she smelled, saw or heard seemed to remind her of him in some way. She reached into her pocket and fingered the Zippo lighter and wished she hadn't packed in smoking seven years ago. More than anything she'd like to feel the pacifying smoke drawn down her throat and into her lungs, perhaps with a vodka and coke to wash it down. But no, she was stuck out here in the pouring rain in some godforsaken abandoned mining village in the back of beyond.

This would have to go down as one of the shittiest days on record. Hell, she would rather be back in the dusty, arid shit hole of Iraq where a suicide bomber almost succeeded in taking her life. Two years on and she still recalled the sound of the explosion, the bright flash of light, the relentless ringing in her ears before the body parts rained down. Two women, one child and five men died in the blast, bits of their bodies strewn hundreds of yards, unrecognisable lumps of charred meat, food for the Egyptian Vultures and the Eurasian Buzzards that haunted the skies above, their portentous shadows signalling that lunch was served.

Even now, she thought that carrion eaters seemed to be the only victors in the long running war.

Most of the people on the circuit, which was what those involved called the security business, were men, and half of those had never grown up, caught in a Peter Pan syndrome. Civilian life wasn't an option for them. They could no more settle in a factory or office as a nun could in a brothel. They craved excitement. Hungered for the thrill of a life on the edge, a life where a wrong move might be your last. Always more a tomboy, Amber felt right at home in their company.

"Cover me," she said. "I'm going to head towards that building across the road. Once I'm there, I'll cover you so you can come across." She indicated a building that seemed more intact than most. If the kidnappers were anywhere—it would be there.

Keeping her head low, she charged across the track and dived behind the cover of a low garden wall, the plants of which had long since been overtaken by weeds and thistles.

Once in position, she signalled Eddie to come across while she covered him with her gun, eyes peeled for the slightest movement, ears pricked for the slightest sound.

Eddie ran squelching across the track and crashed into the wall beside her. Despite his bravado, she thought she saw a slight trepidation in his features and he kept licking his lips.

"You okay?" she asked.

Eddie nodded. "Couldn't be better."

With no time to question his answer, she thumbed her microphone. "Anyone see anything?"

"Nothing," John said.

"Zilch," Lars added.

"Hunter, you seen anything?" Amber said.

"No. I don't think there's anyone here."

Amber took a couple of deep breaths. "Okay, Eddie and I are going to check out a building. The rest of you, keep looking." She turned to Eddie. "Right, let's go."

She crawled along the side of the wall towards the front door. Entering buildings was always hazardous, anyone inside easily able to hide and lie in wait. With stairways, hallways, basements, doorways, closets, attics, nooks and crannies, the odds lay in favour of the hunted. Even though she suspected the place to be deserted, she knew complacency would be tempting fate.

Once she reached the door, she said, "Think attack, expect attack. Keep 'em peeled, Eddie."

Amber reached out and tested the handle. Finding the door unlocked, she pushed it open and Eddie entered. Amber followed him, her heart hammering. She feared the sound of a gunshot, the pain of a bullet. Eddie took the right wall, making his way towards the top-right corner. Amber followed the left wall, scanning the room with the barrel of her gun.

Grey light cut across the floor, filtered through the single window. From what she could see, the room seemed empty. Old floorboards creaked underfoot. Movement caught her eye. She spun and saw a rat scurry through the doorway on the far wall. With that the only other door in the room, and the single window facing the track out front, neither Eddie nor Amber needed to worry about crossing open doorways or unprotected windows.

"Clear," Eddie said once he reached the far wall.

The door stood open, the space beyond filled with beckoning darkness. Amber edged towards it, switched on her torch, and shone it through the doorway, revealing a small, narrow passageway lined with peeling wallpaper.

Taking one careful step at a time, she crept along the passageway. Her dry throat yearned for moisture, but her glands seemed incapable of producing saliva. She tried to swallow, but gave up when the action proved too difficult. The air in the building smelled damp and stale, but it was far more palatable than the terrible aroma circulating outside.

A staircase at the end of the passage disappeared in shadow. Before the stairs were three doors, two of which were shut. Amber and Eddie placed themselves on either side of the first door. Amber pressed her ear against the wood, then nodded, turned the handle and pushed it open, allowing Eddie to rush inside.

Amber followed him in to find the room empty, devoid of fixtures and fittings. Their footfalls echoed around the walls.

Eddie shrugged. "Clear."

Amber motioned him out. They returned to the passageway and headed towards the next door. She pressed her ear against the cool wood and prepared to turn the handle when she heard a noise inside the room. She stiffened. Her heart missed a beat. She placed her finger to her lips, indicating silence. She felt her heart restart, thumping inside her chest, heard the sound of her breath burst from her flared nostrils.

Eddie frowned.

Ignoring his quizzical expression, Amber cupped her hand around her ear and pressed it back to the wood. She heard a soft thud from inside the room.

Heart in her throat, the sound of blood pumping through her ears masked any further sound from inside the room. She straightened up, licked her lips, gulped, then motioned to Eddie that they enter on the count of three.

Using her fingers to do the count, she lowered each digit one at a time. Once her hand resembled a fist, she kicked the door open and charged inside. The beam of her torch chased away the darkness, cast gargantuan shadows of the abandoned furniture dotted around the floor. She scanned the room, eyeballs flicking left and right, took in the wooden table and chairs covered with dust, the display cabinet with the abandoned crockery.

Two windows let in the dull light. One faced her, the other at her left. One window stood open, allowing in the rank smell from outside. She wrinkled her nose, wanted to gag.

A sound reached her ears. A susurrus that drew her torch beam to the corner of the room. She tensed her finger on the trigger of the gun, her heart hammering like cannon fire in her chest.

Movement.

Quick and agile.

A hiss.

Multiple eyes stared back at her, their lenses illuminated in the torch light.

Amber let out a long breath. Stared at the black feral cat. It stood protecting its litter of kittens, hackles raised, teeth bared, hissing. After a moment, the cat's fur smoothed out and it licked its chops.

"Fuck's sake," Eddie said. "It's only a bastard cat." He raised the barrel of his gun, pointed it at the feline and her litter.

Amber swatted his weapon aside. "Don't be stupid."

Eddie glared at her. "You can push someone too far, you know. When this is over—"

"Grow up. You'll give our position away if you open fire."

The cat proceeded to pick up one of its litter in its maw to carry it across the room and hide it behind the cabinet.

Then it returned to repeat the procedure. Amber watched it for a moment, then said, "There's no need to worry, we're going now."

"You're speaking to a cat," Eddie said, shaking his head in disgust.

"A cat with more brains than you."

The cat stopped in the middle of the room, stared at Amber, then turned its head towards the window. Its hackles rose again, teeth bared as it let out a long hiss that chilled Amber's blood.

"Now what?" Eddie said.

Amber watched the cat return to its litter, collect another of its offspring and carry it to the cabinet.

"I don't know," she said, "but I don't think it's us the cat's afraid of."

TEN

Hunter shouldered the Dragunov sniper rifle and stared through the image-intensifying scope at the village below. TJ hunkered down at his side, his gun propped between his legs.

The wind rustled the leaves and Hunter shivered. Soaked to the skin, the wind only deepened the chill.

He'd been in worse situations. He recalled sitting in a tree in a fetid, godforsaken third world jungle, soaked to the skin with perspiration, the bugs and ants biting him relentlessly as he waited for his target to arrive—a rebel leader. And it was a long wait. Rebel patrols wandered by only feet underneath where he sat hidden, and he knew that the slightest rustle could give him away. He never moved a muscle.

His patience was rewarded three days later when his target arrived at the ramshackle collection of wooden huts the rebels had been using as their base. They had decapitated the resident population and left their heads on poles, the stench hanging in the air like a physical presence, and the rebel leader had given them an appreciable glance as they escorted him to one of the huts.

The smoke from cooking fires hung in the damp, humid air, and Hunter had often worried that he was going to cough and give himself away. By the time the target arrived, he was keen to complete his mission and make his escape, but he knew that rushing now would be fatal. So he waited for the perfect opportunity—and took the shot.

One bullet. The man's head exploded, sending the rebels into a frenzy as they opened fire, shooting at shadows.

Hunter slipped away in the ensuing mayhem.

Being wet for a few hours was nothing compared to that.

To him, killing was a profitable business.

He glanced at TJ. "So what you going to do with all that money?"

"First thing's a holiday. Somewhere bloody warmer than here."

Hunter nodded. "Sounds good."

"What about you?"

"My girlfriend, Alice, will probably have a few ideas. She can shop for England."

"Does she know where the money comes from?"

Hunter shook his head. "No way. She thinks I'm something big in the city. When I go on assignments, I tell her I'm on a business meeting." If she knew the truth, that would be the end of the relationship. Not many people could cope with their partner making money out of killing people. Of course, not every job he accepted involved killing, but the majority did. He was good at it. And he made the most of his ability.

"Well, when the pay is as good as this…" TJ chuckled.

Hunter nodded. "It does seem a lot."

"No shit. Whoever's hired us must be loaded. Perhaps we should have asked for more money."

"You're all heart."

"Fuck me. You smell that?" TJ said, wrinkling his nose.

Hunter nodded. He recognised the smell straight away. Had endured it for three days when holed up in that tree in the jungle.

He tightened his grip on the rifle and peered through the lens.

This time the smell was more pungent. A lot more pungent.

It was the smell of death.

ELEVEN

Amber stepped out of the building, eyes and ears alert. Having found nothing inside, and with no trace of anyone in the vicinity, her assumption they were in the wrong place seemed confirmed. She kept getting the tang of rotten meat in her sinuses. It made her wrinkle her nose in disgust. But the smell kept dispersing on the wind and she couldn't get a fix on its source.

"Anyone seen anything to suggest there's anyone around?" she said into the microphone.

Negative responses filtered back. Amber shook her head. *Now what?* The only course of action she could think of seemed to be to ask Finch to ascertain the intel he supplied, although of course he should already be listening in and would be up to speed, which didn't make any sense. For the sake of the kids, she hoped to God there hadn't been a mistake. Those poor devils must be half out of their wits with fear. She didn't want to let them down.

"Finch, this is Big Red, over." She released the button.

Silence.

Amber frowned. She tried again. "This is Big Red, over."

"You sure you're using it right?" Eddie said.

"Of course I'm using it right."

"Well it don't seem to be working."

Ignoring Eddie, Amber tried again. "Goddamn it, Finch, answer me."

A sick feeling spread through her stomach.

She stared through the pouring rain, watching for anything suspicious or out of place, when she heard a loud clanging sound like metal being struck repeatedly.

Drawn to the source of the noise, she gazed at the mouth of the mine farther up the hillside. The clanging became a loud squeal, like something opening, and in the feeble light, she saw movement.

"What's going on?" Eddie asked.

Amber pointed up the hillside. "There's someone up there." She clicked the button on her microphone. "TJ, Hunter, what's going on at the mine? Can you see anything?"

"Shit. People are coming out of the entrance," TJ replied.

"This is fucked up," Six-pack muttered through her earpiece. "They're not registering on the thermal goggles."

Just like the man she saw earlier that Eddie shot. What was going on here? How could they not register, unless they didn't have a heat signature? And the only things that didn't have a heat signature were what, dead things? Amber grimaced at the thought. "How many?" she asked.

"Jesus, there's dozens of 'em," Hunter said.

"Exact figures. How many?"

"I don't know," Hunter said. "They just keep coming. I'd say forty, fifty. Make that shitloads."

Amber clenched her teeth. *What the hell was going on?* She watched the dark shapes running down the hillside. A low, throaty moan like that of the wind reached her ears, a painful sound that chilled the marrow of her bones. Although too far away, she targeted the figures along the barrel of her weapon, but couldn't make much out in the near dark.

Shit, she thought.

"Talk to me. Anyone. What's going on?" she asked.

She felt a hand on her shoulder and jumped. Turned and saw Eddie. "I thought you were supposed to be in charge," he said. "Well, prove it—do something."

Amber chewed her lip. She didn't know what to do. She felt out of control. Events had taken a turn for the worse when she wasn't looking.

"What we going to do?" TJ asked.

Amber knew they were looking to her for answers, but she didn't have any.

"They're almost at the edge of the village," Barry said.

She didn't think the crowd were in any way associated with the kidnappers, which left the question: *Who the hell were they, and what were they doing here?*

Something about the way the people moved didn't seem right, too mechanical, rigid, even despite their speed. The rank smell grew stronger, more pungent, enhanced by the surging throng—the smell of death.

She saw two people ahead, about forty feet in front of what she could only describe as the black swarm. After a moment, she recognised the figures as John and Barry.

"John, get the hell out of there," she screamed into the microphone.

John turned tail, but Barry stood his ground. Next moment, she heard Barry speak in her earpiece.

"I don't believe it," he gasped.

"Barry, withdraw," Amber said.

The approaching figures continued on, all heading in the same direction: towards Barry. From a distance, she couldn't tell if the crowd were armed or not, but their intentions sure seemed hostile.

Through the veil of rain, Amber saw a muzzle flash, followed by the sound of gunfire as Barry opened fire.

The figures at the front of the crowd bucked and twisted in the air, the volley of automatic fire punching them back, cutting through flesh, severing limbs and appendages like a scythe through wheat.

"Cover him," Amber shouted, running forwards and levelling the barrel of her weapon at the crowd. Using controlled bursts, she opened fire, picking off the people at the front. More gunfire opened up from the hillside, the swarm caught in the crossfire.

Amber still didn't understand what was happening. She couldn't understand why the figures seemed so intent on surging forwards even when they were under attack.

Bodies lay on the ground, but the rest of the crowd seemed oblivious as they continued to surge forwards, trampling across the fallen as though it was a macabre assault course. Barry retreated, still firing as he went. Gunfire opened up beside Amber, and she heard Eddie whoop and holler.

Why weren't the hostiles stopping? Why weren't they running from the bullets? This didn't seem right. All of these people couldn't be involved with the kidnappers, could they? It didn't seem feasible. So who the hell were they? And why the hell didn't they cry out in pain when they were shot?

She fired another volley, targeting what appeared to be a woman who bared her teeth and rushed towards Barry, arms raised, fingers fashioned like claws, oblivious of the bullets striking her body, tearing out pockets of flesh

After another couple of shots, the woman pirouetted in the air and landed face first in the mud. Amber didn't feel any sense of satisfaction at the kill. A sick feeling swelled in her stomach. *What was a woman doing here?* As she pondered the situation, she saw the woman twitch, and then sit up. Although her left arm dangled on a strand of purple, bruised-looking skin below the shoulder, she raised herself, opened her mouth, and made a sound that was lost within the cacophony of the crowd's lion-like roar.

Amber looked out across the carnage, saw another fallen corpse move and regain its feet, oblivious of the fist-sized hole through its chest. Then another corpse rose, and another and another. A couple of bodies with their legs severed started to crawl through the mud, pulling themselves along, their mouths open, making a terrifying groaning sound.

"What the fuck?" Six-pack said. "They're getting back up. They're fucking *getting back up.*"

Amber remembered the person Eddie shot earlier. Fear penetrated her body. Her hands started to shake, the barrel of the gun wavering. Having thought she might be going mad, suffering from posttraumatic stress, now she wished that was true, as the reality seemed a thousand times worse. Despite cutting the figures down, bullets weren't stopping them. She had never seen anything like it, and she wondered whether there was something wrong with the ammunition. Every fibre of her body seemed to tingle in dread. Gooseflesh spread along her arms.

More gunfire rang out, but the bullets seemed to have little effect as the downed targets stood right back up and continued.

A number of expletives rang in Amber's ear as her team realised the horror, the futility, of the situation.

"Fall back," Amber shouted, back-pedalling towards the main street. She flicked her weapon to full auto as she went, changed the magazine and opened fire. Hungry bullets gnawed into flesh, obliterated a man's cheek and shattered his lower jaw. Another man advanced with his eyeball hanging down his face like a bloated leech. She'd never seen so much carnage. So much horror. The advancing swarm seemed oblivious, unstoppable, moving faster than she believed possible considering the condition they were in.

A middle-aged woman wearing a dirty overcoat shuffled forwards. Her right foot was missing; she hobbled on a nub of bone that kept sinking into the mud. Amber aimed and fired at her, saw a bullet tear a chunk out of her thigh, and another volley punch a hole through her chest, out of which her organs slopped like a nest of snakes.

"Will someone tell me what's happening?" TJ said.

No one replied. No one knew.

Amber's gun fell silent as she emptied another clip. She ejected the magazine, about to replace it when a man charged towards her. Of solid build, he had short dark hair and might once have been handsome, but now the left side of his abdomen was missing and his face contorted into a vicious snarl, either a rictus of pain or anger, she couldn't tell which. A tattoo of a snake on the back of his hand flexed as he fashioned his hands into claws. He bared his teeth, the chasm of his mouth rank with the smell of death and decay.

With no time to reload, Amber withdrew her Beretta M9 pistol and fired. Her hand was shaking and her first few shots missed. The third or fourth bullet struck the man's shoulder—but he didn't stop. He shambled towards her with surprising speed for someone riddled with bullets, reached out and grabbed her shoulders. Unable to stop the man, she stumbled. A small cry escaped her lips. The man crashed down on top of her like an avalanche, forcing the air out of her lungs. She could see his open mouth, could smell the reek of death, spotted what appeared to be strands of flesh dangling between the man's teeth.

Acting more in a state of panic, Amber raised the gun, pressed the barrel to the underside of the man's chin and pulled the trigger, once, twice. The bullets ripped through the man's head, sending brain matter and shards of bone into the sky like a gory firework display. Strands of cold skin and gore splattered Amber's face. She grimaced and wiped them away.

The man slumped aside and lay still. Breathing fast, Amber sat up and stared.

When he didn't move, Amber jumped to her feet and shouted into her microphone, "Head shots. Take head shots. That's the only way to kill them."

A word entered her thoughts: *zombie*. The undead. The more she looked at the people, the more she realised some of them showed signs they'd been dead for quite some time, their skin possessing a greenish tone. For others, their skin acquired a marble-like appearance, the veins in their bodies closer to the surface and more visible—they'd been dead the longest. But it seemed impossible. This couldn't be happening. Zombies weren't real. They were the stuff of legend and bad horror movies. Dead people were supposed to stay dead.

Another figure ran towards her. She aimed and pulled the trigger, only to find the magazine empty. Her heart stopped and she chastised herself for having forgotten to reload.

"Eddie," she shouted, hoping he would take the figure out. When he didn't answer, she lifted her gun by the barrel, prepared to use it as a club if she needed to, when the figure's head exploded in a shower of bone and fatty matter.

"You okay, Big Red?" Hunter asked in her earpiece.

Amber stared up at the hillside. Although unable to spot Hunter with his Dragunov 7.62 mm sniper rifle, she felt relieved he was up there, watching her back. The stopping power of the bullet went without saying as she stared at the stump of neck.

She raised her hand to the unseen sniper and then reloaded both her weapons. The amount of people swarming along the track between the houses seemed never-ending, and Amber knew the only form of offence was defence.

She turned to bollock Eddie but he was no longer beside her. She bit her lip and took a breath. *So much for him covering me*, she thought. *I should have listened to John.*

She keyed the microphone. "Everyone listen, we're going to have to make a run for the evac point."

She caught sight of Lars and Six-pack ahead, and started to make her way towards them when she saw a dishevelled man charging their way. She shouted a warning, but the figure was moving too quickly, and she watched in horror as he grabbed Lars from behind and sank his teeth into the ex-serviceman's neck.

Even from a distance, Amber heard Lars scream. The sound curdled the blood in her veins. She levelled her weapon, but couldn't get a clear shot without hitting Lars.

On hearing his partner's cry, Six-pack turned and started trying to pull the attacker off. When that failed to work, Amber watched him remove a knife from his belt and start hacking. She saw the blade of the knife sink in and out of the man's neck and shoulder, the serrated edge trailing strips of flesh like obscene party popper streamers each time Six-pack ripped it back out.

After a moment, the man's head tilted, the flesh and muscle on one side of his neck hacked away. Bizarre and terrifying as it seemed, the man was still alive, or at least as alive as someone dead could be.

"Sever the head," Amber said into her microphone. "You've got to sever the head to break the spinal column." Even though she didn't know how it worked, she remembered reading or hearing somewhere that a zombie could be killed by a bullet to the brain or decapitation. So far, the folklore seemed to ring true.

Upon hearing her instructions, Six-pack started to saw through the zombie's neck. Even from a distance, Amber thought she heard the rasp of metal on bone, a sound that set her teeth on edge, making her wince.

Five figures appeared in front of Amber. Ravaged by bullets, they looked worse for wear, their already decaying bodies made all the more hideous by the wounds. But instead of continuing to advance, they stopped and stared at her. Somehow those stares were more terrifying than anything else, more blood curdling than if they'd charged straight for her. Despite the lack of light, there was something in their eyes, something cognizant.

What the hell are they waiting for?

Although she seldom heard of flies flying at night, a number alighted on the walking corpses, having made themselves at home among the festering flesh, no doubt woken by their hosts' movement; they buzzed excitedly through the air.

Amber wrinkled her nose. "Six-pack," she said into the microphone, "get Lars inside a building and maintain a defensive position."

"I'm okay," Lars rasped.

Amber shook her head. "That's an order." She didn't want to let anything happen to the men under her command. "I'll double back and make my way to you."

She watched Lars drape an arm over Six-pack's shoulder and stumble towards one of the derelict buildings, then she turned her attention back to the four men and one woman blocking her path. She couldn't be sure of taking them all out with headshots, and although she knew they moved fast, she felt confident she could move even faster when fuelled by fear. But why weren't they advancing? What were they waiting for?

"You want me, then come get me," she snarled. A sound caught her attention and she turned, jaw dropping when she saw another three zombies rushing towards her from behind.

In a classic pincer movement, the zombies had her trapped.

TWELVE

"This way," Lofty said. He watched the guard's torchlight sweep towards where they sat hunched behind the pile of earth at the end of the road. His throat was dry, heart pulsing, breath coming in short bursts.

"Where?" Jill whispered.

Lofty pointed down at a manhole cover partly covered with soil from the mound

Jill grimaced. "Are you mad? I'm not going down there."

Ignoring her comment, Lofty slid the metal bar into a small slot in the cover. Pressing down on the end of the bar, the cover rose enough for him to slip his fingers underneath and slide across.

"We aren't doing anything wrong," Jill said. "We won't get into trouble."

"Perhaps *you* won't. I'm on probation, remember. They find me anywhere near this place, they're going to throw the book at me. I can't take the risk. We'll just hide until he's gone."

Jill stared at him as though he had a point, then she shimmied across, lowered her legs into the hole and descended the ladder attached to the wall.

As she went, she whispered, "This is typical of you."

Lofty put the bar in his rucksack and scampered after her, dragging the cover back over just as the guard reached the mound and shone his torch around, the light broken into numerous narrow beams by the holes in the cover.

Lofty took each rung one careful step at a time so as not to make any noise. About ten feet down he found himself crouched in a narrow tunnel.

Although too dark to see well, he heard Jill breathing. He took the small Maglite from the rucksack and turned it on, dazzling Jill in its beam.

"Get it off me," she said.

Lofty wished they'd never come. This wasn't how he hoped things would turn out.

He shone the torch along the tunnel. Judging by the water running around their feet, it seemed to be a storm drain of some sort. The tunnel walls were smooth concrete and the air smelled of stagnant water.

A sudden howl echoed along the pipe, making both Lofty and Jill jump.

"Jesus." He shone the torch in the direction of the sound, chasing shadows along the pipe. He felt as though he were in the barrel of a gun.

"They've got guard dogs down here," Jill whimpered.

Lofty shook his head. "That wasn't a guard dog. It was the same howl we heard outside. What the hell are they doing to them in there?"

"I don't know, but as soon as the coast's clear, I'm going."

Lofty stared along the pipe. By the looks of it, the drain ran right beneath the building. "We can't just ignore it," he said.

Jill shook her head. "You said it yourself, we can't get caught."

Lofty pursed his lips. "Just one quick look."

"No way. We're not going anywhere."

Lofty took the van keys out of his pocket and held them out. "I won't be long."

Jill snatched the keys from him and then turned away, arms folded across her chest as she rounded her back to lean against the wall.

Lofty hesitated. He stared at Jill's profile in the torchlight. He really did love her. Perhaps he shouldn't go. If he left her on her own, he would only worry about her. He wouldn't be able to live with himself if she got caught and ended up in trouble. And Jill's parents would never forgive him either. No, perhaps he should wait with her until the guard left, then run back to the van and drive away. That seemed like the best idea.

The dog howled again, making the hairs on his arm stand on end. He started crawling along the pipe.

"Hey, where do you think you're going with the torch? You're not leaving me in the dark on my own."

"But I've only got one torch. You'll be all right. The ladder's just behind you and your eyes will adapt to the dark after a while."

"Oh, great. So now you're abandoning me."

"You'll be okay. Trust me."

"*Trust you?*" Jill said. "Look at the mess we're in already."

"*Shhh.* Keep it down," he said, wary the guard might hear them. "Just wait here. I won't be long. I promise."

Jill looked about to protest, then thought better of it.

He didn't know how far the tunnel extended, but he hoped it didn't get any narrower because it was already a squeeze. Although he felt guilty about leaving her, he put the torch in his mouth and crawled away, knowing the quicker he found out what was going on, the quicker they could leave. Another howl echoed along the tunnel and he heard movement behind him.

"If you think I'm sitting there in the dark on my own, you've got another thing coming," Jill said.

Lofty didn't know whether he felt happy or sad that she decided to accompany him, but he grinned to himself anyway.

The water running down the middle of the pipe sloshed around Lofty's hands and feet. Every now and then, he lifted his head to illuminate the path with the torch in his mouth. He hoped the guard hadn't guessed they'd descended down the storm drain, otherwise they could find themselves trapped if the pipe came to a dead end. He remembered reading somewhere about Urban Explorers, people who ventured into places normally off-limits, such as abandoned buildings, catacombs, tunnels and storm drains. As he crawled along the pipe, he understood the thrill they experienced being in places where they shouldn't be, exploring places they weren't meant to see. He didn't expect Jill would feel quite so excited. Although she dressed down in a grunge style, she always liked to look her best, what he called *grunge-chic*, so her present dishevelled state would cause her to feel angry and annoyed, and he knew who that anger would be directed at.

"Typical, just typical," Jill mumbled.

Lofty tried to think of a quick retort, something amusing to lighten the mood, but he guessed that by the way Jill was feeling, whatever he said would be frowned upon, so he remained tight-lipped.

He tried not to think what they were doing to the poor dog in the facility somewhere up above, but the intermittent howls made it hard. The last time he heard a noise like that from a dog was when he ran over one in a car many years ago. The animal had run out in the road, and with not enough time to hit the brakes, the car smashed into it, the front offside wheel leaving the road as it rolled over the body.

Lofty had stopped and jumped out of the car to find the dog still alive. It lay curled in the road, a hideous howl emanating from its bloody maw. Next minute, the animal staggered to its feet, stared at Lofty, growled and then limped away, howling in pain. Although Lofty chased after it, the dog scampered through a hedge and disappeared. The memory of the incident haunted Lofty's dreams for weeks after, and now the sound issuing along the storm drain brought it back to the surface.

He peered ahead, the torch in his mouth illuminating the tunnel for quite a distance. So far, there seemed to be no way out. The thought that there might not be an exit up ahead made his heart sink. The sounds from the dog grew louder, each howl and bark cutting him to the core. Why were people so goddamn cruel? There were plenty of other ways to test drugs and cosmetics without using animals. He didn't know how any self-respecting person could inject shampoo into a cat's eyes, or sew a pipe into a monkey's mouth and then continually insert cigarettes, leaving it no choice but to inhale the smoke. And as for battery chickens and fur coats— if people were supposed to wear fur, they would have been born gorillas.

The more he thought about things, the angrier he became. He felt his breath sharpen, his muscles bunch. There had to be a way inside, there just had to.

Even though he doubted his wishes had anything to do with it, he spotted a dark patch in the roof of the pipe ten feet or so ahead, indicating a gap. When he reached it, he sat underneath and shone the torch up to illuminate a ladder leading up a narrow pipe to a grid above. Barely large enough to fit inside, he knew he had to check it out.

"I'm going up to have a look around," he said.

Jill snorted. "And I suppose you want me to wait here. Well stuff that. If you're going, then I'm coming too."

"You don't have to. I'm just going to look, that's all."

"I said I'm coming, okay?"

Although she posed it as a question, he knew she wasn't seeking his permission. He nodded, put the torch in his mouth, grabbed the bottom rung of the ladder, and began climbing.

There was a grid at the top of the ladder, and all he could see through it was a ceiling high above. He paused, listening. When he didn't hear anything, he placed his elbow against the cover and pushed.

Although heavy, the grid moved. Lofty pushed it aside, wincing at the loud, reverberating clatter it produced once it hit the ground. He hesitated, crouched inside the drain, breathing fast. A pungent smell of faeces and urine hit him, and he wrinkled his nose.

When it seemed no one heard the sound, he reached up, grabbed the lip of the drain and pulled himself up to peer out.

A sudden loud growl emanated from his rear. He twisted his body and turned his head as the salivating maw of a mangy German Shepherd lunged for his throat.

THIRTEEN

Trapped on all sides, Amber raised the barrel of her MP5, aimed it at the smallest group and pulled the trigger. Bullets sprayed out and drilled through flesh. Rank, rotting skin disintegrated beneath the onslaught. The bullets animated the man and two women, making them dance to the silent tune of her gun. One bullet took a chunk out of the man's throat. Another ripped a portion of his shoulder away.

Beneath the folds of rotting flesh, she discerned chiselled features—a real ladies man taken in the prime of his life. His eyes looked vacant, face devoid of expression, his muscular body now a breeding ground for maggots.

The two women beside the man bucked and jumped as though having a fit as the bullets tore into their flesh. One of the women was topless, her sagging breasts marbled with veins and weeping sores. Bullets smacked into her body, creating viewing ports into her internal organs that slopped and jostled as she moved. Both women looked old, at least mid-fifties. Blood speckled the topless woman's grey hair. More blood decorated her chin, the sanguine fluid long since dried and resembling a gory scab. Her left breast had exploded, leaving a sagging pouch of rotting skin out of which tumbled a trickle of maggots.

Although repulsed, Amber kept her finger on the trigger. The terrifying situation threw her aim out, made all her training seem useless as the bullets flew in all directions. She felt on the verge of madness.

When the magazine ran empty, she grabbed a fresh one from her webbing, almost dropping it in the process. Trying hard to regain her composure, she ejected the spent magazine and replaced it, her hands shaking uncontrollably. She knew she had to aim, otherwise she was wasting her time. She glanced over her shoulder, saw that the other group still hadn't moved. Their stillness and objective scrutiny unnerved her, reinforcing her theory that they possessed some form of intelligence, as they didn't just rush in mindlessly. Fear coursed through her veins, spreading throughout her body.

Working on autopilot, she snatched a grenade from her belt, pulled the pin and threw it at the smallest group. She watched the grenade tumble towards them, and then threw herself on the ground. As she waited, she kept expecting to feel sharp teeth crunch into her legs or arms. Although it only had a five second delay, it seemed to take ages before she heard the explosion shatter the air and felt the ground rumble beneath her. With the bang still ringing in her ears, she jumped to her feet and without looking back, she ran towards the source of the blast.

Bits of body parts lay strewn all around, a human abattoir. The topless woman's legs lay twitching against a low wall, her torso close by. Still alive in some form, she seemed unconcerned by the loss of her limbs, dragging herself through the mud with her hands, towing her entrails in her need to reach Amber. Vicious cuts scarred her body from the blast, the puckered edges of the bloodless lesions resembling the underside of a sea slug.

The young man seemed to have taken the worst of the blast. The front of his chest lay open as though undergoing an autopsy. His shattered ribs resembled a broken cage, his innards escaping through the gaps. A stick protruded from his eyeball. The other woman sat about five feet away, one side of her face devoid of flesh, leaving her with a grotesque, toothy grin. Still alive, she picked at the remnants of skin on her cheek, as though remembering what she looked like before, and now appalled by her present condition. Was this another sign that they were aware? Did they know who, or what, they were?

Amber dodged around the topless woman, avoiding the clutch of her clawed fingers. She stepped over the downed man with her right leg, careful not to slip in the mud and gore. Her left foot sank a little as it took the brunt of her weight, and she made to pull it free when the man grabbed her ankle. Amber's heart leaped into her throat and she almost jumped out of her skin. The man yanked her leg towards his mouth and gnashed his teeth together as though anticipating the bite. Using her like a rope, he started to pull himself up, causing his innards to slop out of the gaping chest cavity and slither around his waist. Clear, gelatinous liquid oozed from his punctured eyeball and slid down his cheek. Despite his dishevelled appearance, he was remarkably strong.

Amber fought to contain the scream building within her chest. She yanked her leg, trying to free herself, but the man's grip remained tight. Not wanting to trip and overbalance herself, she leaned as far away as she could. Behind her, she heard rabid grunts, the noise rising in pitch. She glanced back, saw the zombies moving. A shiver of fear ran from her head to her toes. She gnashed her teeth, twisted the gun around, pointed it at the man who had grabbed her and prepared to pull the trigger when one of the approaching zombies smashed into her side, sending her sprawling into the mud, the man's hand still attached to her leg and denying her the release she craved.

"Need a hand?"

Amber snapped her head up to see Eddie leaning nonchalantly against a wall a couple of feet away. He grinned, seeming to relish her distress. Rain splattered her face, the cold drops seeming to sap what little strength remained within her battered body.

Before she replied, Eddie pointed the barrel of his Steyr Aug at her and pulled the trigger. The bullets slammed into the zombie.

"In the head," Amber screamed, kicking at the man holding onto her ankle, keeping him at bay.

Eddie swept the barrel of his gun up, stitching a path of gore towards the man's head. Bullets smacked through his skull.

Amber saw bone fragments fly out like shrapnel and turned away, shielding herself.

A second later, she turned back and saw Eddie slam his foot down on the man holding onto her ankle, driving the stick that had pierced his eye farther into his head. The man bucked, made a grunt and then lay still. Amber snatched her leg from his hand and pushed herself to her feet. Then she joined Eddie and opened fire at the remainder of the group that had tailed her, although in her present state of mind, she thought Eddie lucky she didn't turn her gun on him instead.

Moments later, what remained of the zombies lay on the ground, their bodies finally at peace, but another group advanced fast along the main road, a never-ending march of the undead, forcing Amber and Eddie to retreat.

As they ran, she said, "Where the fuck did you get to?"

"You think you were the only one in the shit? I had to make a run for it. A group of those sons of bitches were sneaking in from the side wanting to make a main course out of me."

Although Eddie sounded sincere, Amber had her doubts. Nothing she could put her finger on, but she felt he wasn't telling her the whole truth.

Although she didn't like the thought of him watching her back, she didn't have any other choice at the moment. The sooner she met up with the rest of the team, the better she would feel.

But first, she had to help Lars and Six-pack.

FOURTEEN

Lofty let out a small yelp as the salivating dog lunged for him. The torch fell out of his mouth and clattered down the pipe below. The creature's hot breath stank of rotten meat, making Lofty cringe. He ducked. His hands turned sweaty in an instant and he almost lost his grip on the rung of the ladder, making his stomach lurch as though on a big dipper. Knowing the safest place was down, he descended quickly. The dog's savage, throat-searing barks followed him down.

"What's going on?" Jill shouted up.

"*Down. Go back down.*" He heard the clank of her feet on the metal ladder as she descended. Lofty followed as quickly as possible, careful not to step on her fingers. When he reached the tunnel, he reclaimed the torch, glad that it still worked, and crouched down to sit hunched against the wall. "Fuck me," he gasped, breath rapid. "That was close. There's a rabid dog up there."

"Rabid dog!"

Lofty stared back up the ladder, saw the dog staring down at him, drops of saliva dripping from its maw. "What else would you call that?" He aimed the torch up the pipe, the bright light illuminating the dog's eyes, making them glisten.

Jill slid across and leaned over him to stare up. "Jesus. What have they done to it?"

"God knows. They must be sick to do something like that. Its bloody fur was dropping off."

"Poor thing."

"Well the *poor thing* nearly had my head off."

"It's no wonder. You probably scared it half to death popping out of the floor like that."

"*I* scared *it*?" He shook his head. "Have you seen the teeth on that thing?" He looked up again, saw the dog snarling down at him.

"Well, I thought that was what you came here to rescue."

"Are you mad? The thing's beyond saving. It's savage. The way its ribs are sticking out, it hasn't eaten in days by the looks of it."

"So what are you saying? That we should leave it there?"

"I'm saying if you offer that dog the hand of friendship, it'll bite the bloody thing off."

Jill looked unconvinced.

"I'll take a picture of it, show it to someone that might be able to help."

"You're all heart."

"Jesus, Jill. Look at it."

"You can't leave it like that."

Lofty agreed, but he didn't know what to do. This wasn't what he expected to find, and faced with the sickening truth, he felt powerless to do anything. He gritted his teeth, stroked his goatee and cursed the people involved in reducing man's best friend into the slobbering beast above.

"We're going to have to free it," Jill said.

Lofty shook his head. "Don't be stupid. The thing's probably infected with God knows what."

"Don't call me stupid."

"I didn't mean it like that. I wasn't calling you stupid."

"Then what were you calling me?"

"I wasn't calling you anything."

Before Jill responded, Lofty heard the faint sound of a door opening somewhere up above. Seconds later, a distant voice shouted, "What's that bloody racket for?"

Lofty wasn't too concerned that they would be discovered, until he remembered he'd removed the drain cover. He gulped, rolled his eyes and silently cursed.

The dog stopped barking and growling. The only sound now, that of its claws clicking against the concrete floor as it started traipsing the room.

"I'm going to have to go back up to replace the drain cover, otherwise they'll know we're here."

Jill reached out, grabbed his arm and squeezed. "Be careful."

A warm feeling settled in Lofty's stomach. He grinned. "You can bet on it."

He passed her the torch, and then started up the ladder, the rungs of which felt cold beneath his fingers. Some of the rungs felt wet. He didn't like to think where the wetness originated, but considering the smell of piss that filled the pipe, he could take a guess.

When he reached the lip of the drain, he popped his head up enough to peer out, almost putting his nose in a rank smelling dish of raw meat. The dog traipsed back and forth in front of a row of floor-to-ceiling bars that created a caged enclosure, separate from the white-walled, clinical looking room filled with computers and laboratory equipment, among which the only things he recognised were test tubes and microscopes. The other equipment looked like something from the deck of a spaceship, the use for which he couldn't begin to imagine. Some of the equipment made soft beeps, other equipment seemed to be scrolling through calculations. Complicated medical charts adorned one wall, scribbled notes on a large marker board on another. Lofty noticed lots of algebra—all that 'x,' 'y' stuff that used to give him headaches and nightmares at school.

Whatever experiments were being conducted here, they sure didn't seem short of money. Lofty looked back at the dog. Strands of muscle were visible where its fur had been scraped off and it looked malnourished. He found its appearance sickening and heartbreaking. How could anyone calling themselves *civilised* do such a thing?

Although gentle by nature, Lofty could strangle those responsible.

As quietly as possible, he leaned out and grabbed the drain cover. The last thing he wanted was to alert the dog to his presence—although he felt sorry for it, the dog would view him more as something to sink its teeth into than an ally. The cover felt heavier than it looked. Lofty cringed. He licked his lips and leaned farther out to get a good purchase.

Bracing himself in the hole, he lifted. The cover clanked as one edge struck the ground. Lofty turned and stared at the dog. The dog turned and stared back, its ears pricked, teeth bared.

I may as well have rung a bloody dinner bell, Lofty thought.

With the dog alerted to his presence, he had to work fast. Although it looked unsteady on its feet, he knew it would be upon him in a couple of strides. Now unconcerned about making a din, he dragged the cover across, ducked down, and let it clatter into the recess in the concrete above. He hoped the dog's loud barks and growls were enough to disguise the noise, because seconds later, he heard a door open.

"What's all this noise about?" someone shouted.

From where he gripped the ladder in the hole, Lofty could see the dog standing above him, looking down.

"Hey, mutt, what you looking at?" the gruff speaker said.

Lofty guessed the man sounded middle-aged. He peered up through the drain cover, praying the dog would move away, but it remained in place, teeth bared.

"Hey, mutt, if I have to come in there, you'll be sorry."

The dog continued to bark. Lofty heard something strike the metal bars, heard it drawn across them to create a loud *tatatatatat.*

The dog stopped barking and lifted its head to look at the man on the other side of the bars. Then it turned back and started barking and growling at Lofty.

"I warned you," the man said.

Lofty heard a clank of metal, and what sounded like a bolt being drawn. He tried to swallow, but his parched throat made the act too difficult. If the man came into the cage and spotted him...

He felt like a rat in a drain.

Wary of losing his grip or slipping, Lofty started to descend, placing each foot carefully on the rungs to minimise any noise. The dog's attention on the drain would alert the man to a problem, and if he looked down...

A shadow fell over the drain as the man approached. Lofty froze on the spot, breath caught in his throat.

Any second, the man would spot him.

Lofty heard the dog growl. Then bark. Then he heard the crackle of an electrical buzz, and the dog fell silent.

Squeezing his eyes shut, Lofty prayed. He didn't want to go to prison.

He heard the man approaching, his footsteps seeming to reverberate through the ground. Any second now...

A door opened and another voice said, "Mack says he saw someone outside, but he lost them. He wants us to help him look."

"Jesus Christ. I'm not a security guard. Don't they get paid enough?"

"Suit yourself. I'm only passing the message on."

Lofty heard the man grumble and walk away. He let out a sigh of relief as he heard the cage door shut and the door to the room slam. That was too close.

"What's going on?" Jill asked.

Lofty peered down the ladder and saw Jill staring up at him, her face shadowed.

"Nothing. Everything's fine. He's gone."

"And what about the dog?"

Lofty hadn't heard a peep out of it since whatever the man did to it. "I'll go and look."

Lofty climbed back up the ladder, and pushed the cover aside, leaving it within easy reach if he needed to replace it fast. He peered into the room, saw the dog lying motionless less than a foot away. He could only guess, but he thought it looked stunned. Its tongue lolled from its maw, and its legs kept jerking as if it were running in its sleep. Puss leaked from one of its eyes, leaving a slug-like trail. For some reason, it appeared more pitiful lying comatose than when awake.

Lofty climbed out of the hole and crouched down next to the dog. Although out for the count, he was still wary of it, and he made sure that if it awoke, he could jump aside.

"Jesus, is it dead?"

Lofty turned and stared at Jill as she poked her head out of the drain.

"No. I think it's been stunned."

"Why would anyone do that to a defenceless creature?"

Lofty didn't think it looked too defenceless when it had its teeth in his face, but he knew what she meant. Not knowing what to say, he shrugged.

"Well we can't leave it here like this."

"There's nothing we can do. Like I said, I'll take a picture of it and report what we've seen."

"And what good's that going to do? Judging by how it looks, the poor creature's probably in pain."

Lofty shrugged again. "I don't know. What would you suggest?"

Jill fixed him with her gaze. "You're going to have to kill it."

FIFTEEN

Six-pack helped Lars through the front door of the abandoned building, gently lowered him to the ground, and then slammed the door shut. Turning on his torch, he scanned the room. The torchlight revealed a couple of dining chairs, a threadbare rug, a broken table and an old china teapot. From what he'd seen of the village, it seemed everyone upped and left, leaving behind some of their property. The most useful thing in the room seemed to be the chairs, one of which he rammed under the door handle to provide extra security.

Groaning sounds emanated from outside the door. Whatever those things were out there, he didn't want them in here.

Satisfied the door was secure, he turned to Lars and shone the torch in his friend's face.

Lars raised a hand to shield his eyes from the glare.

"How you doing?" Six-pack asked.

Lars nodded and then coughed. "I'll live. It's just a scratch."

Six-pack nodded and lowered the torch, but he wasn't convinced. Although naturally pale, Lars looked paler still, the prominent veins in his hands like a relief map of roads in the South Pole.

Six-pack leaned across. "Let me have a look then."

Lars tilted his head and Six-pack shone the torch at the wound on his neck, recoiling at the severity. He hoped Lars hadn't seen his reaction, but man, that gash looked as though someone had scooped some of his flesh right out. He could see where individual teeth had chomped through the skin, and although he'd seen horrendous wounds in Angola where he was employed to assist the Angolan army in regaining control of the Soyo oilfields from Unita rebels, it always turned his stomach to see prominent veins exposed. There seemed to be little blood considering how bad it looked, but Six-pack knew if he didn't dress the wound, then infection would soon set in—perhaps he only imagined it, but he thought he could smell it decomposing already.

A sudden bang at the door made him jump. He turned and stared across the room. A low groan reverberated outside, a throaty sound that chilled the marrow in his bones.

"They know we're here," Lars moaned.

Six-pack watched the handle turn, saw the door rattle in the frame, but the chair held it in place. But for how long?

There were two windows set into the walls of the room, the thin glass of which would allow easy access.

He switched the torch off. Darkness descended as his eyes took time to adjust. Lighter outside, he saw movement beyond the window. They were coming.

"You okay to walk?" he asked.

"Walk? I'm going to fuckin' run, my friend."

Despite the situation, Six-pack grinned. "Right, let's go."

He helped Lars to his feet, assisted him through the door at the other end of the room. The door led to a narrow corridor, at the end of which he spied the stairs. Knowing it would be easier to defend from a higher position, he helped Lars along the corridor and up the stairs. Once on the landing, he sat Lars on the floor by the newel post.

Flowery wallpaper decorated the landing, a sign that perhaps the former occupants leaned more towards old age. The landing extended about eight feet, then turned a corner. There was a door at the end of the landing.

Lars unslung his gun from around his shoulder and pushed the barrel through the banister posts to aim at the corridor downstairs. Six-pack heard him breathing, the sound laboured as though he struggled to catch his breath.

He took the small first aid kit out of his webbing and opened it. His biggest worry was bacteria from the mouth of the man that had bitten Lars, so he needed to clean the injury. He poured water over it from his canteen, dabbed at it with a clean cloth from the kit, then applied antibiotic ointment before dressing the wound by wrapping a bandage around it. Although he expected Lars to shout out or complain from the pain, he didn't make a sound. It was unnerving.

With Lars being as big as a bull, Six-pack knew he would struggle to lift him if he couldn't walk. He stood and stared down at his friend. Outside, the dead legion moaned and groaned. Fists pounded against the door, rattling the wood in the frame. Six-pack didn't know how long the barricade would last. He imagined them hammering until their fists were raw, sloughing off dead flesh until bare bone remained.

"I'm gonna see what's going on out there," Six-pack said.

Lars didn't respond.

"You listenin'? I'm just gonna have a look out the window."

Lars nodded, the movement almost imperceptible as he kept his gaze directed down the stairs.

Six-pack fingered the flask on his hip. He didn't like being sober—not at a time like this. At least in a drunken stupor he wouldn't feel so vulnerable, wouldn't feel anything at all. He guessed he inherited his alcohol dependence from his mother, who often became violent while under the influence, but unlike her, he could handle it—at least that's what he kept telling himself.

He could still see her in that hospital bed. Cirrhosis of the liver they'd said, but even then the old coot asked for a drink and threatened to punch their lights out if she didn't get one. He remembered her ranting, "How you supposed to handle news like that if the bastards won't give you a drink?"

Six-pack stepped back and pushed open the nearest door. The room beyond seemed empty. Bare floorboards creaked as he walked towards the window opposite. Moth-eaten curtains hung across the glass, diffusing the wan outside light.

Six-pack parted the curtain enough to look out, wrinkling his nose at the dust that wafted from the old material. Although the monsters outside—because that's surely what they were—knew his location, he didn't want them to see him, so he peeked through the gap he made in the curtains. Down below, he saw a group of about twelve people battering on the door and walls. One of them, a woman, showed remarkable intelligence by lunging through the window, heedless of cutting herself on the glass.

Diverting his gaze, he stared along the street where hordes of the undead wandered aimlessly. He saw others charging into the trees in pursuit of his teammates.

He thumbed the microphone. "This is Six-pack, can someone tell me what the fuck's going on?"

"Glad to hear you're okay," Amber said. "How's Lars?"

Six-pack didn't want to broadcast the truth, knowing that Lars would hear his response, so he said, "He's fine. Tough as an ox."

"Good. Eddie and I are trying to circle around to help you. Where you holed up?"

"We're in one of the houses on the east side of the village. I've barricaded the door, but they're coming through the window. Now tell me, what the fuck are they?"

He heard Amber cough, then heard her mumble something unintelligible.

"Say that again," Six-pack said.

"My best guess is that they're zombies."

Six-pack took a sharp intake of breath. Had he heard right? *Zombies?*

"Which house are you in?" Amber asked.

"How the fuck should I know. You think I looked for a number on the fuckin' door?" He knew he shouldn't be getting angry at Amber, but he couldn't help it. Zombies! He noticed the curtain twitch, stared at his hand holding it and saw it shaking.

"Give us a sign then. Flash your torch out the window if you can."

Six-pack pulled the torch from his belt and pointed it at the window. He switched it on and off a few times.

"Hey, amigo," Hunter said in his earpiece. "I've got a bead on you. There's a building in front and I can't see the bottom of the house from where I am, otherwise I'd pick the buggers off."

"I can see you, too," Amber said. "It's going to take a while for us to reach you, as the street's full of those monsters."

"Well I'm not going anywhere," Six-pack replied.

"I'd help if I could," Barry said, "but we've got our own problems on the edge of the village."

Six-pack let the curtain drop back into place, and then sank to the floor to sit with his back against the wall, his Colt Commando assault rifle wedged between his legs like a lethal erection—a thousand-round-per-minute love machine.

Spraying those outside with bullets would be useless, unless he managed a kill shot, he would only be filling them full of holes. So he sat in the dark, waiting.

No amount of money in the world was worth this shit. But he knew greed made fools of everyone.

How did dead people manage to walk? It didn't make any sense. Seemed more like something from a nightmare. War was hell, this something worse. Give him any war zone in the world, and he'd feel at home. But this...

The smell of death and putrefied flesh lingered everywhere. It permeated the house, made it feel like the inside of a corpse-filled coffin. Every breath he took made him want to gag.

Deciding he'd left Lars alone for long enough, he stood and walked back out onto the landing—only to find Lars gone.

Six-pack stared at the spot where Lars had been seated. "Lars, where are you?"

When Lars didn't answer, Six-pack stared down the stairs. What if the zombies had gotten him? What if they lurked in the shadows below?

Surely he would have heard something if any of those things occurred, but he couldn't help peering into the shadows.

"Lars, speak to me, buddy. Where are you?" When Lars didn't respond, he thumbed the microphone and repeated his question.

"Problem?" Amber asked through his earpiece.

"Nothing I can't handle. You just concentrate on getting your ass over here."

Six-pack turned on his torch and shone it along the landing. Motes of dust hung in the air like radioactive fallout. A dirty carpet cushioned the floor, dampening any sound. Six-pack crept along it, heading towards the second door. Perhaps Lars had gone in search of a toilet. He expected to push open a door and see his friend sitting on the crapper taking a dump. He didn't know which he preferred, the thought of that, or the undead horde outside. Neither seemed very appealing.

Gun in one hand, torch in the other, he pushed the door open. It swung around and slammed against the wall. Six-pack cringed and shone the torch around the room. Newspapers yellowed with age decorated the bare floorboards. He illuminated them in the light for a moment, and then shone the beam around the walls. Bright light stung his eyes and he lowered the torch and raised the barrel of his gun. At the same moment as he lowered the torch, the bright light dropped away and he saw a figure opposite, aiming a gun at him.

Dazzled by the after-effects of the light, he couldn't see clearly. His eyes went wide, heart missed a beat. Adrenaline flooded his system. Something about the figure made him hesitate, his finger tensed on the trigger, ready to open fire. He wanted to speak, but a lump caught in his throat. What if it was Lars?

He tried to swallow, but his throat felt constricted.

Feeling like a cowboy in a showdown, he raised the torch to illuminate the figure and the torchlight shone straight back, blinding him again.

"Shit," he said, lowering the torch, watching as the figure did likewise. He raised the torch a fraction, waved it from side to side and realised he was looking at a mirror on the wall opposite.

"Goddamn idiot," he said, angry with himself for mistaking his own reflection for someone else.

He stepped into the room and crouched down to inspect one of the newspapers. The headline read: GOTCHA, and was from The Sun, dated May 4th 1982, and told the story of the sinking of the Argentinean battle cruiser, General Belgrano during the Falklands War.

Six-pack snorted. Same shit, worse situation.

"Goddamnit, Lars, where the hell are you?" he said into the microphone. He didn't like the way his voice seemed to echo throughout the building, making it seem deserted. Outside, gunfire rang out like firecrackers.

Standing up straight, Six-pack turned and headed towards the door. But then he heard a floorboard creak outside.

He sighed and stepped onto the landing. "About fucking time, I've been—"

It wasn't Lars.

Six-pack choked on a breath. The woman that had lunged through the window stared back at him with dead, feral eyes. Skin hung in ribbons from her cheeks. A shroud of dirty, limp black hair dangled across her forehead. Puss-filled lesions adorned her bare arms. Her hands rose up, fingers fashioned into claws.

Caught off-guard, Six-pack started to raise the barrel of his gun, but the zombie batted it aside and parted its bloated lips, revealing blood-stained teeth that seemed to chatter in anticipation of munching on flesh and bone.

Unable to get a clean shot, Six-pack dropped his gun and punched the zombie in the face. His fist struck rotting flesh that split as it compacted against bone. The skin felt cold, almost like rubber, but the punch achieved nothing. The zombie's head flew to the side for a brief instant under the impact, then it faced forwards again.

The creature groaned, the ragged sound coming from deep within the bowels of its rotting body. Six-pack punched it again, once, twice, three times in quick succession—to no avail.

The zombie grabbed his arms, seemed to possess a strength far beyond that implied by its decomposing state as it wrestled him to the ground. Then, inch by terrible inch, it lowered its head towards his neck, teeth primed like a gruesome mantrap, ready to clamp down and tear through flesh.

Six-pack grunted and dug his elbows into the zombie's chest to apply leverage, holding it at bay. He felt his strength ebb, the bunched muscles in his biceps straining to save him from being savaged.

The creature's fetid breath clung to the back of his throat, smelled worse than the drains of any abattoir. Six-pack gagged, as though he was about to vomit.

He tried to manoeuvre his leg underneath the creature, hoping to roll it off. The zombie may as well have been a former wrestler for all the good it did. Every move he made, the zombie seemed able to counter.

The handle of the knife attached to his belt thumped against the floor. If he could reach it he would slice the motherfucker's head clean off. He tried to wrench his arms from the zombie's manacle-like grip, but found it impossible.

Movement caught his eye beyond the zombie's shoulder. He imagined another zombie arriving for a late supper. He cursed. No one should have to die like this. Gooseflesh peppered his arms and his cheeks prickled as he strained one last time to break free.

A sharp crack rang out and the zombie's head erupted. Bone and brain matter splattered across Six-pack's face, coating his gritted teeth. He spat the foul tasting substance out. The zombie collapsed, what remained of its strength failing with the loss of its brain. The cumbersome corpse lay motionless across his chest, a ragged Cyclopean hole in the middle of its forehead, from out of which dripped feculent matter.

Six-pack rolled the body aside and reached for his knife. He grabbed the handle, slid it from the sheath and stared up, his eyes refocusing. Lars stood above him, the barrel of his gun wavering.

"Lars, Jesus, I thought you were dead."

Lars stared down, eyebrows narrowed and brow furrowed as though he didn't recognise Six-pack. A moment later, his expression softened and his awareness seemed to return.

"It fuckin' hurts," he said.

Six-pack sheathed his knife, scrambled to his feet and helped Lars settle against the wall. He lifted the bandage to check the wound, wrinkling his nose.

"Man, it smells like something crawled inside your arse and died." He regretted the words as they left his mouth.

"That bad?"

Six-pack wanted to tell him the truth, that his neck looked like chopped liver, but he couldn't bring himself to do it. Positive affirmations—that's what this man needed. "You're going to be fine. Big Red'll be here soon, then we can get out of this shit hole and get you to a hospital."

Lars nodded. He coughed, bringing up a clot of blood that Six-pack didn't like the look of. Tales of zombie folklore circled in his head. Once bitten, you don't stand a chance, would become one of them sooner or later. Looking at Lars, he guessed it to be sooner. He should kill him now, put him out of his misery. But what if there was a chance he wasn't infected? What if he killed him for no reason? He wasn't a murderer, had never killed anyone in cold blood. Perhaps the zombie stories were wrong.

"I'd better check the building's secure," he said. "I'll be back as quick as I can. Just hold in there." He passed Lars a canteen of water then stood up.

A series of loud bangs continued to emanate from all around the house, as though the creatures outside were taunting them.

He wondered how many more had snuck inside. All that banging would mask the sound of anyone creeping up on him. Perhaps that was the idea. Perhaps these creatures were a lot more intelligent than he gave them credit for.

Six-pack didn't want to switch his torch on in case it drew any unwanted attention. He stared towards the shadowed doorway leading out of the room, his eyes narrowed, penetrating the dark. The groaning and banging from outside jarred his nerves. Why couldn't they just shut the fuck up to give him chance to think?

Gun barrel leading the way, he stepped towards the door. Holding a gun gave him confidence, made him feel omnipotent, but knowing only a head shot killed the zombies lessened the feeling, took away some of that power. Only one thing would give him the confidence back. He hesitated, licked his lips, fingered the flask on his hip and pulled it out. He undid the top, raised the flask to his mouth and took a long swallow. The Jack Daniel's burned his throat and started a fire in his belly. He took another drink, then another, feeding the burning sensation until he felt numb to it.

What he would give for a bottle rather than a couple of measures...

He drained the last of the alcohol from the flask and shoved it back in his belt. The gun felt a little more reassuring, more like the death bringer he knew and loved. He patted the stock, slipped his finger through the trigger guard and crept towards the doorway, his steps now more assured.

The lack of background light found in most towns and villages made the darkness look like a physical barrier, impenetrable. Six-pack approached the doorway, his back slick with sweat. His finger itched to switch the torch on, but he resisted the urge and stepped into the dark.

SIXTEEN

Lofty looked at the dog and scowled. He couldn't kill it. That would go against everything he stood for. The one time he ran over that dog by accident had been bad enough, but this...

"You've got to," Jill said. "Look at it. The poor thing must be in agony."

"You do it then."

Jill pulled a lemon-sucking grimace and shook her head. "I can't."

"Well, what makes you think I can?"

"You're a man. Hunter-predator, that sort of thing. It's in your genes."

Lofty didn't agree. "And what would you suggest I kill it with, my bare hands?"

Jill pointed through the metal bars into the main room. "There must be something in there."

"And how am I supposed to get through the bars? Squeeze?"

Sighing in exasperation, Jill stretched her arm through the bars, lifted a catch and swung the door open. "Anything else?"

Lofty tried to ignore her condescending tone and walked out of the cage into the room beyond. Numbers scrolled across various monitor screens and intermittent beeps emanated from hi-tech machinery. On a table, he spotted what he recognised from television as a handheld stun gun: a handle with two metal prongs through which a current travelled. He guessed the man used it to stun the dog and he picked it up, turning it over in his hands to study it. More as an act of rebellion to stop them using it again, he put it in his rucksack.

A locked metal cupboard sat against the back wall. Next to that was a set of metal drawers. He pulled the top drawer, and it slid open, revealing manila folders. He wondered whether there might be something in them he could use against the company, but he didn't want to hang around. Someone might come back at any moment. He closed the drawer.

One of the monitor screens appeared to be hooked up to a microscope. The image on the screen showed tiny squiggling alien-like organisms. Lofty stared at the image, intrigued. He couldn't begin to comprehend what he was looking at—science and chemistry were never his best subjects at school.

He looked around the desk, rummaged through a couple of drawers, but nothing he saw seemed useable as a weapon.

"What about this?"

He turned at Jill's voice and stared at the Phillips screwdriver in her hand. "And what do you expect me to do with that? It's not a broken engine."

"You know what you can do with it." She did a quick impression of the killer in Psycho, jabbing down with the screwdriver.

Lofty tugged on his goatee. He didn't need to ask whether she was serious, her expression said it all.

She held the screwdriver out like a high priestess offering up a sacrificial blade. Lofty hesitated. He stared at the screwdriver, the six-inch steel shaft becoming something menacing. After a moment, he accepted the makeshift weapon, held it point down, ready to strike. The plastic handle fit snug in his palm, almost as though designed for a more sinister purpose.

"Hurry up," Jill said.

Lofty kept his tongue in check. It was alright for her to egg him on. She wasn't the one being asked to kill an innocent animal.

He trudged back to the cage, his shoes feeling as though they'd turned to lead. He stopped in the doorway and placed his free hand against the cold metal. The pungent aroma now seemed unimportant, more a slight distraction than an overpowering sensation.

I can't do this, he thought. *I can't kill it.*

He stared down at the beast, its tongue hanging like a slab of meat from the mantrap jaws. Jill came up beside him and put a hand on his shoulder.

"It's for the best," she said.

Lofty knew she was right. Cruel to be kind and all that. But why him? Why did he have to kill it? Hell, he balked at killing wasps, spiders and flies…but a dog?

He swallowed, trying to quell the sick feeling rising from his stomach to his throat. His palm felt sweaty, lessening his grip on the handle. He switched the screwdriver to his other hand and wiped his palm on his trousers before transferring the implement back.

"Someone could come back any time," Jill said. "You've got to be quick."

Easy for you to say. He stared back at the dog, saw its leg twitch the way canines do when they're asleep, as though chasing cats in their dreams.

He took a step forwards. The gravity of what he planned to do pressed down upon him, made his shoulders slump in resignation that it was for the best. *At least if it's asleep, it might not feel the pain.*

When he reached the dog, he stood above it and stared down. A trickle of sweat ran down his forehead and along his nose. He wiped it away, felt his heart pounding within his chest like a timer on a stick of dynamite. His throat felt dry, his tongue glued to the roof of his mouth. The bald patches in the German Shepherd's black and tan coat revealed raw-looking wounds. The dog's eyes were open, but they appeared glazed, lifeless.

A smell like rotten food emanated from the dog. Lofty kneeled beside it and placed the tip of the screwdriver against its head. He paused, couldn't kill it. No matter what pain the animal suffered, he couldn't take its life.

He removed the screwdriver, heard Jill mutter something, then saw the dog's leg twitch again. Its tongue moved, sliding back into its maw like a moray eel seeking shelter. Next moment, its head moved, one beady eye swivelling in its socket and fixing him with a hungry glare.

Lofty swallowed and edged away from the dog. He saw its gaze follow his movements. Next minute, the German Shepherd scrambled to its feet. Its claws scratched across the cold stone floor, and a low growl rumbled from its throat. Its lips peeled back, revealing sharp teeth. It took a faltering step, still unsteady on its feet.

Knowing Jill screamed blue murder at the sight of a spider, he expected to hear her scream now, but to her credit, she stayed quiet. Lofty glanced back, saw her standing at the gate, eyes wide and shaking her head as though to dismiss what she saw.

Her lips moved, but no sound came out.

Lofty turned back to the dog, saw it preparing to attack, swaying slightly as though still dazed. The hair along its back bristled, its ears slowly standing at attention, and its tail disappearing between its legs.

Feeling sick at the thought of the dog biting him, Lofty stumbled away, his legs shaking. Didn't it realise he was on its side?

"Good dog," he said. "Sit."

"Jesus, you're not Barbara Woodhouse," Jill said.

Although surprised she even knew the deceased dog trainer, at this moment, he would give anything for the old lady's uncanny affinity with dogs.

"There's a good dog," he said, unable to keep the tremor from his voice. He literally tasted the dread oozing from his pores, and knowing dogs could smell fear, he knew this one would be having an olfactory orgasm.

He took another faltering step back.

And the dog launched itself at him. Out of instinct, Lofty raised his hands. The dog's front paws, almost as big as hands, struck his chest and pushed him back. Lofty stumbled, struggling to stay on his feet when he stepped in a puddle of urine and lost his footing. He fell hard, his back hitting the floor with a loud smack, knocking the wind out of him. The contents of the rucksack fell out and rolled across the floor. He saw the stun gun and grabbed hold of it. The dog didn't hesitate. It pounced on his chest, teeth inches from his face.

It growled, the sound deep and throaty, and for the first time, Lofty heard a series of barks and howls emanating from outside the room, issuing from the other animals within the facility as if in sympathy with their brother.

With hesitation meaning certain pain or even death, he used all his strength and rolled the dog off, pushed the stun gun into its neck and pulled the trigger. At the same time, he rammed the screwdriver into its side. He stabbed again and again, felt the pointed tip pass through meat and muscle, striking ribs.

Jill screamed, the sound echoing around the room.

Lofty kept stabbing, too afraid to stop. A moment later, the dog collapsed.

Sickened by what he'd done, Loft struggled to his feet and looked at the screwdriver in his hand, saw tufts of fur and gore decorating the shaft. He dropped it, along with the stun gun, and backed away, his legs shaking more than before.

Jill stopped screaming and started sobbing.

"You've…killed it," she said.

"No shit. That's what you wanted me to do."

"Not like that. Jesus, Samuel, you…you butchered it."

"It was going to bite my fucking face off, what did you expect me to do?"

"But not like that."

"Well, I'm sorry, but fucking hell, Jill—I didn't have a choice."

He walked out of the cage and slumped into a chair to catch his breath and recover his senses. His hands wouldn't stop shaking. He threw up, splattering the floor with vomit.

Jill came up beside him and rubbed his back. "I'm sorry, you know, for what I said. I know there was nothing else you could do."

Lofty ran the back of his hand across his mouth. His stomach felt as though it had been turned inside out and his throat burned. The vile taste in his mouth made him feel worse.

"It's okay." He forced a smile.

"I've never seen you like that before. You were…wild."

"I just wish it hadn't come to that, that I could have saved it somehow."

"I don't think anyone could have saved it. You did the best thing for it."

Lofty wasn't convinced. Guilt played pinball in his mind, overriding all other thoughts. If only there was something he could have done. He knew deep down there wasn't, but it didn't help. But what if he could do something now? What if it didn't die in vain? He thought about the other dogs he'd heard howling. What if he could help them? He didn't have to free them, just had to find some evidence that they were being mistreated, then present it to someone able to help. Even animals used in experiments had rights that said they shouldn't suffer discomfort or undertake any procedure that interfered with their health.

He thought about taking pictures of the German Shepherd, but then dismissed the thought, realising he could get in trouble for killing it. He stared at the door leading out of the room, wondered what else lay out there.

"Hadn't we better go?" Jill said.

"In a minute." Lofty opened his rucksack and withdrew the Olympus digital camera. Opening up the metal case, he started taking a few shots of the room, making sure to avoid the dead dog.

"Okay, David Bailey, now can we go?"

Lofty scratched his head. "I've just killed a dog. I dunno, but I want to make its death mean something, you know?" He shrugged, felt sheepish.

"What are you saying?"

Lofty looked at the door. "You saw what they'd done to that dog. Well, there are others out there. If I could get a photograph—"

Jill held her hand up. "Hold it right there. Don't you think we're in enough trouble if we get caught? I'm going nowhere but back down that drain."

"Jill…babe, I've got to do this. I *killed* something. You know, I feel guilty enough without just running away with nothing to show for it."

"We can tell people."

"And what good do you think that'll do?"

"Well, I'm not going to let you go traipsing around out there. Anything could happen."

"I'll be okay."

Jill cupped her face in her hands. "I think my mother's right about you."

Lofty's heart sank.

"But God help me, I love you, and if you think I'm going to wait around here, not knowing what's happened to you, then you don't know *me* very well."

Lofty smirked. A warm glow settled in his stomach. He leaned forwards to kiss Jill, but she pushed him gently away.

"I may love you, but not enough to kiss those lips after you've just been sick."

Lofty smiled, then turned and headed towards the door.

SEVENTEEN

Amber ran along the muddy main street, firing indiscriminately at a zombie that stumbled around the corner of a building. The rain hampered her vision, and she knew that if she stopped, she could get a better shot, but adrenaline-fuelled fear drove her on. Lars and Six-pack needed her help. She couldn't let them down. She let loose a small volley, and saw its head explode.

She ran to the edge of a building, hunkered down, and stared in the direction of the house Lars and Six-pack were holed up in. She let out a sharp breath.

"You're shitting me," Eddie said. "There's no way we can get past all of them."

Amber surveyed the zombie horde surrounding the building: too many to count. She raised her gun and prepared to fire when Eddie knocked the barrel aside.

"You want to commit suicide, do it when you're on your own. You open fire now, them fuckers are going to swarm all over us. Besides, they're not doing anything, just standing there."

Amber turned on Eddie, eyes narrowed and teeth gritted. She knew he was right, but it didn't make it any easier to accept.

She thumbed her microphone. "Lars, Six-pack, hold your position, I'm going to see if there's another way to reach you."

A muffled affirmation returned through the earpiece.

Eddie spat on the ground. "You ask me, we leave 'em and get the fuck out of here."

"When I want your advice, I'll ask for it. Now button it."

Eddie shrugged. "Don't say I didn't warn you."

Amber glared at him. "What part of *button it* don't you understand?"

"Women," Eddie mumbled.

Amber raised the stock of her gun, felt like slamming it into Eddie's face. She took a breath and then lowered her weapon. "We need to find a way to clear them away."

"You could always run bare-ass naked towards them shouting, 'dinner, come and get it.'"

"Or I could hogtie you to that tree and see how long it takes them to spot you. But then I guess even zombies have got standards. Knowing my luck, they'd ignore you."

Eddie winked. "You know you don't mean that. I've seen the way you've been looking at me."

Amber cringed. "Stop talking bollocks. Let's rescue our men."

"The lady doth protest too much."

Amber tried to ignore him, but he was getting on her nerves. *Again.*

She'd met his type before. They were all talk. If she called him out on any of it, he would run a mile. But she just hadn't got time for his ego theatrics now.

She pointed along the track. "Cover me, I'm going to see if I can get across to that building to get a better look."

She didn't wait for Eddie to respond before she started moving, didn't want to listen to him spout more crap from his foul mouth.

Unearthed roots protruded from the ground, natural snares that tried to trip her up as she ran. The building she headed towards looked about to collapse, and wouldn't be somewhere to hole up if the zombies saw her and decided to give chase.

The windows were broken and there was no front door in the frame—just a shell of crumbling brickwork and rotten timbers. Many of the tiles lay on the ground around the outside of the structure, most of them broken. Amber picked her way among the debris and scurried through the entrance. The first floor had collapsed, creating an obstacle course on the ground. Amber stepped through the wreckage, heading towards the rear of the building, where she'd be able to better see the building Lars and Six-pack were trapped inside.

With most of the roof missing and one wall collapsed, the building offered no shelter from the rain. In fact it seemed worse. Large, accumulated drops dripped from the structure above. A virtual cascade ran down one wall—overflow from something up above. The sound was loud enough to mask any noise from outside, and Amber shivered when she realised she might not hear anyone creeping up on her.

She picked her way across broken timbers, testing where she placed her feet in case the debris shifted, trapping her foot or worse.

But why are they just standing there? What are they waiting for?

She strained her eyes to see through the darkness. The sky was a patchwork of black and grey, a virtual cauldron of malevolence swirling high above. She prayed for a letup in the deluge and a break in the clouds to allow the moon's baleful glow to shine through.

With one of the outer walls collapsed, Amber questioned how safe the structure was, especially if it was a load-bearing wall.

She scrambled over a collapsed ceiling beam lying horizontally across the middle of the room, made her way towards the doorway at the rear of the house

A sound like that of a herd of cattle emanated from the zombies. Amber wondered whether they were communicating or in pain.

Once at the doorway, she pushed the door, wary it might destabilise the building's precarious condition, but it didn't move. She pushed again, using her shoulder, but still the door wouldn't budge.

Judging by the state of the room, she imagined more debris blocked the door from the other side, and no amount of pushing would move it. With no other way to open the door, she started back across the room. She clambered across the fallen beam, heard it creak, and then felt it shift beneath her like a bucking bronco. She instinctively wrapped her arms around it for support. The movement of the timber acted as a catalyst. A noise like distant thunder cracked from the wall next to her, and next minute it collapsed. Age-old bricks cascaded across Amber. The backpack helped cushion her back, but the weight of the bricks forced the air from her lungs. She fought waves of pain as the bricks pinned her legs and buffeted her chest.

An overhead beam broke free and swung down like a pendulum. Amber tried to move her head aside, but she didn't have enough room. The jagged end of the beam tore across her face, leaving a gash in her cheek that felt as though it was on fire. She saw the beam reach the end of its swing and start its return journey. Knowing it would strike her again, she raised her hand to stop its momentum. The beam slammed into her wrist, sending a blast of pain through her body, another one to add to her collection.

Amber gritted her teeth and swore. The beam creaked. She saw it was hanging by a few splinters of wood. It could fall anytime.

She tried to pull her legs out but found them pinned by another beam. She grimaced, pulled harder, sending a shaft of pain through her leg.

A sound drew her attention. She lifted her head and gazed across the room. Someone approached. She saw the figure scramble across the rubble. Eddie? Unsure, she bit her lip, raised the barrel of her gun and aimed towards the figure's head. Her finger tightened on the trigger, almost at the point of no return.

"Amber, you okay?"

Amber let out a breath and removed her finger from the trigger. "TJ, what are you doing here?"

"I heard what you were saying about rescuing Lars and Six-pack, and I came down to see if I could help, when I saw part of the building collapse—"

"You're a life-saver. My legs are stuck under a beam."

"I've got it." TJ unslung his gun and   squatted down to grab a hold of the beam. Getting a good grip, he started to lift, grunting with the exertion. Bricks toppled aside and the timber creaked and shifted.

The pressure relaxed on Amber's legs, made them feel as light as air and she started to pull them out. She hoped nothing was broken. From what she could tell, apart from a few scratches and bruises, she was fine.

There was a loud clatter as TJ dropped the beam. He took a deep breath before crouching down. "So where's Eddie gone?" he asked, rolling her trouser legs up to inspect the damage.

"He's supposed to be watching my back."

"From the other side of the village?"

Amber frowned. "He's at the end of the track out front."

"Not any more he's not. I saw him scooting around the perimeter. Can you move your legs?"

Amber closed her eyes and bit her tongue. *What the hell's he playing at?* She raised her legs and bent each one at the knee and ankle.

"Well, you'll live," TJ said. "You'll probably be a bit sore tomorrow, and there are a few scratches, but I don't think there's any permanent damage."

"I'm sore now, never mind tomorrow." She rubbed a wound on her leg, wincing at the resultant sting. Satisfied she was okay, she rolled her trouser legs back down and struggled to her feet. Shooting pain emanated from her calf and thighs, but as she moved around, hobbling across the debris, the pain subsided to a dull throb.

"Where's Hunter?" Amber asked.

"He's scoping the village from the hillside, picking off one or two zombies when he can. Not that it seems to do much good. There's hundreds of 'em —all over the place."

"Well, as soon as we've got Lars and Six-pack, we're out of here."

"Then let's get a move on. Dead people shouldn't walk around like that, it's just not right. I mean, how's it possible?"

Amber shook her head. "I wish I knew."

"If you ask me, we haven't been paid enough for this shit."

"That's just it though, what have we been paid *for?*"

TJ frowned.

"We're supposed to be on a rescue mission, but paint me red and call me stupid, the only people that need rescuing are us." She ran a hand through her hair, her fingers coming away covered in grit, dirt and God knows what.

"So you think we've been set up?"

Amber nodded. "Hook, line and sinker."

"What for? What's the point of all this?"

"When you find out, make sure you let me know. One thing's for sure though, when we get out of this, I've got a few things I'd like to say to that Finch bloke that recruited us."

TJ picked up his gun. "You won't have chance to ask him anything if I get to him first."

Then I'd better make sure you don't, because I want some answers. But first, I want to find out just what the hell Eddie's up to. "Okay, let's get out of here before the rest of the place collapses." She gritted her teeth, gun an extension of her arm as she returned to the nightmare awaiting her on the street.

EIGHTEEN

Hunter lay behind a log and peered through the ATN scope of the Dragunov sniper rifle. He made a couple of adjustments to the rangefinder reticle that allowed him to gauge the target's distance, made another couple of adjustments to compensate for elevation and wind, took a deep inhalation, exhaled until the moment of natural respiratory pause, then squeezed the trigger. The rifle kicked in his hand, but he kept his head in firm contact with the stock, kept the trigger pulled all the way to the rear, continued to look through the sight, and only released the trigger when the recoil stopped. Through the sight, he watched the bullet strike its target with unerring accuracy and the zombie flew back to lie spread-eagled across the ground, its head blown apart.

Hunter couldn't afford to feel remorse when he took someone out, but knowing the targets were already dead made it more monotonous than anything, like shooting inanimate objects. He found another target, a woman this time, readjusted the sight and then went through the previous breathing procedure before he pulled the trigger. The 7.62x54mm bullet struck home, spinning the woman like a top.

Rain trickled through the leafy canopy above, the foliage providing a little relief from the downpour. Despite having a good view of the village, the layout and the buildings provided too many obstacles. From what he could see, the zombies were everywhere. Some were running around like wild things in search of fresh meat, others just stood in ominous silence. He could just about see the building Lars and Six-pack were holed up in, but couldn't help from where he was. With the rest of the team scattered, all leadership seemed to have gone out the window. It now seemed to be every man for himself. Hunter could deal with that, could work well enough whether acting on his own or under orders. Sometimes he found his own company preferable to that of others. Those three days in the jungle when he had waited for the rebel leader had shown him that. It took a certain sort of person to be a sniper.

His girlfriend Alice, on the other hand, would probably say he couldn't cope too well on his own, considering the mess he left their flat in on the rare occasions she went away without him to visit relatives or friends. In the army, he had to keep things tidy, had to look smart and follow orders to the letter. Once he left the armed forces, a rebellious streak manifested, and he took a more slovenly approach to his general appearance. He liked to think of himself as laid-back and chilled, a surf bum with a gun who followed the tides of war instead of the waves.

He slotted into the personal security way of life without too much trouble. There were plenty of opportunities for the right people. Sure, there was danger, but that was part of the thrill. He couldn't see himself opting for the quiet life, stacking shelves in the supermarket like his brother, Tony. Getting a rollicking for stacking the cans of baked beans too high wasn't the same as making life or death decisions.

He retargeted, adjusted the range, took a respiratory pause and fired another round. The bullet struck home with devastating effect, taking a man out and almost severing the leg of a man standing a few feet behind. The crippled zombie flopped to the ground and started crawling, pulling himself along like a slug. Hunter decided not to bother wasting a bullet dealing the deathblow, preferring to save each round for those who looked capable of doing damage.

A branch snapped somewhere behind him. He felt his heart kick like a mule as he swung the gun around, targeting the trees. The sudden adrenaline rush made him feel light-headed as he scanned the area. When he failed to spot anything through the sight, his heart went from a gallop to a trot and then relaxed. Unsure if it was sweat or raindrops on his forehead, he ran the sleeve of his jacket across his brow to wipe it away. He exhaled a shaky breath, couldn't believe how spooked he felt.

He turned back to view the village, grateful for the distance and the rain which helped to dampen the zombies' groans. He felt the darkness pressing at his back and a shiver went down his spine. The hairs on the nape of his neck bristled. He glanced over his shoulder—the darkness absolute. At least it helped as much as it hindered, because if he couldn't see, he couldn't be seen either—or could dead people see in the dark? They couldn't in any of the films he'd seen, but this wasn't a goddamn film. As he equated death with darkness, perhaps they could see as they existed between two worlds, that of the living and that of the dead. The thought sent another shiver coursing through his body.

The sooner they were out of here, the better. This was fucked-up with a capital F.

Although loaded with plenty of ammunition to last a while, he knew taking out one or two zombies wasn't going to help when there were so many of them. A sniper in the field took out selected enemy personnel. But here, no one stood out as a selective target. To Hunter, it now became a case of if-the-face-fits.

He scanned the streets, spotted John and Barry at the edge of the village, hiding behind a low wall. Further movement caught his eye and he saw a large, topless man charging towards their position. From where they were, they wouldn't be able to see the man, drapes of belly fat swaying from side to side as he ran.

Hunter targeted the man, but fired too fast. The bullet missed. He fired again, not taking the time to sight the target, and missed again.

He thumbed his microphone. "John, Barry, there's a man running towards you. Seven o'clock. Coming in fast."

He watched through the scope as Barry poked his head above the bricks in time to see the man plough through the wall at his side. Startled, Barry fell back, his gun sent flying in the confusion. John jumped aside and raised the barrel of his gun to target the zombie, but it straddled Barry, causing him to hold fire, afraid he might hit his companion. Hunter watched Barry wrestle the zombie while John battered its head with the stock of his gun.

Strong and resilient to pain, the zombie seemed unperturbed. The force of John's blows caved half of its head in, but it didn't seem to make any difference. He guessed it didn't feel anything in death.

While watching the fight, Hunter adjusted the scope. He aligned the sight on the zombie, but couldn't take the shot for fear of hitting Barry.

Despite the damp conditions and the rain trickling through the leaves, Hunter's lips felt dry. As he licked them, he thought how Alice liked kissing them. He didn't think she would feel that way now, would no doubt say they felt like sandpaper.

Although he acted macho and a little aloof around Alice, thinking about her caused a slight pain in his stomach. Unused to the unfamiliar sensation, his hands started shaking, disturbing the image through the scope. Hunter released the polymer foregrip and wiped his hand along his trousers before resuming his hold. It took him a couple of seconds to retarget on the zombie.

John had moved aside, was crouched by the wall, fiddling with something Hunter couldn't make out. Next second, the zombie seemed to freeze, its head aloft as it straddled Barry.

Hunter prepared to take the shot. He regulated his breathing, relaxed his muscles. Water trickled into his eye, whether sweat or rain he didn't know. He blinked, blurring his vision, removed his trigger finger to rub his face, then retargeted. With no time left to hesitate, he pulled the trigger, saw half the zombie's head disintegrate.

The sound of breaking branches made Hunter jump. He snapped his head around, saw a figure darker than the surrounding night rushing towards him. He started to bring his weapon around to fire, but the figure crashed into him, knocking the Dragunov aside. It brought with it the smell of death and putrefying flesh. Hunter gagged. Strong hands with sharp nails gouged his face, scoring the flesh from his cheeks. Hunter grunted. Leaves, mulch and clods of earth fell onto his face from the creature. The sweet smell of the mulch entered his nostrils, but the fetid odour of decay proved too overpowering.

He couldn't tell whether it was a man or woman, didn't care. All he knew was that it was trying to kill him. Although he couldn't see clearly, he heard its teeth click together, primed to tear a chunk out of his flesh. The thought spurred him on, fuelling his muscles. He released the gun and threw a punch, his fist striking cold, compliant flesh that felt like the congealed skin of a rice pudding. He grimaced, his stomach as queasy as if he'd awoken from a night of heavy drinking.

The zombie groaned, a sound of anger or pain—Hunter couldn't decide which.

He tried to rise, but the zombie pushed him over the log he'd been using to support the gun. He landed in a mulch of leaves that felt slimy against his skin. He struggled to his feet, pulled the Colt M1911 pistol from the holster around his waist and cocked the hammer, fired blindly into the dark. The pistol bucked in his hand, the automatic movement of the slide cocking the hammer for each subsequent shot. The trees swallowed the roar of the gun. He heard the thud of bullets striking targets, but didn't know what those targets were. The magazine ran dry, all seven bullets fired.

Hoping and praying he'd hit the zombie, he reached for the Maglite on his belt when he heard a groan to his left. He turned, switched on the torch and shone it into the ravaged face of his adversary, taking an involuntary gasp as he surveyed the creature.

Dead eyes stared back from what turned out to be a man's sunken sockets. His skin looked waxy and pale. Leaves and dirt protruded from his black hair, one of his ears looking as though it had been nibbled by a rat, or blasted by a bullet. At a guess, the man hadn't been dead too long. The Colt's bullets had ripped holes in his once white, now filthy, ripped shirt. No blood poured from the wounds, but an internal organ protruded from one, like sausage meat squeezed from a machine. The man's corpse was bloated with gasses, the release of which tainted the air with an even more disgusting aroma.

Hunter ejected the magazine from the pistol and reached for another, but the zombie moved too fast. It lunged forwards.

Unable to react quickly enough, Hunter dropped the gun and torch, freeing his hands to wrestle the zombie. But it was too strong. He smelled its fetid, stomach churning odour wash over him, felt its teeth bite down on his wrist as he tried to protect his face. White-hot pain seared through his body, made him feel as though he had been dunked in liquid nitrogen. He gasped, felt the zombie crunch through skin and connective tissue, then bite into bone. He felt its teeth gnawing. Felt bone splinter and break. He squealed. Kicked out. But the zombie didn't react.

He felt warm blood run along his arm, seeping from the cold, dry kiss of the zombie's lips against his flesh.

Hunter punched with his free hand, screamed, kicked, but none of it helped. The zombie shook its head like a dog, tore a chunk of meat from Hunter's arm. He heard it spit the chunk out, making room for more as it pressed itself forwards, knocking Hunter to the ground as his feet slipped in the mulch. His breath blasted from his mouth as the zombie landed on his chest, compressing his lungs. He groaned, felt the zombie lower its head, its teeth finding the fresh meat around his throat.

Tears rolled from Hunter's eyes. In his mind he pictured Alice. He wished he could tell her how much he loved her.

For the first time in his life, he envied his brother. Stacking shelves didn't seem such a bad career after all.

NINETEEN

The MP5 spat bullets at an alarming rate as Amber shot at three zombies coming onto the main track from a gap between two buildings. Although many of the bullets missed, a few hit their respective targets, carving out chunks of flesh and bone. TJ opened fire at her side, doubling the firepower.

Her body ached all over from numerous bruises, cuts and scrapes, and the gun's recoil only accentuated the pain. TJ was spattered in blood and mud, and she imagined she would look the same—probably worse if how she felt was any indication.

A couple of bullets smacked into a middle-aged man's left leg, severing it at the knee. He dropped to the ground, dragging himself along like something possessed. A volley of bullets hit a teenaged female zombie in the stomach, opening her up like a tin can. Meat and bones sprayed from the cavity, but she continued running towards Amber regardless.

Amber found the way they didn't feel pain disconcerting. As she retargeted on the teenager, TJ fired a round from his M16 Assault Rifle, downing the girl with a single bullet to the head.

The third zombie succumbed to the bullets, its head obliterated, no longer recognisable as male or female. Amber stood above the now one-legged man crawling towards her, placed the barrel of her gun against his head and pulled the trigger. The man's torso flopped to the ground, his arm still outstretched where he tried to reach for her.

Groans and shouts emanated from around the village. A series of loud shots came from the hillside. Amber glanced up but couldn't see anything.

She thumbed her microphone. "Everyone report. Over."

"Still here," Lars wheezed

"Me too," Six-pack said.

"John, Barry, how you doing?"

"We had a bit of a problem, but Hunter sorted it for us," John said.

"Hunter, come in, over."

No one replied.

"Eddie, do you hear me? Over."

Another gap of silence.

"What do you think?" TJ asked.

Amber pursed her lips and exhaled slowly. "I don't know. They might be out of range. Their equipment might be damaged—"

"Or they're dead," TJ interrupted.

"As far as Eddie's concerned, that might not be such a loss." She thumbed the microphone again. "Hunter, can you hear me? Over."

When he didn't answer, Amber busied herself replacing the MP5's magazine, trying not to think of the worst-case scenario. "Okay, let's go," she said.

She ran towards a large pine tree, its natural aroma tainted by the smell of death and decay choking the village, and skidded into the earth beside the trunk, breathing fast. The layer of needles beneath the boughs wasn't as uncomfortable as she imagined. She closed her eyes for an instant, dreaming of being home in bed. A second later, TJ dropped down beside her.

The rain had lessened, and the cloud cover thinned, allowing wan moonlight to filter through.

Amber peered above a low pile of earth providing a little cover, almost wishing she hadn't bothered. The horrific scene of the dead running rampage through the village looked like a scene from hell. She ducked back down.

"I don't know how we're going to reach Lars and Six-pack without a bloody tank," she said.

TJ leaned against the tree. "If only."

Under conventional circumstances, she knew they probably had enough ammunition to take on a small country, but when the enemy refused to die, every bullet counted and her magazines were being emptied at an alarming rate. She couldn't afford to rush out, guns blazing. Not when the dead would fall over themselves, fighting tooth and claw to return the attack.

TJ peered over the mound then ducked back down. "What if we follow the tree line and come back in around the back to try again?"

Amber wiped moisture from her forehead. "As far as plans go, it's the only one we have." She peered over the mound. "Okay, let's go."

She stood and ran back towards the trees, negotiating the rubble of a fallen wall. The uneven ground made running dangerous, and with the risk of twisting her ankle prominent in her mind, she slowed her pace. The thought of the dead creatures made her skin crawl. If she hadn't seen them with her own eyes, she would never, ever believe such creatures existed.

She noticed a figure ahead at the edge of the trees: a zombie, a man, his face deathly pale, almost like the glow of the moon. He turned and lurched towards her as though fitted with a fresh meat radar.

Amber raised the barrel of her gun and fired as she ran, stitching his body with a line of bullets. The man jerked, his limbs moving as though operated by an unseen puppeteer.

Having missed his head, the man continued to run towards her. With the magazine empty, and with no time to reload, Amber performed a flying kick. Her booted feet struck the man's chest and he flew back. Pain shot up Amber's legs, emanating from the cuts and bruises obtained when the building collapsed. Unable to land on her feet, she dropped on her side. Pain exploded from her ribs.

She winced and gritted her teeth. Expecting to see the zombie recover from the attack, she reached for her pistol.

"Nice," TJ said as he arrived at Amber's side and reached down to help her to her feet.

Puzzled, Amber looked up to see the zombie impaled on the broken branch of a pine tree, its arms flailing in the air.

She accepted TJ's hand and pulled herself to her feet.

The zombie thrashed and struggled, gnashing its teeth like a rabid dog. Amber raised the silenced MP5 and fired a single bullet through its forehead. The zombie flopped forwards, snapping the branch.

Amber wondered who the man was, where he'd come from, and how he'd ended up here. Dishevelled in appearance, his clothes consisted of turned-up trousers held tight with string, and an ill-fitting, mismatched jacket.

"He looks like a tramp," TJ said, voicing her own thoughts.

"Come on, before any more come." She ran into the trees. Tall ferns slowed her down as they wrapped around her limbs like grasping hands. She waded through them as best she could. The forest felt primordial. Strange hoots and shrieks filled the night air.

Still soaked from the downpour, Amber felt uncomfortable. The added weight of wet clothes taxed her energy reserves and she readjusted the backpack to alleviate the pain in her shoulders. She brushed the ferns aside, wishing she had a machete to clear a path. Beneath the trees, the darkness seemed even more oppressive, making her wary that anyone could lie hidden in the undergrowth.

Moving as fast as she dared, Amber led TJ around the perimeter. She could see the village through the trees, figures running in wild abandon. Some were semi-naked – death obviously removed all inhibitions. She wondered if they were even aware of what had happened to them, if they knew they were dead.

The smell of fresh pine and foliage mingled with the awful smell of decay, creating a foul aroma.

Bushy Common Juniper and thick bracken made progress difficult. She changed course, ventured deeper into the trees, looking for an easier route. Within the dense thicket, the moans and groans from the village died out, replaced with the babble of a mountain torrent, and the haunting sound of a curlew somewhere in the night. For a moment, she imagined none of it had happened. That the dead weren't stalking her team. But she knew that was a false hope, a pipedream.

The thick undergrowth eventually thinned, and Amber increased her pace. She checked her GPS a couple of times, just to make sure she was going the right way. Navigating a forest could be difficult in daylight, but at night...

The sound of movement up ahead attracted her attention. She stopped, held her arm up to relay the problem to TJ, glimpsed him squat at her side.

Although she knew the darkness helped as much as it hindered, she crouched behind a thicket and peered through the fronds.

Eyes now adapted to the dark, and with the added help of the moonlight filtering through the canopy above, she saw a figure crashing through the foliage like a stampeding bull.

She gripped her gun, raised it to her shoulder.

Only someone already dead would be stupid enough to make so much noise.

And now they were about to stay dead.

She put her finger on the trigger, aimed, prepared to fire, when a bullet slammed through the thicket, inches from her face.

TWENTY

"What's going on?" TJ said, dropping flat on the ground. "God help us if they've learned how to shoot."

Amber wished she knew. She fired though the fronds, the bullets making them dance as they cut a path. The figure rolled out of the way and disappeared into the undergrowth. A moment later, return fire echoed through the trees. The awl-shaped needles of the Juniper beside Amber rained down around her. Bullets punched into the tree's thin trunk, releasing a heady sap.

"Shit," Amber said, rolling aside. A line of bullets struck the ground where she'd just been lying and she thanked every God she could think of that she'd moved aside in time.

"*What the hell's going on?*" she shouted.

The gunfire ceased.

"Fucking hell, I might have known," the figure said. "Hold your fire, I'm coming out."

Amber stood at the same time. "Eddie! What the fuck are you doing?"

Eddie slouched towards her, shaking his head. "I almost killed you. You're supposed to be in the village. I thought you were one of them dead things."

"And *I* thought *you* were watching my back. What are you doing out here?"

"We're waiting," TJ said, getting to his feet, "because I want to hear this as much as she does."

"Those dead fuckers were everywhere. I was surrounded—had to scarper before they got me."

"So why didn't you reply when I radioed you?"

"Didn't hear you."

"Do you think I was born yesterday? You were doing a runner."

Eddie visibly bristled. "Fuck off I was!"

"You got spooked and decided to cut loose. Only problem was, you got lost out here."

"Bollocks. I'm not scared of anything."

"Tell that to the zombie behind you."

Eddie spun, firing into the undergrowth as he did. Realising there was no one there, he turned on Amber. "Think you're fuckin' funny, don't cha? Well fuck you, and fuck this mission. I'm off. You're just lucky I didn't hit you when I opened fire. From this close, I won't miss." He levelled his gun at Amber's chest. "Now move out of my way, because I'm going."

Amber stepped aside. "You want to get yourself killed, be my guest."

"You're not going to let him go, are you?" TJ said. "I'll stop him if you want."

Amber placed a restraining hand on TJ's arm. "Just let him go. We'll be better off without him anyway."

She watched Eddie traipse away through the undergrowth, then consulted her GPS. Satisfied she knew the way back to the village, she replaced the GPS in her pack and withdrew the water bottle from her hip. She took a long drink, savouring the chilled water as it slid down her throat.

"Right, let's—"

Gunfire roared from the direction Eddie had taken. Amber stared through the foliage, watched as Eddie burst out of it, back-pedalling, firing into the trees as he went.

"They're fuckin' here," he said. "They're all around us. You've brought them here."

The moans of the undead drifted through the trees, a dark chorus. Next minute, figures thundered through the vegetation. Amber tried to count, but there were too many of them. She opened fire, bullets scything through foliage and flesh alike, but it seemed futile.

"Go!" she shouted.

She snatched a grenade from her utility belt, pulled the pin and lobbed it towards the zombies. Seconds later, an explosion filled the night and a bright flash scorched her retina. In the instant of the flash, she saw zombies caught in the blast, saw bodies explode like pustules, throwing gobs of meat and bone in all directions. Some of the gore struck her face, cold and slimy.

She turned, started to run, leapt over a fallen tree, slammed through a bush, almost tripped on concealed vegetation. Fear fuelled her muscles, made her feel turbocharged, almost invincible.

They slid down an embankment into a small gulley. Eddie took point, followed by TJ and then Amber. Trees lined the banks and rainwater cascaded through the middle. Amber splashed through the water, felt her foot slip and grabbed a branch to stop from falling.

She heard the zombies in pursuit, crashing through the undergrowth. Their inability to feel pain and obvious disregard for their own safety made them quicker. Amber heard them getting closer, hunting like a pack. She wished Eddie and TJ would move faster because she didn't want to be first on the menu.

The tops of the trees lining the gulley intertwined overhead, making it seem like an oppressive hallway that stopped the moon's glow from illuminating the path. The steep sides of the gulley didn't help. She knew if any of the undead rushed towards them from the front, they'd be trapped. Their only means of escape was to try scrambling up the banks. She hoped it didn't come to that.

Amber snatched a grenade from her belt, pulled the pin and dropped it behind her. A couple of seconds later, she heard a muffled explosion as it erupted beneath the water, felt the concussive blast as though part of it had exploded in her chest. The force of the detonation and debris struck her back, almost knocking her over. The blast shook the trees, made leaves rain down, nature's ticker-tape parade. Although hard to tell, she saw what appeared to be a foot bounce off the bank in front of her and splash in the water.

The noise of the explosion rang in her ears, muffling the sound of pursuit, so she didn't know if it worked to slow the zombies down but she wasn't going to turn back to look. Every second counted, and to look back, she would have to slow her pace.

She felt her heart pound, her muscles ache, her ankles jar. Breath blasted from her mouth, and she took quick inhalations to replace it. A break appeared in the darkness ahead, indicating the end of the tree-lined gulley. The sight filled Amber with renewed strength.

"Get a move on," she shouted. Eddie and TJ increased their pace, either spurred on by the sound of her voice, the prospect of getting out of the gulley or the thought that the zombies were catching up.

With the increase in pace, Amber exited the gulley within thirty strides. Tall fir trees stood sentinel near the exit, their trunks grouped together like bars. She jumped clear of the water and ran faster, overtaking TJ to exit the trees. She scrambled and skidded down the grass and shale bank alongside the small stream, finding herself about forty feet below the mouth of the mine. The clouds had now nearly all dispersed. The village was nestled below, bathed in moonlight. Eddie came to a stop in front of her and doubled over, coughing and choking. Amber stopped beside him, fighting to catch her breath.

Sweat dripped from her forehead. She felt uncomfortable and sticky beneath her clothes. *What I'd give for a hot shower and a bed,* she thought.

TJ came up beside her, holding his side and wincing in pain. "Talk about being in the shit."

Before Amber responded, the zombies burst out of the trees behind them. "They're like bloodhounds," she said, opening fire.

Bullets scythed through the approaching throng, and although she tried to aim for their heads, most missed. The ones that did hit their targets bowled the zombies over, causing them to collapse, hampering the movements of those behind.

At her side, Eddie and TJ joined in the attack, and for a moment, Amber thought they were holding their own, but then she heard a series of loud grunts and groans, and she looked back to see another horde of the undead scrambling up the hillside from the direction of the village to reach them.

"Shit," she said, realising they were trapped.

The narrow railway track that led into the mine caught her eye. Standing out in the open, she knew they couldn't maintain a defensive position, but the mine would give them a chance to defend themselves, assuming the zombies had vacated it.

"Follow me," she said, starting towards the mine.

She scrambled up the sleepers embedded into the hillside, using them like steps. Eddie and TJ followed close behind. For once, even Eddie didn't argue.

Still wet with rain and overgrown with moss and weeds, the sleepers were slippery, but there were grooves in the earth between them where countless feet had trodden over the years.

As the zombies didn't feel pain, didn't have to breathe, and seemed unstoppable, they careered up the hillside behind them without slowing, the only sound they made an incessant groaning.

A couple of overturned trucks lay beside the track, and the remnants of tools protruded from the ground: pickaxes, spades and rusted buckets.

The ground levelled out before the mine. A building with a tall chimney and a large, jagged crack down its walls stood near the entrance. The flat ground came as a welcome relief to

Amber's aching legs, but she didn't have time to stand around. Above the mine stood a wooden frame with a spoked wheel at its apex. She guessed it to be some form of pulley system to lower the trucks into the village. Trees and shrubs interspersed the space between the buildings. She ran between them and charged into the mine.

At the entrance, she assumed a kneeling position, and started firing at the first of the zombies to make it to where the ground levelled out. Sweat poured down her face and her leg muscles screamed in agony, but she couldn't rest. An overpowering stench of death wafted from the mine.

TJ and Eddie joined her in firing at the zombies, their combined firepower bowling the undead over, only for them to reappear seconds later when they'd picked themselves up.

"It's no good," Eddie squealed. "We can't stop them."

"Shut it," Amber said. Talk about morale boosting. If it was left to Eddie, they may as well give in now and accept their fate.

The mine entrance was about five feet wide and shored up with rotten wooden posts. Amber glanced back into the mine, but couldn't see anything in the dark.

The relentless zombie assault seemed never ending, and like soldiers going over the trenches, they kept coming, gaining ground.

"They're going to be on us soon—like flies on shit," TJ barked.

Amber changed her magazine and started firing again, but TJ was right. If they stayed here, they were sure to be overrun. Where else could they go? She was too tired to carry on running.

With TJ and Eddie providing cover fire, she withdrew her torch and shone it back into the mine. The beam glinted from deposits in the rock, lighting the railway track that descended into the depths. About to turn back, she noticed new fixtures on either side of the entrance. On closer examination, she saw a motorised gate, recalled the sound she'd heard before the zombies flooded from the mine: that of a gate opening.

Who had opened it, and why?

With no time to ponder the ramifications, she said, "Eddie, TJ, into the mine—quick."

"What, and get trapped?" Eddie said, continuing to fire. He shook his head. "I'll take my chances out here, thanks."

"If you stay here, you'll die. Now get inside."

"You can't order me around anymore," he said, cutting down the front row of zombies and ejecting the magazine from his weapon.

"When the lady *says* get inside, the lady *means* get inside," TJ said as he pushed the barrel of his gun under Eddie's chin. "Now get inside."

Eddie scowled at TJ. He held his ground for a moment, but with no alternative, he scuttled into the mine. TJ followed him, with Amber bringing up the rear. The cold air inside the mine made Amber shiver, but the temperature was the least of her problems.

"Here, there's a gate," she said. "Help me close it."

TJ ran up beside her and tried helping her push, but the gate wouldn't move.

With the zombies approaching fast, she didn't have time to find out what was blocking it. "Get back," she shouted, retreating into the mine. When she thought they had gone far enough, she withdrew a grenade and pulled the pin.

"Are you fuckin' crazy?" Eddie said.

"Probably." Amber threw the grenade towards the entrance. "Now if I were you, I'd run."

Amber followed them into the mine, running as quickly as she could. All three of them switched their torches on, the beams chasing strange shadows along the walls. Seconds later, the ground shuddered and a loud blast roared through the mine. Amber threw herself on the ground as rocks and dust fell from the ceiling. She covered her head with her arms as the ceiling crashed down behind her.

As the sound receded, Amber picked herself up. Dust filled the air, swirling in the torch beam like smoke rising from the bowels of hell. She coughed and put her hand over her mouth and nose. She aimed the torch back at the entrance to see it blocked by rocks.

"Is everyone okay?"

"You stupid cow," Eddie barked, picking himself up. "We're fuckin' trapped now."

Amber shone her torch in his face. Apart from a couple of small cuts, he looked okay. "TJ, how you doing?"

"I've been better."

She spotted him squatting against the wall a little farther along the mine, dusting himself off.

The stench she'd smelled at the entrance was stronger than ever. It mingled with the dust, became almost tangible.

"We're gonna die from bloody oxygen starvation," Eddie said. "That's if that stink doesn't suffocate us first." He wiped dust and debris from his bald head then thumbed his microphone. "Can anyone hear me? Hello, is anyone out there? Christ almighty, there's no reception. We're well and truly in the shitter."

Before Amber responded, she heard TJ scream. She swept her torch towards where he crouched, and her stomach flipped when she saw him surrounded by a mass of writhing corpses coming out of a side tunnel. Too decomposed to walk, they pulled themselves along with their hands—if they had them. Some were limbless, more like maggots than people, and they shuffled along, teeth snapping. Others were desiccated husks of flesh and bone. A couple of them grabbed hold of TJ and dragged him to the ground. He punched and kicked as he tried to bring his weapon around to fire, but one of the zombies latched its teeth onto his leg and bit down—hard.

TJ screamed.

Shots rang out as Eddie opened fire. "Fuck me, fuck me, fuck me," he said.

"Hold your fire," Amber shouted. "You'll hit TJ." But Eddie seemed unconcerned. He gritted his teeth and wrinkled his brow as he continued to fire, the bullets just missing TJ and hitting the surrounding zombies. He only stopped when the magazine emptied.

Amber took the opportunity of a lull in firing to help TJ. She ran forwards and smashed the heel of her boot into the nearest zombie's head. She heard a crack as its skull hit the ground. Numerous hands reached for her, their desiccated fingers wriggling like maggots. Close enough that she knew she wasn't going to hit TJ, she aimed the barrel of her MP5 at the head of a man with one leg and arm. Strips of dead skin trailed from his ragged stumps. The bullet smacked through his skull and the man flopped to the ground.

Amber saw TJ pinned down by numerous zombies. He was still screaming, although the sound had dropped a notch or two. Blood poured from bites in his hands and neck. One of his ears had been bitten off, the ragged remains pouring blood. A couple of zombies sated themselves on his flesh, their lips smacking loudly.

Amber shone her torch at TJ's face. He stared back, a pitiful look etched across his pained features.

"Shoot me," he said, grimacing as a zombie bit into his ankle. He booted it with his free leg, but lacked strength behind his attack.

Amber kicked the ankle biter away and put a bullet in his head. She shot a couple more of the undead to clear a path.

"I'll get you out of here," she said.

She heard Eddie at her back. "How? You've trapped us in the mine, you stupid bitch."

"There's got to be another way out," she said, shooting another zombie.

"Why has there?" Eddie said, firing a couple of shots as he spoke.

Amber swallowed. "That man you killed in the woods when we arrived. Well, I didn't say at the time because it seemed stupid—I thought I'd made a mistake—but with what I know now, I know he was dead before you shot him. He was one of these *things*."

"And you only think to mention it now! Jesus on a fuckin' moped."

"He was outside before that gate at the entrance opened. That means there might be another way out."

TJ cried out, the sound echoing along the mineshaft. Amber shivered, gritting her teeth. She had let the men down. Just like she let her brother, Simon, down.

More zombies crawled and pulled themselves from the depths of the mine, too many to count, no doubt attracted by the sound of the explosion and subsequent gunfire.

Amber targeted the zombies crawling towards them and opened fire, aiming for their heads.

"Perhaps that man I killed wasn't trapped down here at all," Eddie said. "Perhaps some of them were lurking around outside already." He shook his head. "I can't believe you didn't fuckin' mention the stiff was already, well, *stiff*. You laid a big guilt trip on me, and for what?" He spat on the ground. "I knew a woman shouldn't be in charge. Didn't I say that, TJ? Now perhaps you'll fuckin' agree with me."

TJ groaned. Amber didn't know if it was assent or pain.

"It hurts," TJ said. "Feels like fucking ants crawling under my skin."

Amber bit her tongue. Fingers snatched at her boot and she kicked the hand away before putting a bullet in the zombie's head, a putrid mass of brains splattering the ground.

TJ caressed his left hand in his right. Three fingers had been bitten off. Blood pumped from the stumps. He shut his eyes as though riding out another wave of pain.

"Poor sod," Eddie said, staring down at TJ.

"Give me a hand to get him up," Amber said.

Eddie shook his head. "I ain't touching him. Have you never watched a zombie film? One of those fuckers bites you, then you become infected. You become one of 'em. Putting him out of his misery is the best thing you could do."

"I'm not going to kill him."

"Well if you're not…" He aimed his gun at TJ's head, but Amber batted it away. "Fuck me. Can't you see he's in agony? If it was you, wouldn't you want someone to take away the pain?"

"There must be something we can do. We'll get out, get him to a hospital."

"You're livin' in a fantasy world, lady. We ain't getting out of here, and even if we did, no one could help."

"He's right," TJ said. He coughed, the action making him wince in agony.

I can't do it, Amber thought. *I can't kill him when there's a chance he can live.*

Eddie shot at a couple of zombies that were getting close, splattering chunks of bone and brain matter across the ground.

The cold mine added to the chill generated by Amber's wet clothes. She shivered. A slight breeze blew along the shaft and caressed her cheek, bringing with it more of the noxious odour of death and decay.

There has to be another way out. Where else would the breeze be coming from?

She turned to mention it to Eddie and TJ, just in time to see Eddie put the barrel of his gun against TJ's forehead.

"Thanks, man," TJ groaned—just before Eddie pulled the trigger. He slumped to the ground, blood trickling from a hole at the back of his skull.

"You bastard!" She clenched her fist and threw a punch. Eddie dodged aside, grabbing her wrist as it sailed past his head.

"I did it for TJ," he snarled in her ear.

"You did it for yourself because you were scared he was going to become one of them."

"Whatever. He's dead. Get over it."

Amber's anger fizzled out. She felt like crying, but knew that she couldn't. It would be a sign of weakness. Her shoulders slumped. Eddie let go of her wrist and she folded both arms across her chest.

The wind howled through the mine, making a noise like a sigh, as if the mountain itself were crying in pain.

TWENTY-ONE

Lofty peered around the door, leaning out far enough to survey the almost antiseptic, spotless corridor of the Strident Industries building. Satisfied there was no one around, he motioned to Jill and she followed him out of the room.

Fluorescent tubes lit the way, their clinical light reflecting off the white walls. Lofty looked left then right, unsure which way to go. He listened for the sound of a dog barking or whining, but heard nothing.

Adrenaline flooded his body, making him feel giddy. He felt his heart pulsing, imagined the blood pumping through it, pouring through his arteries and veins like rocket fuel, priming him for action.

The door clicked shut behind them. A sign on it read Kennel 4. Lofty tested the door, afraid it might have locked itself. It opened without a problem and he shut it again. With the door closed, the smell of the dog faded and even though he took deep breaths to clear his lungs, he thought he could still taste it at the back of his throat. He wished for mouthwash, but the clean aroma of the hallway cleansed his nostrils, felt almost blissful.

Jill grabbed his arm, squeezing hard enough to make him wince. Lofty weathered the pain, felt that he deserved it after dragging her into this mess.

"Which way?" Jill whispered.

Lofty clucked his tongue as he looked left and right. He didn't have a clue. He'd hoped to hear dogs barking to lead the way, but the building seemed quiet.

Knowing Jill expected an answer, he said, "This way," and led her to the right.

Their footfalls echoed on ahead, as though urging them to follow in a game of cat and mouse. Lofty swallowed. Each step he took made him feel more nervous, more vulnerable. His skin prickled, the hairs along his arm seeming to twitch.

Jill still held onto his bicep, sticking to him like a Siamese twin, her feet sometimes stepping on his.

A sign on the wall supplied details of what to do in case of a fire and gave instructions of where to find the nearest emergency exit—a tempting offer. Lofty's temples throbbed.

When he reached the first door along the hallway, he stopped, pried Jill's fingers from his arm and pressed his ear against the cold wood, listening. With it being late at night, the building seemed deserted—he hoped it stayed that way—and unless someone was sitting quietly inside the room…

He tested the handle, moving it slowly, careful not to make any noise. The handle moved and the door swung open. With no marking on the door to indicate what lay beyond, he didn't know what to expect, and was a little disappointed to discover a small rest area with tea and coffee making facilities, a toaster, microwave and fridge.

Shaking his head, Lofty let the door close and stepped back into the corridor.

Jill leaned close and whispered in his ear, "What was in there?"

"Just a small rest room."

"Don't say that word."

Lofty frowned. "What word?"

"*Rest.* My legs are killing me and I'm so tired I could fall asleep on a log."

He knew how she felt. The added anxiety surely didn't help.

"We'd better find some evidence soon, otherwise I'm likely to wet myself," Jill continued.

"There's bound to be a toilet somewhere."

"Let's just hurry. I want to get out of here. This place gives me the creeps."

Lofty took the lead. Jill held onto his arm again, keeping as close as possible. Lofty felt comforted by her presence. Having Jill beside him gave him the conviction to continue. Despite his bravado, if she wasn't here, he didn't know whether he would have the strength to carry on.

At the next door along the corridor, Lofty went through the same procedure, listening to see if he could hear anyone inside the room and then turning the handle, but this time, the door was locked. That piqued his interest. There must be something important inside—but it didn't matter when he didn't have a key.

He wondered why there weren't any security cameras inside the building, presumed that the security outside was deterrent enough.

Continuing on, they reached an intersection, the corridor running from left to right. A sign featuring the figure of a running man and an arrow indicated the way to the exit. Knowing he might need to use it if they were discovered, he decided to head that way. If they ventured the other way, he knew they might end up getting lost.

The corridor ran for about thirty feet. Doors were set into the wall. A picture of a man was stuck to the first door, on the next a picture of a woman.

"I'm going to have to go," Jill said.

Lofty nodded. The door didn't have a handle, and swung in as he pushed against it. The door led to an annex, and they passed through another door to enter the toilet proper. Once inside,

Lofty put his finger to his lips to indicate silence. He noticed four toilet stalls, two sinks, a sanitary towel vending machine and a hand-drying machine. With three of the toilet doors shut, Lofty crouched down and peered through the gaps at the bottom.

"Okay, I think we're safe," he said, getting to his feet.

"It wouldn't matter if we weren't. I've got to go," Jill said as she hurried into the nearest stall.

Lofty leaned against the wall as Jill emptied her bladder. The acoustics of the room made the sound of her peeing seem unnaturally loud and he kept staring at the door, expecting someone to enter at any moment.

When he heard the sound of the toilet flushing, he winced—should have told her not to flush.

Jill stepped out of the stall and crossed to the sink to wash her hands. About to use the hand dryer, Lofty pulled her away. "It'll make too much noise."

Jill looked about to argue when Lofty heard footsteps outside. His heart felt as though it had plummeted into the Arctic Ocean. He put his hand across Jill's mouth and held his breath.

The footsteps drew closer, echoing along the corridor. Not knowing who it was or where they were going, he stared around the room before pulling Jill into the stall farthest away. He lowered the toilet lid and sat on the seat, motioning to Jill to sit on his knee. Then he shut the door and propped his feet against the wall on either side, lifting Jill's legs off the ground in the process. He didn't close the door fully, as that might alert someone to their presence.

The footsteps halted, and he heard the sound of a door opening. Next minute another door opened, and someone walked into the toilet. He put his arms around Jill's waist and pulled her to him.

Lofty wasn't sure whether it was his or Jill's heart he felt pounding, but he felt certain that whoever it belonged to, the other's would drum to the same beat. Sweat coated his palms. He licked his lips and stared around the side of Jill at the door, too afraid to blink in case someone pushed it open.

His breath came in short bursts—almost loud enough to hear. Above the roaring in his ears, he heard the person walk across the room, heard them open the stall door next to theirs, shut the door, rattling the other stalls.

Lofty held his breath. He felt Jill shaking and tightened his hold, trying to offer comfort, her weight on his lap making his legs go numb.

He heard the person start emptying their bladder, spotted their shadow moving under the gap between the stalls. Next minute the toilet flushed, the door opened, and the person exited the stall.

The feeling in his right leg started to go. He flexed his toes, but it was no good, he couldn't feel them either. After a moment, his skin tingled with the first sensation of pins and needles. He kept trying to wiggle his toes, tried to flex his leg to get the feeling back, but Jill's weight on his lap restricted any and all movement.

Jill nudged him in the ribs and nodded her head, indicating the door.

Lofty looked forwards and realised his movements to bring feeling back to his leg were causing the stall to shake a little. The door rattled, started swinging inward.

Just then, the hand dryer burst into life, drowning out the sound of Jill leaning forwards and closing the door.

When the blower wheezed to a stop, he heard footsteps retreating, heard the inner door open and close, then heard the other door swing to as the person exited.

Lofty breathed a sigh of relief and placed his feet on the ground. Jill stood up and faced him. Her face was pale, as though all her blood had drained away.

"We've got to get out of here," she said. "That was too close. What if they'd found us?"

"I still need some pictures. We've come this far..." He wrapped his arms around Jill's waist and kissed her on the lips. "We're doing it for the animals, babe, because they can't do it for themselves."

Jill half-heartedly returned the hug. "I know, I know," she said into the crook of his shoulder. "That doesn't mean I'm not scared to death, though."

"And you think I'm not?"

"I just keep worrying about what'll happen if we get caught."

"We're not going to get caught. Trust me."

"I hope you're right. I've just got a bad feeling about everything, that's all."

Lofty knew what she meant. He felt the same way. He couldn't pin it down, but something just didn't feel right. Whatever experiments they were conducting on the animals in here, he didn't think any good would come of it.

"Come on," he said, "let's hurry up and get those pictures."

Back out in the corridor, Lofty checked the last door to find that it led to a store cupboard. Although loathe to venture deeper into the building, he knew they had to retrace their steps and head away from the emergency exit. The thought sent a shiver down his spine and for a moment, his legs felt devoid of strength, as though about to rebel. He took a deep breath, grabbed Jill's hand for comfort, then started a slow, careful walk back along the corridor.

TWENTY-TWO

"Lead the way, Wonder Woman," Eddie said.

Amber stared at TJ. She knew they shouldn't leave him lying there, but there was nothing else she could do. Deep down, she knew Eddie was right to shoot him, and that was part of the problem: she hadn't done it herself. She'd been more concerned with saving him than thinking what was best for him. In the end, she only prolonged his agony.

She thought about her brother, Simon. Tried to imagine how much pain he must have endured at the hands of those bullies until he couldn't take it anymore. She hated him for what he'd done. By ending his life, he'd escaped, opening up a whole world of pain for everyone left behind. If only he'd talked to her. Told her what was happening. Then she could have done something. She could have helped.

"Goddamn you," she said.

Eddie snorted. "Goddamn you, too, for trapping us in this mine."

Although her statement hadn't been directed at Eddie, she let his reply ride. "Then let's find a way out," she said, walking away.

The rails only ran so far down the mine, then abruptly stopped. A cart still half full of ore sat at the small buffers. Beside it, as though propped up ready to start work again, stood a pickaxe.

Amber's torch picked out places in the mine blackened by fire. She remembered reading somewhere that they used to leave fires burning overnight in some mines, then doused the rock in water to help fragment it.

Body parts covered the mine floor, remnants of the dead that had clawed their way to the exit, their decomposing limbs dropping off along the way.

She tried to step around them at first, but soon gave up and waded through, kicking them aside. The torchlight picked out scars in the rock left by the miners' picks. She couldn't begin to imagine the terrible conditions under which they used to work in order to extract the ore.

The ground underfoot carried the memory of all the feet that traipsed up and down, the rock worn smooth.

So far, the mine had progressed in a straight line, which made navigation easy.

A distant groaning reached her ears, but she couldn't determine whether it was a zombie or the wind. She shone her torch ahead, revealing a larger cavern. As she stepped into it, she noticed movement in the torchlight. Hoping it was a trick of the light, a shadow play woven on the rock face, she shone the torch towards it—and gasped.

Nothing she'd seen so far prepared her for what she saw and she stood rigid, her mouth open, eyes wide.

Putrefied human remains decorated the cavernous space.

Bodies too decomposed to escape slithered, crawled, jerked and writhed across the cold stone. Attracted by the light, a figure flopped towards her, its arms too decomposed to support its own weight, its head kept striking the ground with a loud, hollow thud. A sexless, legless torso scuttled after him, using its arms as improvised legs. Dried entrails followed in its wake like tentacles.

The figure of a young boy detached itself from the wall. As though sensing fresh meat, he dropped the bloodless leg on which he chewed and started across the cavern, his legs little more than bone and sinew. He clawed his way across the ground. With most of his torso either eaten or rotted away only a bony framework remained. Each movement made his knee and rib bones strike the floor, creating a sound like a skeletal xylophone.

"Blow me," Eddie said as he reached Amber's side, shining his torch around.

A teenage girl flopped into the light. Most of the flesh from her face was missing, her jawbone visible. She opened her teeth, revealing a bloated tongue. Her limbs were little more than rotten stumps, what muscle remained flapping uselessly as she humped the ground, unable to move forwards.

Other figures in various stages of decomposition littered the ground. Some, their bodies so decomposed that they were little more than chattering heads, others so devoid of any major motor neuron function used what little motion they had left to bang their heads or remaining extremities against the ground, creating an almost tribal rhythm. With most of their bodies missing, Amber couldn't begin to comprehend how they operated at all. All she knew was that they seemed to have one desire, one basic need: to feast on human flesh.

Eddie opened fire at her side. Amber joined him, knowing there was little she could do but put them out of their misery— assuming they felt misery. Assuming they felt anything at all.

A man scurried across the floor, using the nubs of his shattered wrists to claw at the ground and propel himself forwards while his single leg scrambled for purchase. Amber stitched his torso with bullets, shattering ribs and puncturing internal organs. Pancreas, lungs and bits of heart spewed out of the bullet holes, but the man continued unperturbed until one of her bullets struck his head, punching a hole out of the back of his skull.

Beyond feeling sickened, Amber found the act of killing the zombies almost robotic. Spent casings rained from her MP5 and tinkled on the ground. The bullets slammed into figures, struck walls, pinged from supports—a deathly percussion.

She was a death dealer. An assassin intent on killing.

She ejected the empty magazine and inserted a fresh one, her heart missing a beat when she saw she only had a couple of clips left. She stopped firing.

"Save your ammo," Amber said. The sound of gunfire echoed around the cavern long after Eddie ceased firing.

The number of bodies lying around the mine was impossible to count, especially since many of them had lost their limbs. Body parts lay everywhere. Severed arms twitched and jerked, fingers trying to grab onto something, anything alive.

The light from Amber's torch flashed across the walls, hounding shadows and sending them scurrying deeper into the mine. Moans and groans filled the air. With her sense of smell disrupted, Amber hardly noticed the stench of putrefying flesh anymore.

More figures shuffled and shimmied forwards as though on a conveyor belt of gore.

A sudden shout caught her attention and she turned and aimed her torch towards the sound. There she saw Eddie, pressing himself into the rock, his gun dangling at his side and a knife in his hand as he hacked at the semicircle of zombies surrounding him. Some of the undead had crawled on top of others, making an impenetrable barrier of flesh. They raked their hands in the air, fingers snatching and clawing as they tried to grab a hold of him. Teeth clamped down, gnashing.

"I'm out of ammo," he shouted.

Amber gazed at Eddie hacking at anything that came near, and she felt…nothing. She knew she should help him, but a small part of her didn't want to. He'd done nothing but belittle her, badger and heckle her. So what if he died? No one would know, and the dead don't speak, so who was going to tell?

"Jesus Christ, help me," he screamed.

Amber shrugged. "Why?"

"Because I need *help*," he shouted as he hacked out, slicing a hand off its wrist.

Amber turned and shone her torch into the continuing mineshaft on the other side of the cavern. The way was now clear, most of the remaining zombies more intent on getting at Eddie.

"Sorry, but you're on your own," she said.

Without looking back, Amber jogged away with Eddie's screams ringing in her ears.

TWENTY-THREE

Eddie's shouts followed Amber along the mineshaft, taunting her. She thought about her brother again, and how she hadn't been there for him. Guilt was a heavy burden to carry, and she'd had enough of that without needing to add any more.

"Damn it," she said, coming to a stop. She turned back, shaking her head.

When she arrived at the cavern, she saw Eddie still hacking away at the zombies with his knife. His jaw quivered and his eyes glistened with tears.

She knew her personal feelings needed to be put aside if she were to get out of this mess alive.

Amber waded in, pulling zombies aside and putting them out of their misery with well-placed head shots. Eddie looked at her without saying a word, the relief evident on his face as the last of the zombies was killed.

"Did any of them bite you?" she asked.

Eddie shook his head.

"Catch." She threw him her M9 Beretta pistol and some spare ammo. "This time, don't waste it. Wait for the head shot before you fire."

"I know that," Eddie snapped.

"And you may as well leave the Steyr. Without ammo, it's useless."

Eddie unslung the gun and dropped it to the floor. "Anything else?"

"Yes, next time you run out on me, I'll kill you." She turned and started walking away before he replied.

Water dripped from the ceiling in places and pooled on the ground. The whole mine was freezing, not that the undead would have been bothered. Tomblike conditions probably made them feel all the more at home.

A slight draught wafted her cheeks with the promise of escape. She followed it.

Her breathing laboured as the walls narrowed. She felt nauseous, dizzy, her head spinning—as though she couldn't breathe.

The narrow tunnel seemed to run horizontally through the hillside, and a couple of side tunnels branched off the main shaft. She followed the route along which the breeze blew. The pitted walls bore testament to the backbreaking work that would have taken place below ground. She tried to imagine working down here with only a candle for light, the small alcoves in the walls still visible where the candles had been placed. Judging by its condition, she guessed the mine had been closed a long time ago.

Whether she only imagined it, she felt the weight of the rock above seemed to press down, crushing her spirit. The odd echo and grumble emanated from the darkness, but she tried not to dwell on what might be causing the sound and instead concentrated on controlling her breathing.

She aimed her torchlight straight ahead, creating shadowed patterns that scrolled across the walls. Eyes peeled and ears alert for more zombies. She wished she knew what was going on. How had the people gotten here? And why had they been locked in? It didn't make sense.

No amount of training prepared her for any of this, and she was improvising now.

She heard Eddie traipsing along behind her. He'd fallen quiet since his brush with death, which went to show things always had a bright side.

A groan emanated from up ahead and she tightened her finger on the trigger. Not more of them. Jesus, would they never end? She held a hand up to alert Eddie to a possible problem, then crept forwards. The draught against her cheek grew stronger. The groaning grew louder and she started to suspect it wasn't a zombie at all.

"Eddie, turn your torch off," she said, turning off her own, letting her eyes adjust to the blackness. After a couple of minutes, a faint patch of grey appeared in the black fabric: a hole in the wall to her left, through which the wind groaned.

A faint smile of relief stretched the corners of her mouth. "Eddie, come here."

She turned her torch back on and shone the light into the hole to reveal a tunnel only just large enough to squeeze into that sloped up at a slight angle.

"What is it?" Eddie asked.

"Probably a ventilation shaft. It's a bit narrow, but I think we can squeeze through."

Eddie shone his torchlight up the shaft too. "You are joking. I'm never gonna fit through there."

"It's probably the only way out."

"I wonder why that is."

She didn't need to look at him to see the expression on his face mirror the condescending tone to his voice. "Let's just give it a try."

"Have I got a choice?"

"Sure you have. Stay here or climb the shaft."

"And what if I get stuck?" He waved his gun around and licked his lips, his eyes flicking nervously inside their sockets.

"You won't get stuck. Look, I'll let you go first and then if anything happens, I can give you a push from behind."

"I bet you'd love that. You think I'd trust you at my back?"

"Now I know why they call you 'Crazy Eddie.' I've just saved your goddamned life and you don't trust me."

"You probably only came back because you were scared of being on your own."

"Whatever. Now are you going first, or am I?"

Eddie mumbled something and removed the anti-tank weapon from his back, along with his water bottle. "The water I'll leave, but this baby is coming with me," he said before crawling into the hole, pushing the M-72 before him.

Amber rolled her eyes. It hadn't taken long for the irrepressible Eddie to make an unwelcome return. Perhaps she should have let him die after all.

After adjusting her kit, she removed her backpack and pushed it into the tunnel ahead of her, then started after him along the passage.

Sharp rock stabbed her knees and grazed her palms as she crawled along. Her kit rattled and scraped across the walls and she struggled to breathe in the narrow confines. It was only the prospect of imminent escape that made her keep going. Up ahead, Eddie swore and cursed as he struggled to squeeze through. The thought of him getting stuck wasn't very appealing as it was no doubt easier to go forwards than back, and the sight of Eddie's backside wasn't what she wanted to be left staring at any longer than necessary.

The breeze whistled past Eddie's body, becoming almost musical at times as it blew through any available gap.

"I knew it," Eddie said. "I knew I'd bloody get stuck."

Amber shuffled up behind him and grimaced as she squeezed her hand past the backpack and applied leverage to his backside, pushing as hard as possible. Eddie grunted and strained, popped free, and started moving again. As he did so, a small shower of pebbles rained down on Amber's head.

"Thanks," Amber mumbled when Eddie didn't acknowledge her help.

Eddie didn't respond.

The shaft continued climbing at a steady angle, and although it wasn't steep, Amber found crawling in the confined space sapped her strength even more—and if she'd started to feel claustrophobic before, now she felt positively boxed in.

"I think I can see the way out," Eddie said as though reading her mind.

Unable to see anything past her backpack and Eddie, Amber took his word for it and her heart fluttered with hope.

Up ahead, Eddie cursed and muttered as he clawed his way out of the shaft. Amber pushed her backpack through the opening, clambered out behind him, and took a deep breath, relishing the feel of the cold night air against her skin. She looked back down at the fern-covered hole in the ground, thanking God that they'd managed to find another way out.

Standing beneath the tree canopy, she had a good view of the village. Gunfire echoed through the night.

"Come in, how's everyone doing?" she asked, thumbing her microphone.

"Big Red, good to hear your voice. Where've you been?" Six-pack asked.

"We got trapped in the mine. TJ's dead. How's Lars?"

"Not so good."

"How's everyone else?" she asked.

"We're still hanging on," John said.

The sound of his voice made her pulse quicken. "I'm glad you're okay." She heard Eddie tutting, but ignored him. "How's Barry?"

"I'm still kicking ass, Big Red," Barry said. "Don't you worry about me."

Amber grinned. "Hunter, come in. Over."

Silence.

"Hunter, you there?"

"Hey, isn't that Hunter's rifle?" Eddie said.

Amber turned and watched as Eddie crouched down and picked up the Dragunov sniper rifle from the ground.

"Still half a magazine," Eddie said, checking the gun over.

She shone the torch around, spotting spent shell casings scattered around. About to turn back to Eddie, she saw something move in the undergrowth to her left. Fixing the spot with her torch, she stepped forwards and used the gun barrel to clear the foliage away, jumping back when she saw a zombie sitting among the ferns, hands and face slick with blood. Its flesh appeared blue in the torchlight, and large pink scars marred its cheeks. Once a man, now it was little more than a reanimated killing machine. Hunter lay at the creature's side like a gory banquet. His stomach was torn open, insides looped around the zombie's hands.

Now immune to the stench, Amber could no longer smell the fetid aroma that would undoubtedly emanate from the zombie. The torchlight hit the creature's eyes, but no sparkle radiated back, the lifeless orbs mere windows into a heart of darkness.

Unperturbed, the zombie chewed on a length of intestine. Juices spurted out and trickled down its chin. Judging by the cuts and gashes on the zombie's hands, it had clawed its way along the same tunnel as Eddie and she had, taking Hunter by surprise.

The sight made her gag. A sick feeling passed from her throat to her stomach. Flushed with anger, she aimed and fired before the zombie could react. The bullet cleaved a path through its head and the creature flopped back into the ferns.

Although dead, she fired another four bullets into its skull, turning it into a mushy lump of splintered bone and brain matter.

"I wouldn't waste your ammo," Eddie said. "You never know when you might need it."

Amber spun around and glared at him, her expression more eloquent than any words.

TWENTY-FOUR

Lofty heard the voices first. He stiffened and held Jill back, put a finger to his lips.

Jill's pale face seemed to blanch further, making her appear ghostlike, a shadow of her former self. He watched her swallow, her bottom lip trembling. Tears glistened in her eyes. Lofty squeezed her shoulder and smiled to offer support—not that he felt any less afraid.

The voices originated from farther along the corridor. Having come too far to turn back now, Lofty tiptoed onward with Jill gripping his hand as tight as a limpet.

When he reached the door to the room where the voices originated, Lofty hesitated. Jill pulled, urging him on, but Lofty shook his head and leaned closer to listen.

"I'm telling you, General, Operation Deadfall *will* work," a man with a slight London accent said.

"How can you be sure?" a clipped voice asked.

"That's what the field test is going to prove."

"You're using an unverified virus to reanimate human cells. I should think plenty could go wrong."

"Well, *should* worst come to the worst, we've got a contingency plan," the man replied.

"Which is?"

"We can abort the mission and terminate the subjects—but nothing's going to go wrong."

"And how do you propose to terminate them from so far away?"

"If we should need to travel that road, then we have a way to shut them down."

"Care to elaborate?"

"Like I said, if the time comes—"

"Forget the contingency plan," a gruff-voiced man said. "What I want to know is what's happening now with the field test."

"We've got someone on the inside monitoring the situation and reporting back, and so far everything's going according to plan. As you can see on the monitors, the mission is progressing just as we envisioned."

"And what if the mole doesn't make it?" the General asked.

"Then you'll get to see the contingency plan, but as that hasn't happened, I'd appreciate it if you'd just let us do the job you paid us for."

"That's all well and good," the General said, "but I want to know what percentages we're looking at so far."

Lofty heard what sounded like keys being pressed. Next minute the man said, "So far they've managed to terminate eighty-six zombies."

"Can't we think of a better word than *zombies?* It makes me think of the project as a low-budget horror movie."

Someone coughed. Then the man with the slight London twang spoke. "There's nothing low-budget about any of this. This is state of the art—"

"I know what it is and how much it's cost. Now how many of the team are left?"

"They've suffered two fatalities, and have one man injured."

"Eighty-six to two isn't a very good ratio, Mr. Finch, especially considering there's only eight of them."

"In a normal situation of course you'd be right, but General, we're talking about eighty-six people who were already dead, so where's the loss? Kill them or convert them—either way we win. All we've done is reanimate bodies from the morgue. Now just imagine this virus being deployed in a city."

"I suppose when you put it like that…How much longer are we expecting the test group to last out?"

"Not long. Not long at all."

The General laughed. "It's ironic that to live forever, you've got to die first."

"What happens if word of this gets out?" another man asked.

"It won't," Finch said. "We work with a dedicated skeleton staff. The project virtually runs itself, so those in the loop are kept to the bare minimum."

Lofty clenched his teeth. Although he didn't understand most of the conversation, he got the gist of it, but that didn't make it any easier to accept. Zombies! The scientists had somehow reanimated the dead, and for some reason, they were field-testing them against another group of people. It didn't take Einstein to work out that with the military involved it had a serious—even lethal—application.

Jill squeezed his hand, digging her nails into his knuckles. She must have heard what they'd said, too. He looked around, knowing that his own expression mirrored the look of horror on her face. She cupped her hand around his ear, "Let's get out of here, please," she whispered.

This time, Lofty didn't argue.

He nodded and started to lead the way, but with what he had just heard ringing in his ears, he felt exposed travelling out in the open. He stopped and pressed his ear against the door to another room, cracking it open and peering inside to check if it was empty. "Come on, in here."

Jill shook her head. "The only place I'm going is *out* of here."

"Someone might see us if we stay out in the open. Come on, there might be a window or something we can climb out of." He didn't mention that he guessed if they were prepared to kill a test group, they would no doubt be prepared to kill anyone who interfered—he wanted to get out of sight.

Before Jill could protest, he pulled her inside the room and shut the door behind them. The room was windowless, illuminated by light sources hidden behind opaque plastic panels in the otherwise off-white, false ceiling.

Banks of computers and electronic machinery lined the walls, some of which beeped and whirred. Multiple programs seemed to be running, the purpose of which Lofty couldn't fathom. He approached the first screen and stared at the complex tables scrolling from top to bottom, shaking his head. The next screen showed what appeared to be animated strands of helter-skelter-shaped DNA, but each strand appeared to have things attached to them. He leaned in for a better look, stunned when he realised they were tiny robots.

"Jesus," he said, "look at this."

Jill came across and stared at the screen. "What the hell are they?"

"I think they're nanobots. They're incredible, but I thought they were just something in science fiction stories."

"Nano what?"

"Nanobots. I've read about them in books and things. They're machines constructed from molecules, machines so small you can't see them with the naked eye."

"This is going from bad to worse." She turned away as though sickened.

Lofty stroked his goatee and stared around the room. Rows of fuse boxes lined one wall, out of which snaked thick black cables. There was also a series of junction boxes, and telecoms connections with jack-plug sockets. A blue plastic telephone handset sat on the top of the telecoms box, with two pieces of wire fitted with male connectors running out of it.

Lofty walked across to a cabinet next to the fuse boxes, opened the drawer and leafed through a number of files, none of which made any sense to him. Among the files he spotted a design layout for the building and he placed it on the table next to the cabinet and traced his finger across the page. He worked out which room they were in from what he remembered of the corridors they'd walked through. The rooms were all labelled: animal testing station, analysis room, nanotechnology lab, control centre, quarantine.

Footsteps echoed outside. Lofty tiptoed across to the door and leaned against it. He held his breath and closed his eyes, bright flashes of light exploding behind his eyelids.

His heart drummed inside his chest.

Blood pounded in his ears, the sound reminiscent of waves crashing against rocks. He prayed for the person to keep walking, prayed that the door handle remained still, prayed that he didn't have a heart attack.

If you're listening up there, I promise I'll never do anything like this again, he thought, *only please, please don't let us get caught.*

Outside the door, someone coughed and shuffled what sounded like papers. Jill grabbed his arm, making him jump. Lofty felt his penis shrink, his bladder about ready to burst. He started hyperventilating, felt dizzy. Wanted to scream. Shout. Run. Wanted to feel the early morning air on his face, see the sunrise, feel its warm rays against his skin. Jesus, he just wanted out of here.

He pressed his palms against the cold wood, braced his feet in case someone tried to enter. Continued to pray to any God that might be listening. Feet squeaked across the floor outside, took a step, then another—the person was walking away.

Lofty let out a breath and sucked fresh air into his lungs. At his side he heard Jill sob. This was all his fault. Why did he have to be so goddamn righteous? Nothing Jill said could make him feel any worse than he already did.

The footsteps receded into the distance, became a ghostly echo. Lofty remained tense, his shoulders bunched.

"You okay to carry on?" he asked.

Jill swallowed. "What will they do if they catch us in here? What do you think they'll *really* do?"

Lofty shrugged. "Honestly, I don't know. But we won't get caught." He took her hand and squeezed.

"Great, can we go now?"

Lofty took a couple of deep breaths. He needed to organise his thoughts. "I wonder if the test group know they're being tested."

Jill shrugged. "To be honest, I don't know and I don't care. Did you hear what they said? Do you think they were being serious? I didn't think they were real, you know, zombies. I thought they were just made up for films and books." She kept her voice low, almost a whisper. "And what was that he was on about a virus?"

"I guess that's how they've reanimated the corpses, but I didn't think it was possible, you know, to bring dead people back to life."

"And I can't believe you've gotten us in this mess."

Lofty couldn't either. "Suppose, you know, those people don't know they're being tested. That man said there were eight of them, and that Finch bloke said two were already dead and one was injured. That means six of them are still alive."

"Good luck to them then."

"But we're talking about *real people* here."

"How do you know? They might have been playing a bloody computer game for all we know."

Lofty placed his hand on her shoulder. "Jill, you know they were talking about real people."

"Well…what do you expect me to do about it?"

Lofty didn't know, but being aware people might be fighting for their lives against an undead horde while he ran away made him feel guilty. "Jill, we can't leave. We've got to help them."

Jill stared at him and sucked at her bottom lip. After a moment, she said, "You're right. We'll phone the police when we get out of here."

"It might be too late by then. You heard what they said—they don't expect the test group to last out much longer. Besides, how do we know the police aren't involved? How do we know who we can trust?"

"Jesus, Samuel, what do you expect us to do? We're out of our league with this. Let's just go. Now."

He didn't miss the fact that she had called him Samuel. "People are dying."

"And I don't want to join them," she said, voicing Lofty's own worries.

"Experimenting on animals is bad enough, but now we're talking about people..."

She folded her arms below her bosom. "I feel sorry for them. I really do, but we can't help them if we get caught."

"There must be something we can do. They mentioned having a mole with the test group. That means they must have a way to communicate with them. Perhaps if we can get a message through."

"I think they'll have a pretty good idea what's going on by now, don't you?"

"We've got to do something."

Jill clucked her tongue. "I've put up with a lot before now, but this..." She raised her hands in exasperation. "This is crazy. These people aren't messing around. You aren't Rambo and I'm not bloody Wonder Woman. You've gone too far this time. I always knew this would happen."

"What, that we'd be stuck in a research facility where they've been experimenting with the undead?"

"Don't try being clever. It doesn't suit you."

"And being callous doesn't suit you. We have to do something and you know it. You'll never live with yourself if we don't."

"I don't know these people, and I can quite happily forget that all of this ever happened."

"But your conscience won't."

Jill looked about to respond, but then she exhaled and walked away, sitting on one of the chairs dotted around the room. She put her elbows on her knees and cupped her chin in her hands, her red-painted nails in stark contrast to her pale skin. "We can't do anything. Look at us. You work in the late shop and I'm studying graphic design. We're not exactly Mulder and Scully."

"No, we're not. They dealt with fictional cases. This is real."

"Don't remind me."

"I'm not just a late shop worker, you know. I can do other things." He didn't mean to sound petulant, but he couldn't help it.

"I know. I didn't mean it like that."

"Well, we're not useless. There has to be something we can do. If we can find a way to contact the test group, perhaps it'll help and perhaps it won't, but at least we'll have done something. I can't just leave them, and standing here, we're wasting time. They could already be dead."

Jill swallowed. "Or undead. Jesus, Lofty, it's not as if we can just call and tell them what's happening."

Lofty put his hands on her shoulders, leaned forwards and kissed her quickly on the lips. "That's it."

Jill frowned. "That's what?"

"We can just call them." He grinned. "Trust me."

TWENTY-FIVE

"Hurry up, Eddie. This is no time to get all shy."

Eddie walked towards Amber from under the trees, pulling up his fly. "When a man's gotta go. And I don't want you getting all excited if you saw what I'm packing."

Amber rolled her eyes and whistled between her teeth. "What took you so goddamn long?"

"It had a long way to travel, know what I mean." He winked.

"I guess that's why they call you a big prick."

"Sticks and stones."

"I wish, now let's get a move on, Six-pack and Lars need our help."

Moonlight illuminated the village below, allowing Amber to see the zombies careering through what passed as streets. John and Barry had set up a defensive position across the far side, using part of the structure of a decaying building as a barricade, and she heard sporadic gunfire and the occasional blast as a grenade went off.

The usual principles of combat seemed useless when fighting an impervious enemy, an enemy that didn't need to sleep, and one that functioned on the compulsion to kill, and she knew if they were to get out alive, she had to adapt. This wasn't a war. It was a fight for survival.

Amber knew whatever this was about it didn't have anything to do with kidnap victims. This premeditated plot pitted Amber and her team against the best the undead threw at them. And perhaps that's all it was. A test of some sort. The thought sickened her, but it made a damn sight more sense than anything else she could think of. It would certainly explain the high sum offered to tempt then into accepting the assignment—not that she imagined for a moment any money would change hands. She didn't think they were expected to live long enough to collect.

Taking cover behind a fallen tree, Amber tried to plot the best route to help Lars and Six-pack. At her side, Eddie used Hunter's Dragunov to take shots at the enemy.

"This is some fuckin' weapon," he said, firing another round.

"Well, you'd better save some ammo for when we really need it."

Eddie glared at her. She wondered why they'd assigned him to this mission, as he seemed incapable of taking orders, wondered why any of them had been chosen. "Just what is your military experience, Eddie?"

"What's it got to do with you?" You don't know shit. I proved myself to that Finch bloke who organised all this, that's why I'm here."

"Just *how* did you prove yourself, Eddie? Because from what I've seen so far, it's not for your soldiering skills."

Eddie spun around and pointed the barrel of the Dragunov at her head. "It don't take an expert to hit a target from this close. Now you really wanna know what I'm doing here?"

Amber knew she'd pushed him too far, and the wavering cold eye of the gun made her shiver. Just a little too much pressure on the trigger and her head would become an omelette.

A crackle rang through her earpiece. "I haven't got a clue what's going down, but we could really do with some help," Six-pack said. "At this rate me and Lars are going to be dead before sun up."

Amber swallowed. Eddie glowered at her.

"Just lower the gun, Eddie. We're supposed to be working together. I'm sorry about what I said—I'm sure you're a very good soldier."

"You must think you're so much better than me. Well, you don't know shit."

"I know someone—*two people* in fact—need our help, and if we're to get out of this mess alive, we need as much support as we can get."

Eddie licked his lips.

"Look, whatever beef you've got with me can wait until we're out of here, can't it?" Amber said.

"Why? Not scared are you?" He sneered and prodded the gun barrel into her stomach.

"Of course I'm bloody scared. Scared you might shoot me and scared that we're surrounded by creatures right out of a nightmare. Only a fool wouldn't be bloody scared." She took a breath. "I just saved your life. Surely that's worth something."

Eddie glared at her. "I could kill you."

"I know."

A moment later, he lowered the gun.

Amber looked away and exhaled. That was too close. She had to watch what she said.

"Let's get a move on." She turned and scrambled down the hillside, her skin prickling, fearing she'd be shot in the back.

At the base of the hill, she ran into the village and dodged between the buildings, firing at any zombie that stepped in her way. Bullets smacked into skulls, shattering bone like glass. The sound of gunfire reverberated between the buildings, sounding like a Bonfire Night celebration.

Amber thumbed the microphone. "Hold on, Six-pack, we're almost there." She fired at another zombie, the bullet slamming it over a low wall, its arms and legs waving comically in the air. At her side, Eddie fired the pistol, the loud report ringing in her ears.

She ran around the corner of a building and skidded to a stop when she saw the number of zombies congregated outside the building housing Six-pack and Lars. Still about seventy feet away, she estimated there were at least fifty zombies circling the building. A group of them banged against the walls while others stood back, their heads cocked as though listening out for something. She saw another one crawling through a window, the broken glass of which sliced through its flesh. Another one followed close behind.

"Shit, we've got a problem, guys," she said into the microphone. "There's still too many of them around the building."

"Now tell me something I don't know," Six-pack said. "Why do you think we're still here?"

She heard gunfire from inside the building, obviously Six-pack or Lars dispatching one of the zombies that crawled through the window.

"I need eyes in the back of me 'ead in this place. They're swarming everywhere," Six-pack said.

"If I were you, Six-pack, I'd get to the back of the building and cover your ears," Eddie said. "I'm going to open up a new door."

Amber turned and watched as Eddie dropped to one knee and opened the telescopic tubing of the M-72 anti-tank weapon.

"Hold on," she said. "What good's that going to do?"

"You'll see."

Amber was about to protest the use of an anti-tank weapon against a horde of zombies when Eddie fired. The rocket flew out of the tube with a hollow sound and the stabilising fins popped out of the casing. At the rear of the tube, a jet of flame shot back and licked the wall of the building fifteen feet away. Standing next to Eddie, Amber felt the heat wash over her.

In an instant, the rocket struck the building and exploded with a mighty roar. Amber ducked her head and covered her ears. Bricks and mortar flew through the air and she felt the ground shudder.

"*Jesus,*" she said. Smoke filled the air around the impact site, and as it cleared, she saw that half the building had collapsed, the rubble pinning down a number of zombies. Limbs jutted from the debris, waving like tentacles.

"Six-pack, Lars, can you hear me?" she said into the microphone.

No one answered.

"You've killed them," she said, turning on Eddie.

Eddie shook his head and pointed towards the building. Amber turned and saw a figure scrambling across the rubble. Six-pack.

He charged towards them. When he got close, Amber shouted, "Where's Lars?"

Six-pack looked her in the eye, his expression pained. "He died just before you got here—there was nothing I could do."

"Then try telling that to Lars," Eddie said, pointing to the stout figure charging their way.

TWENTY-SIX

Amber opened fire. The bullets struck Lars' chest with little effect, his death mask face unaltered. His eyes lacked any compassion, the spark of life extinguished. He groaned as he ran, his inelegant movements not slowing him down any.

Eddie opened fire with the Dragunov. The high-powered bullet ripped through Lars' jacket and his shoulder exploded. Pink and purple gobs of skin and muscle flew into the air and the bone shattered, rendering the arm ineffective, but Lars still didn't slow down.

His arm flopping uselessly at his side, he ran on, covering the ground faster than Amber liked. She ejected the empty magazine from her MP5 and fumbled for another one in her kit. A flower of light burst from the barrel of Six-pack's Colt Commando, the accompanying report sounding like a chainsaw tearing through metal at high speed as he emptied a full magazine. The first shell casings hit the floor at the same time as Lars' left leg. Crippled, Lars collapsed. Still unperturbed, he dragged himself along, clawing at the ground, his teeth gnashing at the air.

Not wanting to prolong the agony of the former French Foreign Legion soldier, Amber rammed a fresh magazine home, walked across, aimed and fired. The single bullet smacked into Lars' crown, and he slumped to the ground, his face buried in the mud.

"This is fucking crazy," Six-pack said. "No one should have to die like that." He spat on the ground.

"Unless you want to end up the same way, I suggest we make a move," Amber said, indicating a group of more that ten zombies charging around the corner of the ruined building.

Amber activated her microphone. "John, Barry, it's time to boogie. Rendezvous at the abandoned farmhouse we passed earlier tonight. Double-time."

"Roger," John replied.

Amber fired a couple of random shots at the approaching group, then turned tail and ran towards the trees, zombies in pursuit. Six-pack sprinted in front, with Eddie almost level. Amber noticed that Six-pack carried a couple of anti-personnel claymore mines with the somewhat ironic 'FRONT TOWARDS ENEMY' label printed on the business side. She knew claymores fired shrapnel in the form of steel ball-bearings out to about 100 metres, so hopefully they should help take out a few pursuing zombies.

"Six-pack, when we hit the trees, deploy those claymores to cover our retreat."

"You got it."

"Eddie, you cover him while he sets them and I'll check our coordinates."

For once, Eddie didn't argue.

She hit the tree line behind the other two. Despite the overhead canopy, the light from the moon illuminated the surroundings, painting the damp foliage with a silver hue, making it appear almost magical. "Right, put the first claymore here so it's not obstructed," she said, knowing they wouldn't have to hide it as it wouldn't make a blind bit of difference. As Six-pack rammed the two prongs on the base into the ground, she checked their position with the GPS. Eddie fired a couple of shots at the approaching zombies with the pistol Amber had given him and once Six-pack played out the tripwire, they started up the incline.

The wet fronds of the ferns underfoot felt like hands snatching at Amber's legs. Branches whipped her face and she knocked them aside, ignoring the pain of the sharp pine needles that stabbed her hands.

A flash of light chased them through the trees, and a moment later a loud explosion ripped through the night as the claymore exploded, the ground shaking underfoot.

"Right, place the next one now while we've got chance," Amber said.

As Six-pack deployed the next mine, she covered him, peering back through the trees where shadows lingered. Movement caught her eye farther down the slope, and she saw the after-effects of the claymore on the pursuing zombies lumbering through the trees. Flesh shredded under the impact of hundreds of ball-bearings, some of them little more than obscene caricatures. The woman at the front of the pack had almost lost her jaw, the remains swinging from strands of flesh on her cheek. More ball-bearings had pierced her body, turning her into a pincushion. Further ravaged corpses followed close behind, their lacerated flesh hanging in ribbons and innards oozing from cavities. Their deathly moans and groans sounded even more insidious, as though they were now well and truly pissed off.

Amber took aim and fired, making each shot count. "Make it quick, Six-pack."

"I'm going as fast as I can."

"Well, make it quicker."

She took a grenade from her belt, pulled the pin and lobbed it down the hill. "Fire in the hole!" Next second, the grenade exploded. The blast ripped through the trees, throwing corpses into the air like rag dolls. Body parts already damaged by the claymore broke apart under the explosion. Limbs flew through the air, coming to rest in the surrounding fir trees like macabre decorations in a hellish version of Christmas.

"Ready," Six-pack said, climbing to his feet and starting up the hillside.

Amber followed, using the branches as handholds to help pull her up.

This had to be the worst night of her life, bar none.

She checked her Luminox watch, the luminescent green and purple features now appearing sickly, like undead skin. Sunrise wouldn't be too far away, which would help as much as hinder. The dark masked some of the mutilated corpses, and she didn't know if she wanted to see the zombies in broad daylight.

She heard the coffin dodgers crashing through the foliage at her rear, unstoppable in their pursuit. God knows how many were left. As soon as one lot was dispatched, another rose up behind like a wave of death, surging forwards. The claymore must have disabled a number of them, but it didn't seem to make much difference. That's what made it so scary, the way nothing apart from a bullet in the head seemed to stop them. Amber felt numb, operating on autopilot.

A loud boom shattered the night air as the second claymore exploded. Leaves and foliage rained down from the canopy above. She turned and stared back through the trees where the next wave of undead surged past their fallen brethren, those caught in the blast thrashing around on the ground, their bodies decimated by the ball bearings.

Amber turned away and continued upward. The incline grew steeper, sapping her strength and making her lungs burn. Red-hot pain flared in her thighs as she climbed. The Stairmaster in the gym didn't even come close to replicating the soreness she felt now. The thought that the zombies wouldn't feel tired, wouldn't feel pain and wouldn't alter from their course, urged her on.

Six-pack stayed in front, Eddie bringing up the rear. The branches Six-pack pushed aside whipped back to strike Amber's cheeks, making them prickle, but she ignored the pain, knowing it was nothing compared to what she would feel if the zombies got hold of her. She couldn't think of anything worse than being eaten alive.

She tried to imagine what it would feel like to have someone take a chunk out of her flesh—with their teeth!—and shivered as the thought stirred a memory of being bitten on the ankle by a Jack Russell when she was twelve years old. The dog had been running free in the local park, and she hadn't thought anything of reaching down to stroke it. The dog growled softly, then it struck without warning. She remembered the pinpoint pain as its fangs and incisors punctured her skin, remembered screaming as the dog braced itself, its stubby little body jerking backward and forwards as it fought to hang on. Even with its teeth clamped onto her leg, the dog continued to growl. She remembered feeling its teeth grate against bone, gnawing at her Tibia.

Then she remembered her brother, Simon coming to her rescue. She'd taken him to the park under duress, hadn't wanted to be seen out with her dorky brother during the summer holidays, but her parents insisted that she look after him. He kicked the dog and hit it with a branch until it let go, and then he shouted to drive it away. The dog's vicious attack left a semicircular scar on her ankle. A tear came to her eyes. She never thanked her brother for what he did that day, selflessly risking himself to help her. And look how she repaid him by not even being there for him when he needed her most.

At the top of the hillside the ground levelled out and Amber breathed a sigh of relief. She leaned against a tree and gulped for breath, massaging her thighs to relieve the pain.

Eddie dropped to the ground, panting like a dog and Six-pack clutched his sides, his face screwed up in agony.

"John…Barry…how…you doing?" she said into the microphone.

"We're okay," Barry said. "We heard the explosions. I take it that was you. How you getting on? You sound out of breath."

"Those things…are like bloodhounds," she replied between breaths. "God knows how many there are after us, but…they keep on…coming."

"Just make sure you keep one step ahead of them, then."

"I'd rather be a couple of miles ahead. What's your ETA?"

"About fifteen minutes."

"Make it ten. See you at the rendezvous." She turned to Eddie and Six-pack. "Come on, we'd better move out."

"Jesus, can't I even catch my breath?" Eddie wheezed.

"If you want to stay, feel free. But those creatures are just behind us and they'll be here any second."

Eddie jumped to his feet. "This is seriously fucked-up."

Amber heard the zombies rampaging up the hill, their groans preceding them like a battle cry. "How many more claymores have you got?"

"Just the one," Six-pack said.

"Okay, set it here and I'll string a couple of grenades alongside. We may as well make this one a good one."

She removed two grenades from her webbing and wedged them into the low branches of a couple of trees. Knowing the zombies wouldn't be bothered whether it was a trap or not, she took a length of cord from her backpack and threaded it though the pins, stringing it across the route. When the zombies walked into the cord, it would pull the pins and the grenades would explode at head height, dispatching a few of the undead to their long-awaited grave.

As Six-pack worked, Amber checked the GPS, then when he was ready, she led them through the trees. She took less than thirty steps when the claymore detonated, followed by the boom of the two grenades. At the sound of the blast, Amber hit the deck. She knew what sort of damage a single piece of shrapnel could do.

As the blasts receded, she regained her feet and stared at the carnage. Strips of skin adorned the trees and chunks of meat rained down. One of the trees had split in half. The trunk resembled a white maw lined with jagged teeth. Bodies caught in the blast lay around its base. A woman walked in circles, looking dazed, one side of her face blown away, leaving the skull visible.

The remnants of cloth hanging from her frame couldn't disguise the carnage wreaked upon her torso. Her breasts had exploded, the shredded remains dripping with fatty deposits. Her left arm hung on by a slender thread of tendon and swung at her side like a gory pendulum.

Despite their condition, some of the figures on the ground lurched and stumbled to their feet, dragging themselves if they couldn't walk. And behind those came yet another wave that hadn't been caught in the blast.

"Run!" Amber shouted.

Eddie had already started, his earlier exhaustion no longer evident as his arms and legs pumped like pistons. She found it surprising what the threat of death did to someone's strength and resolve.

In the distance, Amber saw a band of light on the horizon as the sun started to climb. Soon the darkness would recede, revealing the full extent of horror.

She didn't know what they were going to do when they reached the farmhouse, but they needed somewhere to reorganise and take stock.

Colour seeped into the drab grey and black forest up ahead, a fervent green mantel of evergreen foliage that the approaching sunlight brought to life.

Every muscle in Amber's body ached. She dreamed about the luxury of soaking in a hot bath topped with oils and bubbles to relieve the pain, would give anything to have it come true.

Groans and moans followed them through the trees. She wondered if they had some sixth sense that allowed them to pursue their quarry. Whatever it was, they seemed unstoppable and she wondered how she and her team were ever going go escape.

Movement to her left caught her eye and she turned in time to see a figure charging towards them. It took a couple of seconds to focus, and another second or two to realise she recognised the figure: Hunter. Amber gasped and came to a stop.

Intestines swung from the cavity in his stomach, his body a palette of yellow and purple bruises. She'd thought he was dead—hadn't even considered he could come back—and she chastised herself for not putting a bullet in his head earlier.

She started to raise her gun to shoot, but despite his condition, Hunter moved too quickly. As he slammed into Six-pack, she remembered his motto, *Hunter by name, hunter by nature.*

Taken by surprise, Six-pack howled in pain as he crashed into a tree trunk with enough force to shake the foliage. As though they sensed someone in agony, the pursuing zombies' groans increased in volume and intensity.

Amber reacted fast, charging back to help. Six-pack lay slumped on the ground, clutching his stomach and gasping for breath. Hunter dropped down on top of him, curtains of guts slopping either side of his legs as he bit into Six-pack's arm and wrenched a chunk of flesh out of his wrist.

Six-pack grimaced and punched Hunter in the face with his other hand. Blood gushed out of the wound on his wrist. Amber reached Six-pack's side, put the barrel of her gun to Hunter's head and pulled the trigger. The bullet smashed through and exited on the other side, taking half his ear off. Hunter flopped forwards, lying across Six-pack in a macabre embrace.

Amber yanked Hunter's corpse off and crouched beside Six-pack, ignoring the mass of blood and guts covering his body. "Let me have a look," she said, taking a gentle hold of his wrist. She was unable to differentiate between the blood coming out of him and the gore that already covered him.

"Man, you're fucked," Eddie said.

Six-pack looked up and scowled. "You..." He gritted his teeth.

Amber shook her head and glared up at Eddie before turning back to Six-pack. "Just ignore him." Deep down, she knew Eddie was right, and this felt like a bad case of déjà vu. *How many more of them were going to die?* "Are you okay to walk?"

"Walk?" Six-pack said. "I'll fucking run."

Amber snatched a piece of bandage from her kit and wrapped it around his wrist. Blood seeped through immediately. "You'll have to keep it aloft as best you can."

As she helped him to his feet, Eddie said, "We're not going through this again are we?"

Amber knew he was referring to the earlier episode with TJ, but she couldn't kill someone in what amounted to cold blood. She just couldn't. And this time, she wasn't going to let Eddie kill him either, not when there was a chance she could save him. It must have taken a while before Hunter 'changed,' time she could use to their advantage. Besides, Hunter had obviously been dead when he changed, so perhaps if she kept Six-pack alive, he would be okay.

"Let's move out," she said.

Eddie scratched his bald head. "You're crazy if you think I'm letting him come with us."

"Well if you'd rather take your chances with them, feel free to stay behind." She pointed back into the trees where the sound of the approaching zombies grew louder by the second.

"But he's been bitten!"

"Then we'd better move fast," she said through clenched teeth.

Eddie shrugged. "On your head be it." He indicated she should start moving. "There's no way I'm letting him get behind me, so after you."

With Six-pack at her side, Amber started running.

Up ahead, the sun rose into the sky, throwing shadows in their path, but none were as dark as that which trailed in their wake.

TWENTY-SEVEN

In the light of the rising sun, the dilapidated farmhouse looked even more dishevelled. The front door lay on the ground, surrounded by rotten splinters.

Amber helped Six-pack inside while Eddie sauntered in behind them. She propped the door back up, preferring some protection to none. Then she broke some rotten floorboards and used them to hold the door shut as Eddie attended to Six-pack.

"John, Barry, we're at the farmhouse. How far away are you?" she asked into the microphone.

"Be with you in about ten," John said.

"Hello, can anyone hear me?" an unknown man's voice suddenly said through the earpiece.

Amber frowned and looked at her companions. "I can hear you. Who is this?"

"Where are you?"

"Never mind where we are—*who* are you?"

"Yeah," Eddie said. "Tell us who the fuck you are and what's going on."

"Listen, I haven't got much time," the man said. "If you haven't already worked it out, you're being used to test what I think is a zombie army."

"Who are you, and why are you telling us this?" Amber asked.

"We're trying to help. We're in a research facility called Strident Industries."

"*We?* So there's more than one of you?"

"Look it doesn't matter how many of us there are. We're trying to help you."

"Then get us the fuck out of here," Eddie said.

"Yes, who is this and how do you know so much?" Amber heard John ask.

"Aren't you listening to what I'm saying? You're being tested. I can't get you out. We broke in here to rescue some animals and found out about this experiment."

"Well, what good are you then?" Eddie snapped.

"Look, we're trying to help, because there's something else you should know."

"Go on," Amber said.

"One of you is a mole."

"What do you mean a mole?" Six-pack asked before he started coughing.

"All I know is what I overheard. One of you is there to keep an eye on things and report back."

"Which one?" Amber asked.

"Sorry, I dunno. I'd just suggest you all watch your backs."

Amber chewed her bottom lip and stared at Eddie.

"So how we supposed to get out of this shit?" Eddie said.

"Think about it," the man said. "The mole must have some sort of contingency plan to escape. Find the mole and you find your way out. Anyway, we've done all we can. Good luck."

"Wait," Amber said. "We need to know more."

She waited, but the unknown speaker didn't respond.

"I think he's gone," Barry said in her ear.

Amber leaned against the wall, trying hard to get her head around what she'd heard. *They were being used to field test a zombie army.*

It sounded crazy. Yet despite all her doubts, it made a warped sort of sense. Everyone in the group worked in a clandestine world. Recruited at the last minute, they had no time to inform anyone of their whereabouts. Due to the nature of their trades, to all intents and purposes, all of them could disappear without causing too much of a ripple. They were expendable.

She felt sick.

"Well ain't this just great," Eddie said.

"You should know," Amber replied, closing the gap between them so that they stood toe to toe.

"And what's that supposed to mean?"

"So how are you planning to escape?"

"Escape? I'm stuck here the same as—hold on, you don't think…" Eddie snorted. "Listen, lady, if I didn't need the money, I wouldn't have volunteered for this shit, but there's no way I'm a traitor."

"And I suppose you can prove that, can you? You've been shifty from the start and I never trusted you."

He stepped back. "Then your radar needs fixing, 'cause it ain't me."

Sunlight shone through the broken window, highlighting the state of the room. Amber looked around, knowing she might need to act fast if Eddie decided to cut and run.

"My money's on you," Eddie said. "Putting a woman in charge, I always thought that was dodgy. Now I know why."

"You can't talk your way out of this one."

"I'd rather trust Amber than you," Six-pack grumbled from where he sat slumped against the wall.

"And what the fuck do you know? You're dying anyway."

"I know that if it is you, then I'm taking you with me."

Eddie narrowed his eyes, aimed his pistol at Six-pack and said, "I should just put you out of your misery now. At least that'll be one out of the equation."

"Just try it," Six-pack said, "and you'll find yourself reaching those pearly gates before me."

Amber saw Eddie's finger tense on the trigger and she aimed her own weapon at him. "I'd be very careful, Eddie. If you shoot, then you're a dead man."

"We're all dead anyway. You just haven't accepted it yet. I'm *not* the mole." A bead of sweat trickled down his forehead. "Shall I tell you why I'm here? *Shall I?*" he screamed. "My son's dying. The big C—can you believe it? Fuckin' five years old and he's got some form of cancer. Seems they can't treat him over here, but there's a chance overseas, so the girlfriend and me, we've got to take him abroad. Now it ain't cheap, and I need the money. This job might have saved his life. Now look what's happened." He pursed his lips, eyes bristling with tears.

"You have a kid?" Amber said.

"Don't sound so surprised. I just told you, didn't I? Or weren't you listening?"

"How do I know you're telling the truth?"

"You don't, the same as I don't know that you are."

It seemed hard to believe the bigoted self-centred man before her could be putting himself out for the benefit of someone else, but then never having had kids, she didn't know how close the bond between a parent and child could be. Was he telling the truth? He sounded and looked sincere, but could she trust him?

She wasn't gambling just her own life here, but everyone else's too.

"It just doesn't sound like the Eddie I've come to loathe," she said.

Eddie grunted. "There ain't nothing I wouldn't do for my kid."

Six-pack coughed. "Very commendable, now just lower your gun before you do something I'll regret."

Eddie glared at Amber, then turned to Six-pack. "How do I know I can trust either of you? I lower my gun then Annie Oakley over there shoots me."

"It's tempting, but you have my word I won't shoot."

"Ah, well, if you put it like that… What the *fuck* do you take me for?"

"If I can believe what you said, a concerned father who would like to get home to his son in one piece."

Eddie wiped his free hand from his brow to his cheek. The hand holding the gun started to shake a little.

"Just lower the gun, Eddie," Amber said. "We can talk about this."

"Nothing to talk about. You think I'm the mole, I think you are. I'd call that a stalemate."

"We can't stay here all day pointing guns at each other."

"No, we can't," John said, running into the room through a side door. He slammed into Eddie, sending him flying. Barry followed close on his heels.

The gun in Eddie's hand went off, the bullet slamming into the wall and chipping out a circle of plaster. Before Eddie recovered, John leapt on top of him and Barry ran across the room and pinned his arms.

Amber lowered her gun and sighed with relief. "Am I glad to see you," she said.

Barry nodded. "I always thought there was something about our friend here."

"Get the fuck off me," Eddie snarled.

John shook his head. "I don't think so. It's a good job we came through the side. Anyone got any rope?"

"Here, will these do?" Amber said, throwing John a pair of handcuffs that he caught with one hand.

"Why doesn't that surprise me?" Eddie said, rolling his eyes. "Of course you'd leap at the opportunity to tie me up."

John slapped Eddie across the face. "I think it's time you shut your gob."

A trickle of blood ran from the corner of Eddie's mouth. He licked it away. "Lover boy to the rescue. I hate to piss on your parade, but you've got the wrong man."

John raised his fist. "I won't tell you again."

"That's enough," Amber said. "We need to find out how to get out of here, and if Eddie can help, I want him able to talk."

"Lady, if I knew how to get away, do you think I'd still be here?"

"If you want to earn your blood money, then yes, I do," Amber said.

"How many times am I going to have to tell you, you've got it wrong?" He shook his head, swallowed, closed his eyes and let out a loud breath that sounded almost like a sob.

Amber found it disconcerting seeing Eddie break down so easily, but then if he really did have a son dying of cancer...

"What do you want me to do with him?" John asked.

"We need to find out how to get out of here for one, so perhaps you could find out what he knows."

John grinned. "Be my pleasure."

Eddie spat in his face. "Fuck you. I can't tell you what I don't know, so you'll be wastin' your time."

John wiped spittle from his cheek. "Don't worry, hurting you won't be a waste of my time."

A low moan emanated from outside and Amber crossed over to the window and stared out. "Shit, they're here. How much ammo has everyone got left?"

"I've got a couple of full clips, a grenade and some ammo for the pistol," Barry said.

"I'm about the same," John said.

Amber pinched the bridge of her nose. "I haven't got much more." The first signs of a headache throbbed at her temples. She didn't know if it was in response to the terror coursing through her veins or nervous tension—both probably. "We need to set up a defensive position. John, Barry, leave Eddie for now. He won't be going anywhere. John cover the front, Barry the left." John and Barry took up their positions. "Six-pack, you watch that door at the back of the room. *Six-pack*, did you hear me?"

When Six-pack didn't acknowledge her, Amber took a step towards him. Shadowed by the sunlight entering the room at his rear, Six-pack stood with his head cocked.

"Six-pack, you okay?" she asked.

Fists started pounding at the front door like corpses beating at a coffin lid. She didn't know if her attempt at securing the door would suffice for long. "John, I thought I told you to cover the bloody front."

John stood with his back to the window beside the door, watching the proceedings in the room. "Six-pack, man, what's wrong?"

"Just cover the damn door," she snapped.

The banging increased, echoing around the room. Amber's temples throbbed in time with the beats. She closed her eyes and rubbed her brow. The moans and groans from outside seemed to increase in volume, seemed to originate close beside her.

She opened her eyes just in time to see Six-pack lurching towards her, arms extended and the low moan of the dead issuing from his parted lips.

TWENTY-EIGHT

With no time to open fire, Amber jumped out of Six-pack's way, narrowly avoiding the clutch of his fingers.

Six-pack spun around and grabbed at her, snagging her sleeve. Sunlight struck his face, a face drained of colour like a blank canvas. He didn't blink, his eyes dark and soulless.

He opened his mouth, lips peeled back as if about to munch down on a juicy steak. A low, pitiful groan rumbled from the back of his throat.

Amber snatched her sleeve back, grabbed her gun in both hands and rammed the stock into Six-pack's face with enough force to jar her right arm and make her wince. She heard the impact like a slap. Six-pack's head snapped back then forwards as though on a spring. The force of the blow mashed his top lip against his teeth, splitting the skin and shattering one tooth. She hit him again, pummelling his face. The stock crushed his nose, popped one of his eyes. Liquid spurted out and struck Amber's cheek. Repulsed, she rammed the stock into his face again, using all the strength she could muster.

"Move out of the way," Barry said, targeting Six-pack with his Heckler and Koch.

Amber wished she could, but Six-pack grabbed her arm again, grinning as though he knew what he was doing. Working on autopilot, Amber dropped her gun, reached down to her belt and yanked the knife from its sheath. She changed her grip, the vicious-looking weapon now a talon extending from her palm. Gritting her teeth, she rammed the blade through Six-pack's burst eye. She felt the serrations on the blade saw against his eye socket, his eyelid splitting in two as she levered the blade down. Putting all her strength into the thrust, she screamed, felt the blade slide through his brain like cardboard.

Six-pack released his grip and stumbled back, the knife slipping from his socket, trailing skin and brain matter from the serrations. He flopped to the floor beside Eddie, who screwed his nose up.

"Get him the fuck away from me," Eddie squealed.

Amber didn't have time to answer as the banging at the door intensified.

"John, secure that door," she said, seeing that the wood was vibrating.

John sprinted across the room and put his shoulder against the door, bracing his feet to apply leverage.

"Barry, prop that old settee against the window to provide a bit of a barricade, and see if you can draw some of them away from the door."

Placing an unlit cigar between his teeth, Barry nodded and pushed the threadbare settee across to the window where he propped it up. He glanced at Six-pack, shook his head, then leaned around the seat, pointing the barrel of his gun through the broken glass and opening fire.

Eddie shuffled across the floor away from Six-pack. "Jesus," he said. "You can't leave me handcuffed like this."

Ignoring his protests, Amber said, "I'm going to check through the next room, see if the coast is clear so we can get out of here."

"Aren't we better off staying put?" Barry shouted back.

"We'll be out of ammo soon, when that happens…" She didn't need to finish her sentence.

"Let me go," Eddie said as she crouched down beside him and wiped the blade of her knife across Six-pack's chest. She tried to avoid looking at her fallen comrade's face as she re-sheathed the blade and stood up

"You tell me how we can get out of here and I'll let you go."

"Haven't you listened to anything I've said? I don't know how to get out!"

"Then the restraints stay on."

Eddie shuffled into a sitting position and struggled to his feet. "You can't do this to me. I've got a family. If not for me, then do it for them."

Amber shrugged. "I can't trust you. But don't worry, I won't let anything happen to you. I want to save that pleasure for myself."

Eddie's bottom lip trembled. He sucked it in to hide his fear.

Amber stared at him. He looked so sincere. But she just wasn't prepared to take the risk.

"I'll be back in a minute," she said, turning and running across the room before he argued further.

If she didn't know better, the groans of the undead could be mistaken for the wind. She thought about the tale of the three little pigs, with the big bad wolf standing outside the door, huffing and puffing. But for this scenario, she didn't even think a house of bricks could save their bacon. She and her men had to leave. *Now.* At least on foot they stood a chance, however slim. Trapped in here, they were more like prospective meals in a burger bar.

At the back of the building she peered out the kitchen window towards the derelict barn. All seemed quiet. Hopefully, the undead were too intent on the front of the building to have the sense to check around the back—at least for now.

She ran through the house and into the living room. "Right, the coast's clear at the back. Barry, grab Eddie and let's go."

Eddie looked about to protest, but Barry ran across the room, grabbed Eddie by the arm, and started shepherding him towards the back door.

"John, we've got to go," she said.

John nodded, his shoulder propped against the door as he leaned against it. "I don't know how long this door'll last for."

"As long as it lasts until we're out the house, that's all we need."

Amber turned and started back towards the kitchen. As she reached the doorway, she heard the front door crash to the ground and imagined the zombies crushing against one another as they tried to pile into the house.

Barry kicked open the back door and pushed Eddie outside with Amber hot on their tails. The barn door banged in the wind, startling her. She stared at it, saw the overgrown remains of a track leading into the trees, and wondered if the old Land Rover she'd seen inside still worked. She knew it was a long shot, but if they got it going, they could put some distance between themselves and the zombies.

"This way," she said.

Barry pushed Eddie along with John at their rear, the smell of the straw inside the barn a welcome relief after the stench of death. Amber stared at the rusty vehicle. All of its tyres were low and cobwebs lined the windscreen like macabre curtains. Praying it would work, she hurried across and pulled open the driver's door. She slid inside and yanked at the steering wheel to break the lock. When that failed to work, she noticed the pitchfork hanging on the wall and she jumped out of the vehicle and ran to grab it.

"What are you doing?" Barry asked, manoeuvring the unlit cigar around his mouth as he spoke.

"I'm going to try to start the Land Rover."

"*Start it?*" he said. "The battery is going to be as flat as a pancake, and you haven't got a key."

"Then we'll have to push-start it and I don't need a key on an old vehicle like this." Ignoring the rest of his protests, she hurried back with the pitchfork and jammed the handle through the steering wheel, levering it until the lock snapped. "Misspent youth," she said in way of explanation.

Next she slid across the driver's seat on her back and ripped the cowling from around the ignition. She then traced the ignition barrel down to a black cap, which she pried off with her knife. Inside where the cap had been, she spotted a notch, into which she put the knife blade, cracking it in with the palm of her hand. She turned it. As she feared, nothing happened.

"Right, Barry, get Eddie in the car, then you and John give me a push and we'll see, God willing, if we can get this old jalopy going."

Barry shook his head. "I'd be surprised if that thing's even got an engine, never mind if it'll turn over."

"Unless you've got a better idea, I'd suggest we give it a try. And quick, too." She indicated the house opposite where a figure emerged from the back door.

John opened fire with his Colt Commando. The single shot floored the zombie.

She drummed her fingers on the steering wheel and stared anxiously at the entrance as Barry shoved Eddie into the back of the vehicle.

"This is great. Why not just put a sign outside the car saying 'open for lunch,'" Eddie said, righting himself.

"Just shut up, will you?" Amber replied.

Over at the entrance, John fired another couple of rounds and ran into the barn where he joined Barry behind the Land Rover. Amber wiped her sleeve across the rear view mirror to clear the dust and put the vehicle into second gear, putting her foot on the clutch. "Now push," she said.

Both men put their shoulders to the task. The vehicle rolled towards the doors.

The vehicle picked up speed, but the deflated tyres made it harder going than usual and they trundled along at little more than walking pace. She heard either John or Barry curse.

In front, a figure lurched into view, followed by another, then another.

"Meals on fuckin' wheels," Eddie said.

Amber stared at his pale reflection in the mirror. He was terrified.

Realising they weren't going to go much faster, she released the clutch. The vehicle juddered and slowed as the gears came into play, but nothing else happened. "Shit," she said, pressing the clutch in.

With no time to get the vehicle up to speed again, she once more released the clutch. "Come on," she screamed as the vehicle lurched like a wounded animal, almost grinding to a stop before the engine burst into life with a loud bang. She looked in the mirror to see a cloud of black smoke erupt from the exhaust and a jubilant Barry waving his arms in the air.

The first zombie, a middle-aged man with flesh like a desiccated husk lumbered into the barn. Amber floored the accelerator and steered towards him. The front of the vehicle struck his legs, snapping them. The man's torso flopped against the bonnet, his face striking the metalwork with a jarring thud.

Amber slammed the brakes on, throwing the zombie forwards in a grotesque parody of flight. He hit the floor and rolled a couple of times, spikes of broken bone jutting out from his decomposing legs.

Ramming the vehicle into reverse, she drove back into the barn to collect Barry and John. With the tyres almost flat, the vehicle lost a lot of traction, the wheels skidding, making steering difficult.

"I take it back," Barry said as he opened the door. "I didn't think you'd get it going."

"Neither did I," John said, grabbing Barry around the waist. He pulled him back and slit his throat wide open with a long knife.

TWENTY-NINE

Blood spurted from Barry's throat, coating the interior of the vehicle and splattering Amber's face.

Barry clutched at the vicious-looking wound, causing the blood to gush around his fingers. He gagged, coughed, spraying more blood from his mouth.

Amber stared, appalled. She tasted Barry's blood in her mouth, felt the warm fluid running down her cheeks.

"Drive!" Eddie screamed.

Amber hesitated, couldn't make sense of what'd just happened. Blood dripped from the roof like gory stalactites, the windscreen awash with gore.

"Goddamn it, drive!"

Compelled by the sound of Eddie's voice, Amber floored the accelerator. The wheels spun for a couple of seconds, then the tyres caught and the vehicle lurched forwards. Unable to see much of anything through the windscreen, Amber steered towards the light emanating from the entrance. She heard something strike the front, making the vehicle judder. The Land Rover left the ground for an instant as she ran over the corpse of a zombie.

She leaned forwards and wiped the windscreen with her sleeve, smearing the blood. She rubbed harder, concentrating on clearing a small spot through which to see.

The blood made the world look hellish, and the metallic stench filled the car and clogged her throat.

John! She couldn't believe what she'd just seen. Why had he done it?

"Get me out of these damn cuffs," Eddie squealed.

More concerned with driving, Amber steered towards the rough track leading into the trees. The vehicle crashed over every bump in the ground. The speedometer bounced around thirty miles per hour. She didn't dare push it any harder.

She glimpsed in the rear-view mirror in time to see John raise his Colt Commando. "Duck," she shouted, sliding down in her seat.

Next minute, a hail of bullets punched through the back of the vehicle and shattered the windscreen, thudding into the rear door and whining off the side panels.

Amber didn't know whether she'd voiced the scream or whether she'd imagined she did.

The shattered glass created a fractal image, impossible to see through, and she punched the windscreen out, pieces of glass flying into her hair. The cold wind buffeted her face and tears ran down her cheeks, mingling with the blood.

She heard more gunfire at her rear and ducked again, but no bullets struck the vehicle. She steered into the trees, aiming for a tunnel-like opening in their leaves, fighting to keep control as the wheels skidded.

Figures appeared ahead in the track—zombies attracted to the sound of the engine. With no other choice, she steered into them, sending them flying like pins in a bowling alley. The vehicle trundled across the corpses, and above the rumble of the engine, she heard bones snapping like wood.

"Get me out of these so I can help," Eddie said, holding his hands up and rattling the handcuffs.

Amber fumbled in her pocket for the key, but her hand shook too much. "Breast pocket," she said. "You'll have to reach across and get it."

As he leaned across the seat, Eddie said, "Now will you believe I'm not the bloody mole?"

Amber swallowed the lump in her throat. She couldn't believe it. *Not John. How could he?* Her stomach felt hollow and her heart ached.

Rays of sunlight shone through the trees, making the forest appear almost magical. The GPS device was in her webbing, making it easier to grab. Amber pulled it out and checked their position. The track didn't appear on the screen, so she didn't know where it led.

The ground slanted down, so she applied the brakes lightly. Two overgrown grooves in the earth where vehicles once travelled acted as rails, keeping the Land Rover on course. The vehicle ploughed through fresh saplings, the low branches whipping the bonnet, some of which struck Amber through the broken windscreen, making her eyes water as they lashed her cheeks.

"Give me a weapon," Eddie said, "and I'll ride shotgun."

Amber leaned across and grabbed the MP5 from the passenger foot well. She hesitated a moment, then passed it back.

"That was a turn-up for the books. I bet you weren't expecting it to be lover boy," Eddie said as he checked the gun.

Amber didn't answer. She still couldn't believe it. A man she trusted, a man she still loved, who she hoped to rekindle her romance with, had just killed a man in cold blood and then opened fire on her. The pain of betrayal felt worse than anything one of the undead could inflict. John may as well have ripped her heart out.

"So where we headed?" Eddie asked.

"I don't know." Having not seen any of the undead for a while, Amber eased off the accelerator, bringing their speed down to a walking pace. She glanced at the fuel gauge, saw it nudging in the red. "We won't be going much farther in this—the fuel's almost out."

"Great. So you mean those undead fuckers will catch us up soon."

"It's not as if I planned any of this to happen," she snapped.

Eddie put his hand on her shoulder and she flinched, afraid he would try to throttle her. But instead, he squeezed.

"I know," he said. "I just want to get back to the missus and my kid. I know there's not going to be any money to send him abroad, but I want to be there with him...you know, at the end."

Amber sucked her lips in and fought back tears. "I'm sorry," she said.

"It's not your fault. I know that. I didn't mean to rag on you, you know. All of this, it's just...I wanted that money so bad."

"I understand." She placed her hand on top of his and squeezed back. "We'll get out of here. I promise."

Eddie withdrew his hand and slumped back in his seat. "I didn't expect anything like this when I signed up. It's bloody crazy—zombies."

"How *did* you sign up? How did they contact you?"

"I got involved with a company called Stevenson's cleaning services, which was really a front for a recruiting office for security work."

Amber nodded.

"If we get out of this, I'm gonna kill those bastards."

"Not if—when."

The engine spluttered and a cloud of black smoke exploded from the exhaust. The vehicle juddered and its engine stalled, bringing the Land Rover to a stop less than a mile from the farmhouse.

"It looks like we walk from here," Amber said.

"We're miles from anywhere. Where do we bloody go?"

Amber rubbed her forehead, then turned in her seat and stared at Eddie. "We go back to the farm."

"*Back?* Are you crazy? I'm not going back there."

"Whoever that was who told us about the mole also mentioned he must have an escape plan. Well, they're probably right. Knowing John as I do, I know he wouldn't have come out here if he didn't have a way of getting home. He's probably using a scrambled channel, but he'll call for an immediate evac. The helicopter's probably on its way now, so we've got to hurry."

"Why don't I just call someone on my mobile and get them to come and pick us up."

"Who're you going to call? Who would believe any of this?"

"I don't have to mention the zombies. I'll just have them pick us up."

"Pick us up from where? How would they find us if we can't even find ourselves?"

"You've got the GPS. I'll give them directions."

"Even if you could get anyone to pick us up, they wouldn't get here in time to help, and would you really want to risk their lives?"

Eddie grimaced. "There must be something we can do rather than going back."

She reached behind the seat and reclaimed the handcuffs from where Eddie dropped them. "Just think about it. John thinks we're running away. This'll be the last thing he'll expect. We'll have surprise on our side."

Eddie exhaled and exited the vehicle. "Surprises have a nasty way of turning round and biting you on the ass," he said as he started walking back the way they'd come.

THIRTY

Lofty didn't know whether telling the people what he knew had helped, but it made him feel a little better knowing that he'd done something. Having rewired his camper van, he knew how to read circuit diagrams, and he'd found a stack of them in a drawer. By tracing the telecoms plans, he'd found a jack plug socket on the wall that was connected to a satellite uplink. He'd plugged the test phone in and found that he could hear the people speaking. Then he had used a push button on the phone to speak, much like a walkie-talkie.

Now he stood in a recessed area of corridor and consulted the layout map that he'd found in the room, chewing his fingernail and spitting the bits onto the floor. The map showed numerous exits, but he knew none of them would help because the fence surrounding the facility would still block any escape, so the best way to go was probably back the way they'd come. But the thought of going all that way stirred a sickly feeling in his stomach. They'd been lucky getting this far undiscovered, but he wouldn't take bets that their luck would hold out on the return trip, not when the mole informed them that someone had used the transmitter to update the team on the situation.

"What are we going to do?" Jill asked.

"Well we'd better get moving for a start."

Jill stared at him for a moment. "You were right. We did the right thing, staying to tell those people," she said, squeezing his hand.

Lofty shrugged. "I couldn't have done it without you."

Jill smiled. "Okay, enough of the backslapping, you're right, we've got to get out of here." She peered over his shoulder at the layout. "What's that?" she asked, jabbing her finger at the map.

"Just a car park."

"And what might we find in a car park?"

"Cars. Vans. Trucks. What else would you expect to find there?"

Jill rolled her eyes. "Do I have to spell it out? If there's a vehicle of any sort, perhaps we can use it."

"You mean steal it?"

"On top of breaking and entering, I don't think car theft is going to matter."

Lofty grinned. "I'll make a revolutionary out of you yet."

"Well, can we just get a move on."

Lofty folded the layout and shoved it in his pocket. Then he led the way towards the car park, which, judging by their location, would take about five minutes to reach.

The building was larger than it looked from the outside, and the warren of corridors made him feel like a rat in a maze. Sweat coated his body. He kept rubbing his hands up and down his jeans to dry them off.

The sound of voices in the distance made his heart miss a beat and he froze. Jill squeezed his hand, her face a rictus of fear. There was a junction twenty or so feet ahead, and he couldn't tell which direction the voices came from. *What if they were armed? Would they shoot on sight?* He tried to put a stop to the morbid thoughts, but his imagination wouldn't let him. Now in full swing, it threw up different scenarios, none of which ended happily.

What if they reached the car park to find the door locked? Even if it was open, who was to say there would be a vehicle outside? And if there was, where would they find a key? What if there were people out there?

The voices grew louder, getting closer, and the doubts in his head fell silent. A shiver ran down his spine. He found his own thoughts, no matter how morbid, better than hearing the chatter of actual people approaching.

"What are we going to do?" Jill whispered.

They still had a couple of corridors to navigate before they reached the exit for the car park. With time ticking, he needed to make a decision. Fast.

He ground his teeth, skewed his lips, trying to think. Then he spotted the fire alarm on the wall. Without hesitating, he jogged across and smashed his elbow into where it said 'BREAK HERE.' The alarm started ringing straight away and orange lights flashed along the corridor.

"And what good's that going to do?" Jill shouted above the ringing.

"If people think there's a fire, they'll evacuate. The layout showed points to gather in case of emergencies at the front of the building, so they'll hopefully leave by the nearest exit and make their way around the outside."

Jill nodded. "Good thinking, Einstein."

"Come on then, we probably won't have much time." He started walking, the orange lights giving the impression the corridor was the entrance to the underworld, this the final warning to turn back.

He thought he heard voices shouting, but couldn't tell from which direction. Then he heard what sounded like a door banging.

At the end of the corridor, Lofty peered around the corner to make sure the coast was clear, then proceeded towards the car park exit. Halfway along the corridor, he spotted a fire exit, the open door of which swung in the slight breeze. Although tempted to use the exit, he knew they wouldn't be able to escape due to the fence, and he didn't know if he could reach the car park by using it, so he ushered Jill on. Her expression made it clear she'd thought the same thing, but Lofty shook his head. As he passed, he caught a glimpse of daylight through the opening, but he didn't linger. The dayshift would probably be starting soon, which meant more people would be arriving.

Just before the end of the corridor, Lofty stopped and withdrew the layout plan again.

"What now?" Jill said, her eyes forever moving as she looked left and right, wary of being caught.

Lofty pointed to a room on the plan. "There's a locker room up ahead."

"Great. So what?"

"Well sometimes people will leave personal items in their lockers, such as keys, hopefully car keys."

Jill raised her eyebrows and nodded. Then her expression melted. "And what about keys to get in the lockers?"

"We'll get in one way or another. Trust me." He stuffed the plans back in his pocket and led the way.

Although wary of running into anyone, they reached the locker room without incident—Lofty thought his earlier prayer had been answered and he said a silent *thank you.* He pushed the door open and entered, finding himself in a room about twenty feet long by fifteen feet wide. Grey lockers as tall as himself lined the walls and also ran in two rows down the centre of the room, alongside two benches. Some of the lockers stood open, their innards bare apart from one with pornographic pictures taped to the inside of the door.

"Now what?" Jill asked.

Lofty studied the nearest locker, then opened his rucksack and withdrew the bar he used to remove the drain cover earlier. "This should do it. The locks aren't going to be that sophisticated." He jammed the end between the door and frame and pushed. The metal door bent but the lock didn't break. He gave it a hard shove. Straight away, something snapped with a metal ping. Lofty almost lost his balance as the door flew open with a loud clatter, revealing an empty locker.

"Great," he mumbled, rubbing his right triceps.

Knowing he might not have much time left, he approached the next locker and carried out the same procedure, this time taking care to have a good footing so he didn't lose his balance. Yet again, he came up empty. The next couple of lockers contained old newspapers and a couple of jackets—but no keys. The next door popped open and clanged against the locker beside it. The alarm masked any sound he made, so he wasn't worried about the noise.

A jacket hung from a peg in the locker and he rifled the pockets, smiling as he withdrew a set of keys. Among the house keys and other assortments, he spotted a car key with an electronic fob imprinted with the 'S' emblem common to Seat vehicles.

"Bingo," he said, grinning.

Jill smiled back.

The alarm suddenly stopped ringing, leaving an ominous silence in its wake.

"We'd better get a move on before they start coming back inside the building," Lofty said.

He started walking towards the door when the sound of running feet pounded along the corridor outside, getting louder. Lofty halted, eyes wide with panic. He looked back around the room.

"In there," he said, forcing Jill into one of the open lockers. She squeezed herself inside without any argument and closed the door.

Taller and wider, Lofty had difficulty squeezing into the next locker along, and the metal cabinet clanked and rattled as he forced his body into the gap, pulling the door closed behind him and having to nearly dislocate his shoulder in order to shut it tight.

A triple row of vents at eye level allowed him to see out. He focused on the door opposite, saw it burst open and watched a man enter.

Lofty tried to stop his legs from shaking, in case he inadvertently rattled the locker. Sweat rolled down his face, dripped from the end of his nose. His scrunched-up body ached all over and he felt his legs cramping. He bit his lower lip and slowly adjusted his legs to alleviate the pain.

The man outside was about forty years old, his short hair peppered with grey, and he was dressed in a guard's uniform.

A walkie-talkie crackled and a voice said, "It's a false alarm. Everyone back to their posts."

Lofty felt his hot breath circulate around the locker, combining with his body heat, turning the locker into a miniature sweatbox. He started panting, trying to control each breath so that he didn't make any noise.

The guard took his jacket off and sat down on a bench, the wood squeaking. He yanked off his tie and took out a newspaper, flipped it open, and started reading.

Lofty closed his eyes and grimaced. He didn't know how much longer he could stay hidden. If he was stuck inside the locker for too long, he was going to pass out. His thoughts turned to Jill, so near and yet so far.

He was going to get her out of here safe and sound if it was the last thing he did.

THIRTY-ONE

Muscles aching, lungs about to burst, Amber shucked off her backpack and leaned against the trunk of a pine tree

Eddie squatted down against a tree opposite and wiped sweat from his brow.

"So why do you think he did it?" Eddie asked.

"When I see him next, I'll be sure to ask." She couldn't believe that just before this mission, she had been hoping she and John would get back together. "Okay, rest time's over. Let's move out." She picked up her backpack and started walking towards the farmhouse. Eddie fell in step behind her.

The daylight meant she didn't have to worry about unseen tripping hazards, and at least now she would spot any figures lurching through the trees before they were on top of her.

Although they had only covered a mile or so before the vehicle conked out, and even though they followed the track, the rough terrain made progress slower than she liked.

The rising sun chased the last of the darkness away and wisps of steam rose from the forest floor as the temperature increased. Birds began to sing, completing the illusion of another normal day. In reality, she knew death waited ahead.

As they walked, Amber rummaged through the backpack, handed Eddie the last of the magazines for the MP5 and reloaded the pistol that she took back from him earlier. Apart from a few rounds of ammo, she had one grenade and two stun grenades left. A pitiful amount with which to face an undead army.

She walked through the rising mist, watching it swirl around her legs, the threads of vapour snapping like amorphous handcuffs. Dew-covered spider webs decorated some of the lower flora and fauna, a physical analogy to the trap into which they had walked. Some strands of web drifted through the air, undulating like illuminated, spun silk.

The air smelled of pine, ferns and mulch, natural essences that purified the thoughts and helped calm Amber's racing heart. She knew the stench of death would soon permeate the forest once more, so she took a deep breath, enjoying the fresh fragrance while it lasted.

Every part of her body ached, and a tiredness like she had never felt before penetrated down to her bones, but she couldn't stop again to rest.

Her stomach grumbled, and she withdrew an energy snack bar from her backpack. She ripped the cover off, praying that it wasn't going to be her last supper.

THIRTY-TWO

Amber signalled to Eddie to keep low. Up ahead, a trio of the undead skulked through the trees, their rotten stench permeating the air with a foul odour. Behind these, more zombies hovered around the farmhouse, standing perfectly still.

"Use your gun to take those three out," she said, knowing that using the silenced MP5 was a better option than the pistol. John, wherever he was, would hear the shots.

Eddie gave a thumb's up and scrambled through the undergrowth until close enough to open fire without wasting valuable ammo. Almost silent, the bullets thudded home, separating one man's jaw from his skull and severing another's windpipe. The way the undead figures jerked and danced in silence made them seem like spooky marionettes in a silent film. A couple of shots later and all three of the undead lay in the shrubbery, dispatched to the grave from which they'd risen.

Eddie put his thumb up and crouched down beside a bush.

Amber crept up beside him and peered through the undergrowth. The dilapidated farmhouse stood not more than one hundred feet away through the trees. She wondered if John suspected they'd double back, wondered if even now he wasn't watching them, targeting them with a rifle.

Her skin prickled at the thought. A sheen of sweat coated her torso, making her feel uncomfortable. She still couldn't believe he'd turned against her like this. Unsure how to proceed, she felt vulnerable. Low groans emanated from somewhere in the scrub and she scanned the area, finger tensed on the trigger of her gun.

Although unable to see anything, she couldn't relax, her nerves stretched to their breaking point. She heard leaves rustle to her left and spun around only to see a bird take flight.

Exhaling in relief, she returned her attention to the building, looking for any sign of movement. Something caught her eye. She stared towards the barn and saw someone walk in front of a set of doors on the upper floor. *John.*

Having helped on her uncle's farm during the summer holidays when she was a kid, she knew the doors were used to bring in hay bales, and the only other way to gain access to the first floor would be the ladder, which, as she recalled, was rotten and liable to break—which meant John had the advantage. If Eddie and she had more ammo, they could just open fire on the barn—the flimsy shell wouldn't offer much protection, but now every bullet mattered. If they left themselves ammo-less, they may as well sign their own death warrants.

"Now what?" Eddie said. "You want me to take him out?"

"No. If you miss, he'll know we're here and he's in a better position to return fire from high up."

"But I won't miss."

"We can't take that chance."

"So what do you suggest?"

Amber stared at the barn then nodded her head. "We'll smoke him out by setting fire to the building."

Eddie grinned and nodded. "Now that's my kind of plan."

Amber wasn't so happy about it, though. This was *John* she was talking about. A man she'd once loved.

I need to get over it. He just tried to kill me!

"Cover me," she said. Making sure John wasn't looking out of the barn, and that she couldn't be seen by any of the zombies, she ran for the cover of a large bush closer to her objective. The foliage brushed her face as she pushed her head through to see out. With the coast still clear, she made another run for it, this time heading for the base of the barn. Once across, she leaned against the wood and took a few deep breaths to steady herself. Unless John stuck his head out of the door and looked down, he wouldn't see her. A couple of feet to her left she spotted a partially open door in the wall. She sidestepped across to it and peered inside the building.

Amber gripped the pistol with her sweaty palm and wrapped her left hand on top of the right, improving her hold. Then using her shoulder, she eased the door open as carefully as she could and slipped into the barn, aiming the gun at the upper floor, the edge of which was a few feet to her right, in case John should happen to glance down from his perch.

She eased each foot down, taking care not to make any noise. Small piles of straw littered the ground, but a more substantial amount lay piled beneath the upper floor. Pistol aimed high, she tiptoed across, crouched down beside the combustible material and took the Zippo lighter from her webbing. The striker rolled beneath her thumb, sounding too loud within the barn as it scraped across the flint, generating sparks. The sweet smell of the lighter fluid reached her nostrils a second before the wick ignited.

Flame in hand, she hesitated and looked up. The floorboards squeaked and dust and blades of straw rained through gaps as John paced back and forth.

With all that had happened, it was hard to imagine she had once loved him.

Hand shaking, she set the straw alight. The flame engulfed the dry material and she backed away as white smoke spiralled towards the first floor. The straw crackled, the flames dancing.

Amber retreated towards the door, gun trained on the upper floor. Any minute, John would spot the fire, and would have to make a decision. It was obvious he'd know the fire wasn't accidental, so he wouldn't be in any rush to leave, but leave he would.

Smoke billowed upward, becoming thicker, more substantial, almost like a living thing scraping at the floorboards.

Amber backed out through the door and ran to where Eddie waited, aware she might get a bullet in her back on the way. Behind her she thought she heard John cough. When she reached the scrub where Eddie lay, she dove beside him and turned to look back at the building. Flames licked through the side-walls and smoke swirled from the upper doors. She knew John wouldn't be able to stay inside much longer.

"If I ever want anything torched, I'll know who to come to," Eddie said.

Back at the barn, burning wood started crackling and a group of zombies blundered out of the undergrowth not thirty feet from where Amber lay.

The undead troupe stood with their heads cocked, staring at the flames as though mesmerised.

"You want me to deal with them?" Eddie asked.

Amber shook her head. "They're not interested in us at the moment, so save your ammo. You might need it later."

Something exploded in the barn with a muffled bang, drawing Amber's gaze back. She peered through the swirls of smoke, trying to spot John.

Eddie jumped. "What was that?"

Amber shrugged. "There must have been something explosive in there, perhaps a fuel can for the Land Rover."

"What if lover boy goes out the front?" Eddie said.

Although annoyed at Eddie calling John her lover boy, she didn't rebuke him. "The flames will be too fierce under the ladder. If he's coming out anywhere, it'll be there." She pointed at the doors on the first floor.

Eddie settled down and targeted the barn with the MP5. "Bring him on."

More zombies shambled from the tree line like moths attracted to the flame. Afraid some of the undead could creep up behind them, Amber glanced over her shoulder. Even though she couldn't see anyone, an uneasy feeling settled in her stomach.

A crash emanated from the barn and Amber turned back in time to see John flying through the air surrounded by planks of broken wood from where he jumped through the wall itself to escape.

Eddie fired a couple of shots.

"Hold your fire," Amber hissed. "You're not going to hit him in the air."

She watched John land and roll, tucking himself into a ball. Strangely, none of the zombies made a move to attack him.

Eddie started to stand, weapon at the ready. Amber pulled him back down. "If you go out there now then the undead are going to turn on us."

"Those creatures aren't doing anything. Look, I can take him out now."

"I'm still in charge here, and I'm telling you to wait."

She watched John stand and run towards the tree line, passing within feet of the zombies, none of which moved to attack him.

But why didn't they attack? It didn't make sense...

She pressed the transmit button. "John, I know you can hear me. What's going on?" Despite working for the enemy, she felt deep down that a spark of humanity still burned in John's heart, that despite everything, he still had feelings for her.

She saw Eddie frown at her. "Great way to ruin the element of surprise," he grumbled.

She watched John scan the area before he replied. "Amber. Where are you?"

"I don't know what's going on, or what they've offered you, but you're not a bad man. You're not a cold-blooded killer at heart—I know you're not."

"We need to talk. We can get out of this together," John replied.

She watched him run for the cover of the bushes about fifty feet to their left.

"Then talk," she said.

"This is a waste of fucking time," Eddie said. "Let's just kill the son of a bitch."

Amber glared at him. "Look, I don't want anyone else dying. If we can all get out of this in one piece, we can sort things out later. For now, I just want to get out of here—alive."

As she finished speaking, Amber heard something moving through the undergrowth. She looked back in time to see a dishevelled man running towards them. His dead eyes locked with hers, his expression one of pain and hunger. His lips peeled back over dirty teeth and he groaned, arms extended, fingers clutching at the air, wanting to tear the skin from her bones. Acting on pure instinct, Amber levelled her gun and pulled the trigger three times in quick succession, the sound like a peal of thunder. The spent casings flew over her right shoulder, while the bullets slammed into the man's chest, neck and face as she corrected her aim. The bullet that hit his face drilled through his nose and the man dropped to his knees and fell face first on the ground.

Amber took deep breaths. The gun's report rang in her ears.

"Shit," Eddie said.

Sweat ran down Amber's face. Attracted to the sound of gunfire, she saw more zombies turn and head their way.

Eddie opened fire, cutting down the nearest zombie with a line of bullets. Amber took out a woman in bedraggled clothes.

"You shouldn't be here," John said, stepping out from the bushes, gun trained at Amber and Eddie.

Amber swallowed. She stared at John. His expression appeared resolute, but a slight indecision flickered across his face.

"Put the guns down," John said.

"This is bollocks," Eddie said.

"Do it now," John spat.

Amber dropped her gun. "Do as he says, Eddie."

Eddie grimaced, shook his head and then threw his weapon a few feet away.

Amber saw the zombies drawing closer, and she knew they didn't have much time, but she knew if John was going to shoot, he would have already done it, so she felt there was still a chance. "John, we can't stay here. They're coming. Look." She pointed back towardss the blazing barn, the heat from which drew sweat from her body.

John licked his lips but didn't look where she indicated.

Amber thought she heard the faint whir of rotor blades in the distance. "John, for god's sake, they're going to kill us."

John shook his head and pulled a palm-sized computer out of his pocket. He tapped on the screen a couple of times, and the approaching zombies suddenly stopped and stood stock-still.

Amber's jaw dropped and she stared wide-eyed. "How... I... I don't understand."

"I'm sorry," John said. "You shouldn't be here. I shouldn't have let you tag along."

"Much as I hate to break you two lovebirds up," Eddie said, "but I have a job to do."

Unsure what the hell Eddie was going on about, Amber turned and watched as he pulled a small gun out of his waistband and trained it on John.

"The company took out a second insurance policy in case John failed," Eddie said. "Of course he didn't know about me, but I knew about him." He looked at Amber. "You should have trusted your instincts. I'm sorry, but neither of you are getting out of here."

She saw movement from the corner of her eye as John started to lift the barrel of his gun and she screamed.

Eddie's gun barked.

THIRTY-THREE

John released his grip on the Colt Commando and clutched at his chest where petals of blood blossomed around the small hole in his jacket.

He gagged, coughed and stumbled back, dropping the handheld computer. Amber lurched to her feet to help him but Eddie fired another shot, the bullet striking John in the throat. Blood spurted out, a main artery severed. One hand trying to stem the flow of blood from each wound, his legs buckled and he dropped to the ground.

Tears blurred Amber's vision and a pain as though she too had been shot penetrated her chest, but hers was the pain of anguish.

She dropped to her knees beside John and cradled his head in her arms. John looked up at her. He coughed up a glob of blood. "I'm sorry," he said. "You know...I...I love you, Amber."

His head flopped to the side and his chest sank.

"It's nothing personal," Eddie said. "If you had kids, you'd understand."

Amber pursed her lips and fought back the tears and anger as she laid John's head on the ground.

The sound of the helicopter increased, became a raucous din overhead. She knew she had to act fast if she stood any chance of surviving.

With her back still to Eddie, she removed the M84 stun grenade from her webbing. Grenade in hand, she pulled the pin and dropped the device between her legs before diving forwards, hands over her ears and eyes screwed shut.

Almost immediately, an ear-splitting explosion followed a blinding flash of light that illuminated the inside of Amber's eyelids like a supernova. She knew the effects of the grenade lasted about five seconds, so she opened her eyes, picked herself up along with John's Colt Commando and turned to see Eddie covering his face with his hands.

Even if she spoke, she knew he wouldn't hear her as the loud blast would have disturbed the fluid in the semicircular canals of his ear, disorientating him and deafening him for a short time. Even her ears hummed from the blast.

Eddie shook his head and staggered to his left.

"Jesus Christ," he shouted. He opened fire, emptying the magazine.

Amber leaped aside, the bullets from his wild shots shattering the small computer on the ground and sending pieces of plastic flying in all directions. As soon as the machine broke, the zombies started moving as though woken from a spell.

Behind Eddie, Amber saw another group of zombies stumbling towards them. She opened fire, the Colt pumping out bullets that shredded dead flesh like wet tissue paper. Skin, sinew, muscle and bone snapped, cracked and exploded under the onslaught.

Overhead, the leaves and branches stirred as the helicopter swooped down low and passed overhead, the sound of its blades almost as deafening as the stun grenade.

Eddie patted his ears, blinking fast as if to clear his vision. When he opened his eyes, he glared at Amber. "Just get it over with and kill me," he shouted.

Amber pointed the barrel of the gun at him, her finger itching to pull the trigger. She gritted her teeth, narrowed her eyes, took a breath. She knew she should do it for John, but she couldn't. Too many people had died already. Relaxing, she tugged the handcuffs out of her pocket. "You know what to do," she said, throwing them to him.

Eddie caught them in midair and frowned. He rocked, still unsteady on his feet. "What for?"

"Because I'm telling you too. Now fasten the cuffs."

Eddie shook his head.

"At least this way you get to live to see your kid, so just do it."

"To see him die, you mean."

"It might not come to that."

"Hell, I probably won't even get to see him anyway. If you get out of here alive, then we're both dead."

"Not if they don't find us."

"Oh, they'll find us, don't you worry about that."

The helicopter hovered, then disappeared behind the farmhouse.

"Look, enough talking. Put the goddamn cuffs on before I pull this trigger. At least this way, you've got a fighting chance."

Eddie closed his eyes and shook his head. Opening his eyes, he frowned. He fastened the handcuffs around his wrists and stared at her. "Now what?"

"Now we get a ride out of here in the helicopter." As she spoke, she knelt down and relieved John of his remaining ammo.

"And you really think they'll let you? Then it's you they should call crazy, not me."

"They may not want to, but I think this'll persuade them otherwise." She raised the gun. "Now get a move on." She pushed him in the direction she'd seen the helicopter descend, on the far side of the farmhouse.

A bedraggled old woman lumbered towards them, arms outstretched, head cocked like a curious dog. What clothes she wore resembled rags. Her left hand had been snapped at the wrist and a white protrusion of bone jutted from the rotting flesh.

Amber aimed and fired in one fluid motion. The bullet smacked through the woman's eye, knocking her head back and lifting her off her feet before she crashed onto her back.

She didn't like to think the woman could have been someone's mother or grandmother—but she couldn't help it. These weren't soldiers, they were pawns in a sick experiment. They hadn't asked for any of this.

She heard the helicopter idling in the distance and prodded the gun into Eddie's back to make him move faster. More zombies hurtled from the trees with flora and fauna wrapped around them, proof—if any were needed—that they were heedless in their pursuit. A stick protruded from a man's neck where he must have run into a tree and a couple of others appeared covered in lacerations where they had cut themselves on the undergrowth.

At the corner of the building, Amber checked to see whether the coast was clear before pushing Eddie on. She fired a quick burst at the pursuing group, knocking a couple to the ground. Next minute, she watched them pick themselves up and continue the chase.

Not wanting to waste any more bullets, she ran around the corner.

She saw Eddie about ten feet in front, running as fast as he could. Next minute a pair of hands smashed through the window from inside the building and grabbed Eddie by the throat, leaving his feet still running as they left the ground.

Eddie emitted a throat-searing scream that sent a shiver down Amber's spine.

Urged into action, she ran forwards and grabbed Eddie's legs as the zombie tried to drag him into the house. Probably thinking another zombie had a hold of him, Eddie kicked out at her.

"It's me," she squealed.

An arm locked around Eddie's throat so he couldn't answer. He thrashed, slicing his cheeks on the fangs of glass.

A face ravaged by death appeared through the window frame. The creature's sallow skin hung in tatters around its nose and its eyes appeared sunken in pockets of shadow. As it lowered its head, the flesh around its jaw looked like curdled milk.

The zombie sank its teeth into Eddie's cheek, tearing off a layer of skin and leaving a glistening sheet of purple muscle behind. Eddie screamed louder. He tried to punch the creature, but the handcuffs restricted his movements.

Amber aimed at the zombie's head and pulled the trigger. The bullet chipped a portion of the zombies crown out to reveal the grey brain matter beneath. The fragment of skull dangled from threads of skin across the zombie's brow, the tufts of short black hair across its surface resembling a bizarre caterpillar. Amber fired again, this time managing to puncture the man's cheek. His grip on Eddie relaxed as he slumped back into the room, the skin from Eddie's cheek protruding from its mouth like a tongue.

Eddie collapsed to the ground with blood pouring from his cheek. He sobbed, his tears mingling with the blood and leaving a slick sheen on the visible muscle.

"Fuck, fuck, fuck," he said.

"Come on Eddie, we've got to go."

"*Go?* Go where? That fuckin' thing *bit* me. Jesus, I'm gonna become one of them." He bowed his head, the flaps of skin around the wound in his cheek falling open. Blood dripped down. "For God's sake, kill me," he whispered.

Amber pursed her lips. "No, I'm taking you home. They might have an antidote."

"And what if they don't?"

"It's worth a try."

"Why do you care? I killed your fella. I thought you'd be only too glad to kill me." He touched his shackled wrist to his cheek and winced.

He was right, but deep down, she felt he wasn't a bad person—circumstances drove him to do what he did. If there was any chance she could get him back to see his son, then it was worth trying. "Come on, soldier, pick yourself up."

Eddie grimaced, baring his teeth in pain. "Just goddamn kill me."

Amber grabbed the chain between the cuffs and pulled him to his feet. "You did this for your son. Don't make it all for nothing."

Eddie stared at her, the flaps of his cheek hanging down, resembling the jowls of a grotesque bloodhound. Tears ran down his cheeks and he closed his eyes.

"We've got to go—now," Amber said as the pursuing zombies shuffled around the corner, less than thirty feet away. She opened fire, spraying them with bullets, then she grabbed Eddie's arm and pulled.

At the far end of the building, she peered around the corner and spotted the helicopter sitting in a small clearing. An armed man sat in the doorway, but she noticed that no zombies approached. She remembered the device John had used earlier.

Amber knew he would open fire if he spotted her, so she dropped to one knee and targeted the man in her sights, but the end of the barrel kept wavering. She took a deep breath to try to calm herself. Then she exhaled, holding her breath when her lungs were almost empty.

The barrel steadied and she pulled the trigger.

And missed.

The bullet punctured the side of the helicopter, inches from the man's head. The man turned and stared at the entry hole, slipped his finger inside as though unsure of what it was. As the realisation hit home, he turned and raised his weapon, but Amber fired again, and this time she didn't miss. The bullet punched into the man's chest, knocking him back.

"Let's go," she said.

Letting Eddie take the lead, she ran towards the helicopter. Behind her she heard a tumultuous groan. It almost sounded as though the zombies knew their prey was escaping.

The draft from the blades buffeted her as she drew close. She kept her head low and headed towards the doorway. Once she reached the helicopter, she helped Eddie inside, then clambered in behind him. The young pilot turned and stared at her as she thrust the barrel of the gun in his face.

"I suggest you take off—now," she said, "before I paint the cockpit with your goddamn brains."

The pilot gulped and stared at the downed man by Amber's feet, then at Eddie, who sat catching his breath in the seat next to her.

He nodded and turned away. The sound of the blades increased. Amber pulled the door shut, then settled back as the helicopter lifted off and banked over the trees.

Down below, she saw the undead hordes staring up at them and another chill swept over her.

Someone was going to pay for this.

THIRTY-FOUR

Finch reclined in a chair and stared at a bank of monitor screens, each relaying images from the mining village via a series of hidden cameras. Across the other side of the operations room, the General and his cohorts stood in a circle talking amongst one another. Finch knew the General had his doubts, but the results from operation Deadfall would speak for themselves.

"Did you get to the cause of that alarm?" the General asked.

"Someone set off the fire alarm on purpose, but as of yet, we don't know who it was."

"And that's supposed to instil me with the confidence that your *experiment* is going to work?"

Finch laced his fingers together above his head. "I've been informed the helicopter has just landed, so I'll debrief our man to ascertain exact details of battle efficiency."

"How many of those undead creatures were killed in the end?"

"Around two hundred."

The General tutted. "Two hundred taken out by a team of eight! I don't see that as being efficient. If that had been a larger insertion group, they would have annihilated the opposition."

"Yes, but General, you're not taking into account that it doesn't matter how many they killed because they were all expendable—a throwaway army. And in a larger scenario, if we unleashed the undead upon a city, their number would swell to hundreds of thousands within hours. They would literally become an unstoppable force."

The General stroked his moustache and nodded. "I suppose you have a point."

"There's no *suppose* about it. We only have to inject the reanimation virus into a couple of corpses, and like an unstoppable avalanche, before anyone even knows what's happened, half a city will have been recruited by the zombie army."

"That's all well and good," the General said, "but then how do we contain the situation?"

"That's something I'll show you in a while, and I can promise you, you won't be disappointed."

"I should hope for your sake that I'm not. We've invested a lot of time and money in this project."

And you don't think I haven't? Finch's lips rose in a tight smile. *Keep 'em on side*, he thought.

He unlocked his fingers and sat up straight. The General and his ilk would soon see the success of the operation.

The lead scientist, Collins, motioned from across the room. "I've just been told our man on the inside is on his way through."

"Excellent," Finch said. He stood up. "Would you like to sit in on the debriefing, General?"

"Do you have to ask?"

Finch grinned. He couldn't wait to hear the outcome of the experiment.

The door across the room banged open and a figure entered.

"Ah, Mr. Bloor," Finch said, recognising the man as the one they called 'Crazy Eddie.' But something about Eddie's face troubled him, and it wasn't until the people standing nearest the door started backing away that he realised what was wrong.

"Mr. Bloor, what happened to you?" he asked.

Eddie turned his head and stared across the room, revealing a missing cheek, the purple muscle beneath contracting as he clenched his teeth. Finch gasped. At the same moment, he spotted the handcuffs around Eddie's wrists and the length of rope circling his waist.

Another person appeared behind Eddie and the room filled with the sound of gunfire. Bullets penetrated the false ceiling, blowing chunks out of the square tiles. A couple of fluorescent tubes shattered, showering the room with glass.

"Now if I've got your attention—anyone moves and they're dead," the shooter said.

Ears ringing, Finch stared at the woman standing in the doorway and sighed. "Amber Redgrave, what an unexpected surprise."

Amber targeted him with the gun. "I didn't say you could speak, either."

Finch held his hands up. "Just take it easy. We don't want anyone getting hurt."

"Can someone tell me what the hell's going on?" the General said, wiping pieces of the ceiling from his shoulder.

"I'm not going to tell you again," Amber said.

Eddie lurched forwards, tugging at the piece of rope in Amber's hand, causing her to readjust her position so he didn't pull her over.

"Is that what the hell I think it is?" the General asked, pointing at Eddie.

"If you mean, 'is it a result of your sick experiment,' then yes," Amber said. "Now what I need is the cure."

Finch shook his head. "Unfortunately there isn't one."

Amber aimed her gun at him and pulled the trigger. Finch ducked as a volley of bullets smacked the wall behind him.

"Don't lie," Amber said. "You wouldn't have set about conducting an experiment without having some way to counteract the effects."

Finch shook his head and stood up straight. "The effects of death can't be reversed. What's dead stays dead, I'm afraid. At least in the usual terms. What we have in Mr. Bloor is more an automaton. He's no longer alive in the conventional sense, and whatever soul he possessed has now departed, taking his humanity with it."

Amber gritted her teeth. "I don't believe you."

Finch shrugged. "Believe what you want, but I promise you, there is no antidote."

"Now look here," the General said.

"No, you look," Amber spat as she whirled on him. "I want you to take Eddie and inject him with whatever it is you have that'll bring him back."

"How many more times…" Finch said. "We *don't* have anything."

Eddie strained at the leash, his dead eyes fixed on Finch.

"Then it's time to call your bluff," Amber said.

Eddie gnashed his teeth, accentuating the vicious wound on his cheek. At the same time, Amber let go of the rope in her hand and Eddie rushed forwards.

A fair-haired woman across the other side of the room screamed and made a run for the door. Amber targeted above the woman's head with the Colt Commando and opened fire. An arc of spent shells flew threw the air and the plaster on the wall across the room turned to dust.

"There won't be another warning," Amber said.

She watched as Eddie charged across the room, navigating his way around the workstations. People backed away, trying to distance themselves from their creation, their faces drained of colour as though they too had succumbed to death.

Finch pulled a small handheld computer out of his pocket and tapped the screen. Amber recognised it as similar to the one John used—it had the same effect. Eddie came to a stop and stood stock still, a grotesque statue.

"Unless you haven't realised it yet, we may not have an antidote, but we can control the creatures' Somatic motoneurons—which means we can control what they do."

Amber clenched her jaw. "Then you're worse than I imagined. You're a demented fucking puppet master."

Finch chuckled. "Now I think that for the benefit of the General, it's time to reveal our contingency plan, Mr. Collins." He nodded to a man across the room.

The man opened a control panel on the desk in front of him, turned a key, and pushed a button. Eddie disintegrated in a blinding flash of light that radiated from every pore of his body, sending out a wave of heat that singed the hairs on Amber's arms.

Shocked, she stared at the pile of ashes where Eddie had been standing.

Finch scowled and dabbed at his face with a tissue. "I had hoped you were infected so you would go the same way," he said, staring at Amber.

A man dressed in British Army uniform bearing the insignia of a General stepped forwards and poked at Eddie's remains. "Do you mind telling me what just happened?"

Finch dropped the tissue on the desk and wiped his hands together. "You wanted to know how we would contain the situation. Well, that's how. Alongside the reanimation virus, the original corpses were injected with self-replicating nanobots, tiny machines programmed to pass through the mouths of the undead alongside the virus. The nanobots were designed to infiltrate the body of anyone bitten, and then they replicated themselves. These are what we used to control their bodies. When Mr. Collins pressed the failsafe button, a signal was sent down from orbiting satellites that caused them to explode."

"So all the zombies have now been destroyed?" the General asked.

"Yes."

The General took a sudden step back from Eddie's remains. "Won't the virus still be active?"

"No, the nanobots contained small, highly explosive incendiary devices, the heat from which neutralises it."

The General bore an appreciative expression. "I have to say, I had my doubts, but I'm impressed."

Amber couldn't believe what she was hearing. "*Impressed?* You sons of bitches *used* us."

Finch stared across and shrugged. "I'm sorry, but in today's climate of political and social upheaval, we have to be prepared. We need cheap but effective weapons in case we ever need to utilise them against foreign insurgents, and it goes without saying that the weapons have to be field-tested so as to prove their efficiency. Of course, this means there will be acceptable casualties."

"I'll give you an acceptable casualty, you goddamn bastard." She turned to aim her gun at him when a shot rang out and a bullet punched through her thigh, sending a shaft of white-hot pain through her body. Amber bared her teeth and grimaced as she spun around to see the General targeting her with a pistol. She dived behind a desk as he fired again.

More gunfire erupted as the soldiers accompanying the General opened fire with their own small arms. Bullets took chunks out of the wall above her, raining down plaster.

The amount of blood pumping out from the bullet hole in her leg indicated a severed main artery. The pain felt like a swarm of bees stinging her all at once. Amber pressed her palm over the wound. She gritted her teeth and raised her gun above the desk, shooting blindly. The gun kicked in her hand, the recoil hurting her wrist. She heard the distinct crack and fizzle of monitor screens exploding.

Return fire took chunks out of the desk. One bullet passed straight through the wood inches from her face.

Retracting her weapon, she crawled towards the door, leaving a trail of blood in her wake. More gunfire rang out, a deafening percussion.

Knowing she would have to come out into the open in order to exit the room, Amber leaned her back against the desk, took a deep breath, propped the gun on her shoulder, and staggered to her feet, firing wildly behind her as she hobbled away. She crashed through the door with her shoulder, jarring her leg, accentuating the pain. Bright light flashed before her eyes.

Bullets smacked through the door behind her and pinged off the wall. The increased beat of her heart caused more blood to spurt from her wound. She ejected the spent magazine and inserted her last one. Then she staggered away, hopping on her good leg, each movement making her wince.

At the end of the corridor, she fell around the corner as more bullets chipped fragments from the wall behind her.

Amber leaned back around and fired a quick burst of gunfire to deter them from following, but she knew she didn't have much time and that reinforcements would soon be on their way. Anger coursed through her veins like molten lava. She couldn't believe she and her men had been used in such a callous manner.

She hobbled along further corridors, disorientated, firing sporadically. A gory trail of blood splashed the floor in her wake.

Scratching and guttural whining emanated from behind a door ahead and she hobbled towards it. A sign on the door read: Kennel 4.

She turned the handle and pushed the door open a fraction, almost jumping out of her skin as a salivating black and tan German Shepherd lunged at her. She slammed the door shut, but not before noticing the puncture marks decorating the dog's body as though repeatedly stabbed.

By the look of the dog, it was one of the undead. Had been for quite a while. Considering her location, she assumed the dog was an early test subject for the reanimation virus, and because it hadn't died when Mr. Collins pressed the destruct button, either it wasn't riddled with nanobots, or if it was, for some reason they hadn't exploded.

She heard voices from around the corner, signalling the General and his men would soon be upon her. Time was running out.

The dog clawed at the door again, its throaty whine almost pitiful.

She opened the door a fraction, pushed the barrel of the gun into the dog's maw and pulled the trigger. The bullet penetrated the dog's skull and the undead canine slumped back on its legs and keeled over.

Amber put her shoulder to the door and pushed to move the dog out of the way, then entered the room and closed the door behind her.

The dog's tongue lolled from its maw like a bloated leech. A missing chunk in the back of the creature's head showed where the bullet had exited.

She looked around the room, spotted the open cage from where she guessed the dog escaped. On the floor near the cage, she spotted a screwdriver and a stun gun. She wondered if someone had used it on the dog, and if so, whether it short-circuited any nanobots that might have been in its system. It was certainly one explanation as to why the dog hadn't disintegrated in an incendiary flash.

Amber knew she was dying. Tears stung her eyes, further blurring her already hazy vision. She remembered her brother taking his own life, remembered how angry she'd been. Now she realised that sometimes it was the only way.

Fighting the pain in her leg, she crouched beside the German Shepherd and removed the knife from her kit. She dug around inside the dog's skull and sliced a sliver of its brain away, holding the grisly grey morsel up to the light.

With her stomach doing somersaults, she popped the piece of brain into her mouth. It felt dry and rubbery and she swallowed without chewing.

Then she staggered to her feet and hopped towards the door. Finch knew she hadn't been infected with the virus before as she didn't disintegrate, so she hoped he wouldn't feel the need to incinerate her corpse.

She couldn't let them get away with everything they'd done.

Taking a deep breath, she closed her eyes, said a silent prayer, and then opened the door and rushed out into the corridor, headlong into a hail of bullets that took her life.

THIRTY-FIVE

Lofty froze at the sound of gunfire somewhere outside the locker room. The guard sitting on the bench dropped his newspaper, stood up, and ran through the door. When he left, Lofty literally fell out of the locker, sweat bathing his body.

"Jill! Jill, are you okay?" he said, pulling the locker door open.

Jill fell into his arms, panting through heat exhaustion, her face flushed. "I thought he was never going to leave," she said, pulling away from him and stretching her arms.

Lofty rubbed his shoulders and grimaced. He heard the sound of further gunfire like rolling thunder. "Jesus, do you hear that?"

Jill nodded, fear etched across her face.

Lofty couldn't begin to imagine what was going on. "We'd better get out of here while we've still got chance," he said. "Come on." The gunfire reinforced his fears that if they were found, they wouldn't just get a slap on the wrist and a fine, and his already shattered nerves tingled with dread.

Taking steadying breaths, he walked to the door, eased it open, and peered out. Seeing the coast was clear, he took hold of Jill's hand and pulled her into the corridor. He could feel her shaking at his side His heart sank, knowing that he could have put her in such a dire situation.

The gunfire had ceased, and with no idea where it had originated, Lofty knew he could be leading them into the middle of a goddamn firefight, but he also knew they couldn't just sit around. They had to escape.

Lofty started along the corridor, his heart feeling as though it was going to explode with every step. He listened attentively for any noise, the slightest sound making him stop.

He consulted the map as they progressed, constantly double-checking their position. The car park was less than a couple of minutes away now and he increased their pace until they reached the exit.

Lofty cracked the door open and peered through. Various vehicles sat on the tarmac, the rising sun shining from their paintwork. He tried to spot a Seat of any sort among them, but failed to see one. The coast appeared clear, though.

He scurried to the nearest car, a silver Lexus, and ducked behind it. Jill fell in beside him. He sat up and peered through the glass. He still couldn't see a Seat, unless it was hidden behind the other vehicles.

"This way," he said, "and keep low." He moved on all fours, scraping his hands and knees on the tarmac. Overhead, white clouds scudded across the sky.

He glanced back to check that Jill was keeping up and noticed the security camera on the corner of the building. *Shit*, he thought. *How could I have forgotten about the cameras?* From its position, it looked over the car park, and they would be in plain sight. He decided not to worry Jill with the news.

The door behind them suddenly opened and Lofty peered through a car's windscreen. Two men dressed in military uniforms walked out, carrying a blood soaked body between them. Acting quickly, he grabbed Jill and pulled her down behind the car to avoid being seen.

He scuttled to the rear of the car and peered around it, watching the men carry the body towards a green Army Land Rover less than thirty feet away. His heart pounded like a jackhammer as he tried to catch his breath.

From what he could tell, the body was that of a woman with strawberry red hair. She was dressed in some form of military garb, too, but he could see that bullets had torn chunks out of her body.

Another man walked out of the door, dressed in civilian attire. He had straight, shoulder-length brown hair tied back in a ponytail. Sweat glistened on his high forehead and the sunlight made shadows of his eye sockets.

The two men dropped the body unceremoniously on the floor, and one of them proceeded to unlock the back of the Land Rover. Both men were armed with some sort of machine gun slung across their shoulders.

Jill sat with her back against the car. She squeezed his hand. The simple act filled Lofty with courage.

The other soldier was standing, talking to the man with the ponytail. Lofty tried to hear what they were saying, but couldn't make it out. Movement caught his eye. Unsure what it was, he surveyed the scene, his mouth dropping open when he saw the woman twitch, her fingers opening and closing.

Was it some sort of death spasm?

The woman sat up and leapt to her feet—blindingly fast. Lofty almost fell back on his haunches in surprise. He let out a little yelp.

He couldn't believe what he was seeing. Although he had relayed information about the experiment, he hadn't actually believed it was real, had felt it was all some sort of mistake. Now connections came together in his head. Was that the woman he had spoken to earlier?

Jesus. If so, they had killed her, but there she was, moving about.

The woman attacked without preamble. She grabbed hold of the head of the soldier unlocking the Land Rover and sank her teeth into his throat, tearing out a chunk of flesh. A scream echoed around the car park and the man fell to his knees, clutching his throat in an attempt to stop the blood from spurting out. The other soldier stumbled, reached for his gun, but the woman leapt at him. Despite her condition, she moved surprisingly fast, grabbed his head, her thumbs puncturing his eyeballs. The man's scream joined that of his fallen compatriot as she chewed his ear off, tearing at it with her teeth.

Lofty cringed. He heard the sound of Jill being sick, and realised she must have seen what was going on.

Unable to take his eyes off the scene, his stomach roiled as the smell of Jill's vomit reached his nose.

The man with the ponytail backed away, shaking his head, his mouth opening and closing in silence, eyes wide, hands either side of his face, pulling his features into a mask of fear.

The woman released the soldier and turned to look at the man. Although splattered with blood and gore, Lofty was sure the expression on her face was that of hatred and disgust.

As though waking from a living nightmare, the man turned and started to run back to the door. He reached it just ahead of the woman, started to pull it open, but the woman leapt on his back and yanked his hair, literally pulling a whole chunk of his scalp away. Then she started biting, sinking her teeth into his neck, his face, anywhere she could get at.

The man crumpled to the floor, batting at her with his hands, but after a moment, he stopped and lay still.

"We've got to get out of here," Lofty said. He stood up and pulled Jill to her feet. Vomit covered her front, strands of it still hanging from her mouth.

"She's coming," she screamed.

Lofty risked a quick glance back, saw the woman charging towards them, blood and gore dripping from her mouth, her dead eyes like black mirrors.

"Run," Lofty yelled. He pulled the car keys out of his pocket, looking around for any sign of a Seat car. He started pressing the unlock button on the key fob, heard a distant beep and saw the flash of the indicators as the key activated the central locking on a silver Seat Cupra.

"This way," he shouted. When he reached the car, he yanked on the door handle. Then he felt it, a hand on his shoulder. His pulse rocketed, about to make his heart explode. He turned his head, stared into the woman's dead eyes. The smell of death emanated from her gore covered mouth. He saw further blood on her body, long since dried and flaking.

The woman leaned her head in to bite him, and Lofty fought to push her away, but she was stronger than he would have thought. He slipped sideways, fell onto the ground, the woman landing heavily on top of him, making him bang his elbow, pain shooting through his arm.

He struggled, kicked, anything to try to get her off, his fingers clamped either side of her head, trying to restrain her. He grimaced, lips peeled back, using all his strength.

A sudden shot rang out, making him jump, and a fragment of bone and brains shot out of the side of the woman's head before she stopped moving. Lofty pushed her aside, letting her fall to the floor.

He looked up, stared at Jill, the gun she had taken from one of the soldiers shaking in her hand.

Swallowing the sick feeling in his mouth, he staggered to his feet and took the gun off her.

"Thank you," he whispered, fighting to stop the tears from flowing.

Jill nodded, her lips clamped tight.

Lofty threw the gun down and guided her into the car. He darted around the other side, opened the door, jumped into the driving seat and slammed the door shut behind him.

He started the engine, released the handbrake and pressed his foot down on the accelerator. Then he headed towards the exit, driving straight through the barrier, shattered it like brittle bone.

Farther along the road, Lofty pulled into the lay-by where the camper van was parked. He ushered Jill out of the Seat and into their own vehicle. She didn't speak, her expression one of absolute shock and horror.

Once they were both secure, he started driving, nervously glancing in the rear-view mirror, terrified of seeing someone in pursuit.

He glanced across at Jill. She had her head against the window at her side, eyes closed. Tears left tracks through the dirt on her cheek.

He placed a hand on her knee. "We're safe now," he said, squeezing gently.

The action sent a burst of pain up his arm and he withdrew his hand and stared at the small, jagged cut about an inch and a half long on the inside of his wrist that oozed with blood.

Or was it a bite?

In all the confusion that had happened, he didn't know. Fear penetrated him like a knife and his lower lip started trembling, blood turning cold in his veins.

Jill turned and looked at him, her eyes moist with tears. "Are you sure?"

Lofty dropped his arm out of sight. He swallowed, tightened his grip on the steering wheel and focused on the road ahead, the bright lights of the city creating a glow across the horizon.

"I'm sure," he said. "Trust me."

About the Author

Shaun Jeffrey was brought up in a house in a cemetery, so it was only natural for his prose to stray towards the dark side when he started writing. He has had three novels published, including *The Kult* and *Evilution,* and one collection of short stories, 'Voyeurs of Death'. Among his other writing credits are short stories published in Surreal Magazine, Dark Discoveries and Shadowed Realms.

You liked the story, now see it beautifully illustrated in an exciting adaptation of the award-winning Damewood trilogy.
DEMONS OF THE PAST
THE GRAPHIC NOVEL
WRITTEN BY
ERIN DURANTE
ILLUSTRATED BY
JOHN S GROSVENOR

From Erin Durante, author of the *Demons of the Past*
and *Stones of Time*, comes the epic finale to the
award-winning Damewood Trilogy:

RISE
OF THE
DARK SON

Just when they thought their friends were behind them...

After detonating the bomb that destroyed the Ordi's labs,
halting the creation of their engineered army, Nadia and
Vestro embark on their own mission to return home to
Damewood and gain the support of its army while King
Andrew of the Pearl Isles readies his kingdom for the
coming war against Krill.

But the moment of peace before the storm is broken when
Nadia's young child is kidnapped, and in return for the boy's
safety she is forced to betray her allies and the kingdoms
she swore to defend.

October 2010

LEUCROTA
PRESS

The Rocket's Red Glare
David M. Peak

Nearly 350 million quarters are minted each month. In the second after a coin is prpessed, an entire civilization of germs can rise and fall, leaving
behind only their tale of survival.

The Rocket's Red Glare is one of these stories.